To my grandfather
Arthur John Hammond
who fought in the First World War

I wish I had known you

Dearest Maude

LORNA HOWARTH

Plum Stone Publishing

Published 2012 by Plum Stone Publishing
c/o Wellesley House, 202 London Road
Waterlooville, Hampshire PO7 7AN

www.lornahowarth.com

A catalogue record for this book is available from
The British Library.

The front cover image of The Royal Victoria Military Hospital is
reproduced by kind permission of The Army Medical Services Museum,
Ash Vale, Aldershot, Hampshire GU12 5RQ.

ISBN 978-0-9571314-0-8

Printed and bound by CPI Group (UK) Ltd, Croydon, CR0 4YY

Nineteen-fourteen. The year it all began. War.

But there were no thoughts of war in my head as I stood in the queue outside the Union Hall, hugging my arms in close to me to stop the January wind cutting up beneath my coat. For why should there be? The old year had turned, and the troubles may well have been beginning in Europe, but it meant nothing to the likes of me. There was no talk then of trenches being dug, nor battles fought and lives lost. That would all come later.

No, there was nothing in my life to suggest that in a bare seven months we'd all be thrown into a conflict spun by Lucifer himself. All the chatter and gossip at the Emporium at that time was still of hats and hemlines, fallings-out and makings-up, and all of us humming the latest music hall songs. There was no thought in my head of love, neither, for I hadn't even met Hubert then, and as for John, well, the war would be halfway through before all that started. I was a modern woman, a suffragette, and what spare time I had, I spent trying to understand how it was that men had so much sway, and women so little.

It's fair to say, I suppose, that in my own small way I intended to change the world. But in the end I had that done for me.

We all did.

Chapter 1

A gentleman speaker at a suffragette meeting? Goodness, whatever would our Dad say? The wind worries at a corner of the poster above me as more women join the queue, chattering and laughing. There's always a good turnout on a cold night like this when folk are in need of a bit of entertainment and a warm-up.

A young man edges past, the brim of his bowler hat pulled low across his forehead against the wind. A glimmer of light drops onto him as he passes beneath the gas lamp. How handsome he is, with his dark brows and fine-etched lips. He must feel my eyes on him for he glances at me, and I turn away, embarrassed to have been caught so.

'Sorry I'm late, Maude.' Gertie pushes her way in to stand beside me. She turns up her collar and rubs her arms briskly with her hands. 'Blimey, it's cold!' she says, then gestures with her head to the poster above us. 'Should be worth a laugh, eh?'

I'm about to answer that I'm expecting more than just a laugh when the door creaks open, and we move forwards to file into the narrow, chair-filled hall. 'Come on, Gert,' I say as I make for the last two empty seats in the second row. 'We'll get a good view of the stage from here.'

Gertie settles herself, then turns to me. 'Have you told your parents yet? You know, about being a suffragette?'

I place my handbag on the bare wooden floor, and shake my head. 'I tried,' I tell her. Dad's words sound loud in my head. *What do them Pankhurst women want the vote for anyway? Ain't they got any menfolk to think for 'em, then? Clap 'em in jail, that's what I say, the whole bloomin' lot of 'em.*

'If you'd met my parents, you'd understand,' I sigh. 'The world could fall around them and they wouldn't change. Even my mother thinks the Movement's a disgrace.'

'Old folk always find change hard,' she says. She places her hand on my arm. 'You're going to have to tell them sometime, though. It'll be worse if they hear it from someone else.'

I sigh again. 'I know.'

I watch Clara Fotherington as she fusses round a group of women sitting at the front. She's young to be chairman, but she keeps our meetings in order, all right, despite her looks. I'm glad I don't have a long face like that, chalky white as if she's got consumption or something. For all her privileges and position in life, I can't help feeling a bit sorry for her.

When everyone's in, the hall is almost full. Miss Fotherington nods for the door to be closed, and the purple and green ribbons on her hat flutter as she steps lightly up the stairs and across the wooden stage to where a table has been placed. There are two empty chairs behind it. As she pulls back one of the chairs to stand in front of it, the hall falls quiet. Behind her is a picture of Emmeline Pankhurst, hung over the red velvet curtain at the back of the stage, and pinned above it is a banner with bold black letters on it: WOMEN'S SOCIAL AND POLITICAL UNION.

'Ladies and gentlemen,' Clara begins, leaning on the table and looking round. 'Or should I just say – ladies?' she smiles. We all laugh, eager with anticipation. 'We are lucky enough to have a gentleman speaker this evening.' I add my voice to the soft boos that circle the room, a thrill going through me at our daring. 'Now, now,' she remonstrates, 'he's a brave man to come here tonight, I think you'll agree, and he's here to speak out on our behalf, so please remain respectful.' Murmurings buzz like a swarm of bees, and I feel my heart quicken.

'Just one or two points before I introduce him. Firstly, I would like to say something about the acts of violence that are increasingly taking place outside the law, the fire down in Edward Street last week for example.' I exchange a look with Gertie. I knew that would come up. A right old blaze she said it was. You could see the smoke right up as far as the Emporium.

'I can't see anything wrong in strong action if it makes those in authority sit up and take notice,' a schoolmarm voice behind me calls. 'Surely any highlighting of The Cause has got to be good?'

Miss Fotherington shakes her head, which surprises me, for I would have thought she'd be all in favour of it. 'I know many of you think so,' she says, 'and, of course, each of us must do as her own conscience dictates. Exploits like these do get attention it's true, but people will simply stop taking us seriously if we act as common lawbreakers.' She turns her head, sweeping her gaze over us. 'You could even end up in one of His Majesty's establishments!' She smiles which breaks the tension, and there's laughter, but I don't join in. I'm too busy imagining what it would be like being thrown into prison, then having a tube stuck down your throat to force feed you. I feel sick just thinking of it.

'I also want to remind you about the rally in two weeks'

time at the far end of Ladies' Mile on Southsea Common. We need a good turn out, so please come if you possibly can.

She pauses, as if to signify the end of the announcements. 'Now, ladies,' she says, gesturing towards the wings of the stage, 'please welcome our speaker, The Men's Federation for Women's Suffrage's newest member, and my great friend – Mr Hubert Wells-Crofton!'

The stretch of curtain at the side of the stage twitches and a gentleman in his early twenties appears, and strides to the front of the platform. It's him! The young man from outside. I stare at him. We all do. I've never seen a suit cut as smart. Dark, it is, with not a single wrinkle in it, and his shirt's that white, it's almost glowing in the light from the gas lamps. His collar must've had a barrel load of starch in it too, the way it curves round stiff like that. I take in his clean-shaven cheeks, and his thick black hair that's been Macassared firmly into place. I suppose he thinks he's Lloyd George, or somebody, standing up there. He seems to look at each one of us in turn as he moves his gaze across us, and his eyes draw mine. Even from here, I can see they're blue, bright and clear like stained glass.

He rocks backwards and forwards on his heels, clasps and unclasps his hands and clears his throat. 'Good evening, ladies,' he calls in a deep, pleasant voice, and he smiles. A loud cheer goes up. How easily people are swayed by appearances! Where are the boos now? 'Let us get one thing clear straight away,' he continues, as he waits for the rustles and coughs to fade to silence. 'I am on your side!' There's uproar at his words, and a woman in the front row stands up and raises her fist in salute until he holds out his hand, and motions her to sit. He waits till the audience settles once more. I feel Gertie nudge me in the ribs, but I ignore her, absorbed by what is happening on the stage. 'We must decide on the most effective way forward,' he says. *We?* I can't help bristling at that. He might be a member of the Men's Federation for Women's Suffrage, and that's all to the good, but surely he doesn't think he's one of us?

'At Crofton's, we're intent on improving the lot of the women who work for us.'

Crofton's. I know them. They supply us at the Emporium. He's not quite so up in the world as I thought, then, if he's in trade. Suddenly a picture of Mr Arnold, our floor manager, appears in my mind, staring at me across the counter with those watchful eyes of his, and my heart plummets. What if this Mr Wells-Crofton tells him about me being a suffragette? He might use it against me. Women lose their jobs for far less, don't they?

'We already have the best wages for women in the area, *and* the shortest working hours, but it's just the beginning. I intend taking my campaign into other factories and places of work, for I believe that women deserve to be treated fairly, just as they deserve the right to vote in the parliamentary elections.' I watch him carefully, trying to get his measure. Sometimes it seems as if he looks directly at me, then his eyes sweep past and I wish my heart didn't beat so fast.

I turn round as a woman at the back gets up. Her shoulders are stooped beneath her shawl. 'You might pay the best wages,' she challenges, 'but they're still a pittance compared to what the men get, an' that's not much, neither. I know because my cousin works down in your factory. It's all right for you to stand up there with all your fine talk. I'd like to see you bring up a family on what you pay, young man.'

Silence falls on the room, and he looks uncomfortable. I'll give him his due, mind, he doesn't try to duck it. He stares straight back at her. 'I know it's not always easy for the working class,' he replies, but his choice of words make me stiffen. What could someone like him know about the working class? It seems that one minute I'm admiring him, and the next I'm annoyed by him.

'You must understand that it's not easy to run a successful business, especially one that is trying to make radical changes.

If we're not careful, there'll be no jobs at all, and what good would that do anyone?'

'Well, that's true enough,' the woman concedes, but she's still muttering as she sits back down.

'We, at Crofton's, realise that there is still a great deal to do.' He turns to walk slowly along the edge of the stage, reaches the end and turns back again. 'I ask for your patience, ladies. Old habits, as they say, die hard.' He stops centre stage and sweeps his eyes across us. 'But die they must,' he adds cheerfully.

When the time eventually comes for questions, he joins Miss Fotherington at the table. Question after question is asked and answered, until at last she reaches into a pocket of her skirt and takes out a fob watch. 'Time for just one more, please,' she says.

I rise from my seat, and hear a small sound of encouragement from Gertie. The blood rushes in a heat to my cheeks as the chairman points her finger at me. She has beautiful, dove-grey gloves, kid by the looks of them, not like my cotton ones. I tuck my hands into the folds of my skirt. 'Yes?' she says.

I feel the audience's eyes on me as surely as if their fingers were pressing against me, and take a deep breath. 'I wonder if our speaker would be so kind as to explain why a man should be interested in the emancipation of women,' I say in my best voice, the one I usually save for customers. 'What exactly *is* it that has brought him here tonight?' There is murmuring and a rustle of coats and skirts.

'What has brought me here tonight, Miss …?' He raises his eyebrows and looks at me. His eyes do not leave my own.

'Timms,' I say, sitting carefully back down.

'What has brought me here tonight, Miss Timms,' he says, his voice slow and measured, 'is *passion!*' Well, there's a communal intake of breath at that, and you could have heard a pin drop. 'A passion for justice,' he explains, and the room breathes again. 'To my mind,' he continues, looking at me all the while, 'the essential equality of all human beings — and therefore, of course, of the sexes — should be reflected within our legal and political systems. There is too much unnecessary suffering caused by ignorance and inequality. That is my interest, Miss Timms.' He lets go of my gaze then, and his eyes continue around the room. 'The fight,' he says, raising a hand above him, 'is for fairness.' He stabs his finger in the air. 'The fight is for justice.' He stabs it again. 'And … for dignity!'

When he finishes, he looks back at me, and for a moment his blue eyes lock onto my own, then the audience is rising, cheering, around me.

Chapter 2

The sun catches on the tramlines as I walk down Commercial Road. I move quickly to keep warm, making my way past piles of snow shovelled in close to the wall. Above the frosted roof tops of Portsmouth, chimney smoke rises straight as stair rods into the blue sky. Like our Walter always says, it's days like these that make you glad to be alive, even if it is cold enough to freeze your toes off if you stop for long.

I lengthen my steps as I make my way along the edge of the pavement, avoiding the patches of frost where the sun hasn't reached. My thoughts turn, as they keep doing of late, to Mr Wells-Crofton and the talk he gave last week. I push them away and try to concentrate instead on the evening ahead with Gertie. We're off to the Picture-House to see a Charlie Chaplin film that's showing. Charlie Chaplin's her favourite. I prefer *Tilly Tomboy* and films like that myself, though I don't mind, not really. I like anything that gives you a good laugh.

My reflection in a shop window makes me turn and I study myself, pleased with how I look, my tailored coat setting off the narrowness of my waist, and my auburn hair nice and full beneath my hat. I recently changed the ribbons round the brim to green ones and bunched them up at the front and, even if I do say it myself, it looks just the thing. Normally I'd have had dinner with the girls, but Mr Arnold's put me on earlies again. He's always doing things like that, for I don't think he likes me much. Well, I don't mind my own company, not a bit. In fact, I like being alone every now and then.

My thoughts drift back to the meeting last week at the Union Hall. Who'd have thought a man would be interested in women's suffrage? You could have knocked me down with a feather. When he walked on stage and it turned out it was the young man I'd admired outside, at first I was embarrassed, but I soon forgot about that when I listened to what he had to say. If we get more men on our side, it could really change things.

A row of horses stand patiently as their goods are unloaded, snuffing out curls of white air. One of them, a piebald, drops a pile of steaming dung beneath it, and the sharp hay-like scent of fresh manure lifts into the air. Not that I'm one who dislikes such a smell, not a bit, for it reminds me of the farm at Elmford where our Florrie and Tom have gone to live, and where I used to play as a child. For a moment I can feel the dry corn stalks beneath my boots. Crunch-crunch-crunch as we race across the field, my friend Livvy and me. Crunch-crunch-crunch, chasing butterflies. The sun's hot on the top of my head and I know it's time to go home, for my shadow's like a ball that runs with me. Mother will be wanting help with the dinner, but Livvy's running ahead and I can't let her beat me. I put on a spurt and overtake her, despite her legs being longer than mine, then we're between the trees and the shade is cool, like a breeze. Deeper and deeper we run, further and further into the woods.

A tram rattles past as I reach Peterson's Bookshop. I stop, for I always like to look at the titles on display in the window. The sign above the shop announces, in flaking gold lettering,

'Books Bought and Sold'. I glance up the road to the clock high on the Emporium Tower. It's still only twenty-five minutes past twelve, and I haven't got to be back till a quarter to one. Good. I've got time.

I tread up the worn stone step and push open the door. The bell jingles as I cross the threshold into the shop's dim interior, and the low sunshine strikes in through the window, lighting up the books on the wall beside me. I stand for a minute, breathing in the mustiness of the shop. I've always loved the smell of books.

'Is there anything I can help you with, my dear?' Mr Peterson's shaky voice comes from somewhere above me. I look up and see the old man perched at the top of a ladder, gazing at me over his horn-rimmed spectacles.

'I've just come for a look around, Mr Peterson, if you don't mind,' I say, closing the door behind me.

'Of course. Of course. You know your way about. New books to the front, second-hand to the back.'

'Yes, sir. Thank you.'

I move to the back of the shop. The light is dimmer here, as if the books are sending out shadows of themselves. I run my eyes along the titles that are stacked in neat alphabetical order on the shelves, letting my hand hover over a copy of Emily Brontë's *Wuthering Heights* before hooking my finger over the spine, and easing it out. I remember the first time I read it. Mother had given permission for me to stay on at school when I'd reached leaving age, to be a teacher's help-mate for a few months, and Miss Barton lent me her copy. The excitement I'd felt then comes back to me as I open the cover and flick through the pages, stopping here and there each time I catch sight of Heathcliff's name. Why can't there, I wonder, be Heathcliffs in real life?

I am so engrossed that I only dimly register the jingle of the bell and the soft thud of footsteps on the wooden floor.

My back is turned and although I can vaguely feel someone's presence, I don't take much notice for I'm too engrossed. I nearly drop the book when I hear a deep cough beside me and mutter a curse under my breath, but then I nearly drop the book again when I see who it is standing beside me, for it's *him*. I feel my cheeks begin to warm so that I'm glad of the gloom of the shop. He nods to me, lifting his bowler from his head, and I catch a glimpse of his thick, dark hair.

'I'm sorry I startled you. It's Miss Timms, isn't it?' He replaces his hat. 'Perhaps you don't remember me. Hubert Wells-Crofton. You asked a question of me at the suffragette meeting last week?'

Fancy him remembering my name. My heart beats fast. Why was he speaking to me? Had I angered him? Perhaps he'd seen me come in here and decided to take me to task? Well, I'm not apologising, if that's what he's come for! My eyes hold his. They seemed such a bright blue at the Union Hall, but today in the shadowy shop they're darker, more like the colour of dusk. He seems taller, too, than he did up on the stage, a good head and shoulders above me in fact; very business-like with his bowler hat and black woollen coat, his scarf a neat inch of red above his collar.

My mother's voice sounds in my head. *Now, don't you go talkin' to men as you don't know, my girl, that'll only spell trouble. It alus does.* But I push the sound of her away. I'm a modern woman, a suffragette, after all, and I make my own decisions. I don't take any nonsense from anyone, no matter what class they are.

'I was surprised to hear a man speaking on behalf of the concerns of women, Mr Wells-Crofton, that's all,' I tell him. 'It was very unusual.'

'Unusual perhaps, but surely not unique? Why, even in government the women's cause has its champions. Think of Keir Hardie, Miss Timms. Masculine support is growing don't you think? Miss Fotherington is quite certain that it is.'

Miss Fotherington! Jealousy twists me, as unreasonable as it is unexpected. Is she his young lady, I wonder? After all, she did introduce him as her 'great friend', didn't she? I watch as he draws off his gloves and places them in his pocket before reaching out his hand for my book. His fingers are long and slender, his nails manicured.

He steps a little closer and a smell of gentlemen's cologne shifts faintly on the air. 'Ah. Emily Brontë,' he says, looking down at the book I'm holding. 'You're fond of reading, Miss Timms?' Well, I should have thought that was obvious, seeing as how I'm standing in a bookshop, but I bite my tongue. 'And who is your favourite author, may I ask?'

'My favourite?' I stare up at him, a little startled by his interest. 'Well, I like reading the Collins Classics, and I'm fond of Mr Dickens and the Brontë sisters but, if I'm honest, I like Jane Austen best.' I reach out and take the book back.

'Jane Austen? Yes, yes, a wonderful writer. So much beneath the surface, don't you think?'

He pauses, stooping down on his haunches to look at the titles along the bottom shelf, and his coat falls open to the lowest of his coat buttons so that I can see the way his trousers tighten across his thighs. I imagine for a moment what it would feel like to touch him, and shameful desire rises in me.

'And do you read contemporary writers? D H Lawrence, for example?' he continues, looking up at me. I shake my head, feeling a little uneasy. Lawrence is that writer who's rather bold, isn't he?

'I can't say as I have, Mr Wells-Crofton,' I reply, snapping shut my copy of *Wuthering Heights*.

'You really should ignore the critics, and purchase some of his poetry.' I think of how few pence are left over each week from my wages for things such as new books, even with

Nelson's *Sevenpennies* on offer these days. I usually have to depend on the Public Lending Library, even though there's not much between those horrid brown covers that I really want to read, but what would the likes of Mr Wells-Crofton know about that? Judging from the quality of his coat, I wouldn't mind betting that he could buy a whole shelf of books if he wanted to.

The half-hour chime of the Emporium clock makes its way faintly through the shop. 'Goodness me, is that the time?' I say, moving away as he stands up. 'Please excuse me. I'll be late back to work if I'm not careful.'

'And where *is* your place of work, may I ask, Miss Timms?' he asks, walking with me to the counter with its brass till and tumble of books and papers.

'Mason's Emporium at the top of Commercial Road.'

'Ah, yes, I know it. We place some of our goods there.'

I picture him in his factory amongst his goods, the corsets they make, and turn away to hide the blush that insists on rising to my face.

Mr Peterson sees me and comes down from his ladder to shuffle stiffly across the shop. I pass him the copy of *Wuthering Heights*, and he sets the book carefully in the centre of a sheet of brown paper to wrap it before tying the package with a length of string.

'That's threepence then, miss, please,' he says finally, and I give him the sixpence I've taken from my purse. The till rattles as it opens, and he hands me three pennies back. 'There you are. I hope you enjoy your purchase.' I slide my change into the opening of my purse and pull on my gloves.

'Oh, I know I will. Thank you.'

I expect Mr Wells-Crofton to go back to look at the shelves, but he passes in front of me to open the door, and when I step out into the sunshine, he follows me out. 'I hope you will allow me to accompany you, Miss Timms?'

'Won't it be out of your way? Crofton's is at the bottom end of town, isn't it?' The door thuds as he shuts it behind us.

'It is,' he smiles, 'but it's such a splendid day, it's a pleasure to be out and about.'

As he escorts me, our conversation turns on little things, such as the weather, and do I think we're likely to get more snow? He walks as a gentleman should, at the edge of the pavement, but it pushes me into the shadows and it's not long before my foot slips on a patch of frost. Before I know it, he's reached out to steady me. When he leaves his hand beneath my elbow, my heart beat hard at the pressure and the warmth of it.

Too soon, we reach the alleyway leading to the staff entrance of the Emporium. 'Thank you,' I say, stopping and disengaging my arm. 'You'd better not come any closer. Mr Arnold doesn't like us to be accompanied near the shop.'

He smiles. 'Then I'll take my leave.' He looks up at the sky, still clear and bright above us. 'Make sure you take care when you step out this evening, Miss Timms. The frost is sure to deepen. Good day,' he says, and he turns away. He has only taken a step when he stops again, and my pulse flutters up into my throat. What *is* it about this man that affects me so?

'I wonder,' he says, 'if you would care to have tea one afternoon?' Me, have tea with the likes of him? 'We could discuss the Movement,' he says hurriedly. 'The Culver Hotel provides excellent afternoon refreshment. Do you know it?' I nod, my heart racing. I know it all right, for I've seen the ladies arriving there in their fine hats and fur tippets. 'Do you have a half-day?' he asks.

'I do ….' The words are out before I can stop them. 'Mondays, as a rule.' In fact, I have a whole day off each week but I don't tell him that, of course.

'Would next Monday suit you?' he asks, and his brows draw together when I don't reply immediately. 'A quarter past three?' I nod, and his face relaxes. 'Until next Monday then.' He tips his hat, a smile lifting the corners of his lips and reaching into his eyes, before he turns and joins the bustle of people on the pavement.

I watch him as he mingles with them, his athletic stride, and the way he's set his hat just a little to one side atop his head, giving him a distinguished air. But then the quarter hour sounds above me, and I turn down the alleyway, holding my coat close against the icy draught that sucks down between its high walls. If I don't hurry, I'll have Mr Arnold after me again.

Chapter 3

My stomach is like a butter churn as I walk up from the tram stop, my head bent against the wind. I don't know what will be worse, Mr Wells-Crofton not turning up or me having to sit there with him, with nothing more between us than a table. I'm so full of butterflies that I'm caught off-guard by the surge of pleasure that sweeps through me as I see him waiting outside the hotel, the hem of his coat flapping against his legs. He smiles as he catches sight of me, waits until I reach him, then we walk up the shallow steps together.

The light is already beginning to fade from the dull, overcast sky as the doorman lifts his gold-braided hat at us, and holds open the door. In the foyer, I stop and stare. I just can't help it, for I've never seen anything so grand. The floor is made of marble and there are matching pillars and giant ferns in pots, and there's a wide staircase with a pink carpet and shiny brass stair-rods. I take it all in so that I can tell Gertie about it when I get back. But, most of all, I stare at the glittering chandelier that hangs down above us on a chain. Why, there must be thousands of crystal jewels, all strung together. Like little necklaces, they are.

The doorman rings a bell on the desk and a maid in a white apron no bigger than a handkerchief, comes to take our coats. When she asks him for his hat, Mr Wells-Crofton tells her, very politely, that he'll keep hold of it himself, thank you. Then he steps back. 'After you, Miss Timms,' he says, and follows me as we're led through to the room where they are serving afternoon tea. Everywhere smells faintly of polish and a sweet, spicy aroma, cinnamon I think. It reminds me of Mother's fruit cake. More than half the tables in the tea-room are taken, mostly by groups of women in high white blouses and ramrod straight backs, though the large table in the centre of the room is occupied by a couple and three little girls with white dresses and blue sashes. In a corner, an elderly gentleman is playing a piano, his thin hair standing out from his head like a halo and his fingers fluttering like moths up and down the keys as he sends notes tinkling out across the room.

The maid leads us to a table by the fire. 'Will you be comfortable here, sir?' she asks.

Mr Wells-Crofton turns to me. 'Miss Timms? Does this table suit you? You won't be too hot?'

'No, no. I'll be glad of a warm-up. Thank you.' He pulls out my chair for me and I sit down. Then he sits down opposite me, and places his hat on a chair seat beside him. How smart he looks in his suit. I'm glad I put on my best blouse, the one with the Peter Pan collar and the row of pin-tucks at the side of the buttons. I sit up straight, fingering my cameo brooch, which makes me think of Arthur, for it was him as gave it to me. What would he say to see me here, I wonder? I can't help a little smile. He'd tease me most like, and say that I'm getting above my station again, and threaten to tell Mother, like he used to when we were children.

Waitresses glide between the tables with their trays. There's silver everywhere. Each table is set with it: cutlery,

17

jugs, sugar bowls, even the bowl on the window sill that contains a bunch of snowdrops. I let my gaze slip beyond, past the panes with their long damask drapes, to the people hurrying along the street, their heads bent against the wind, their faces grey and pinched. The weather's getting worse. The clouds have turned yellow-grey and so low now that they seem to press against the window. A gust of wind sweeps down the chimney, agitating the flames and curling them around the coals beside me. It'll be a cold journey back, and no mistake.

The conversation in the room is very restrained, not at all like the chatter I'm used to in the Emporium refectory. Mr Wells-Crofton looks across the table at me. 'What would you like, Miss Timms? A pot of tea and some sandwiches?' His words sound tidy and finished, as if he's clipped them with shears.

'That would be nice, thank you,' I reply in my best voice.

'Tea and sandwiches for two then, if you please, and some cake as well I think,' he says to the maid, and she returns almost immediately, placing a teapot on a stand before setting the cups carefully into the saucers. Then she brings a china stand with sandwiches on one tiered plate, and cakes on another above it.

When she has turned away, Hubert says, 'Will you pour?'

I hesitate. Goodness, what if I spill tea over the white tablecloth? Then I tell myself not to be so silly and concentrate on pouring the tea carefully into the fragile china cups before adding a splash of milk in the centre of each. It clouds darkly before it settles, and leaves a little circle of milk skim on the surface.

'Tell me about the Emporium,' Hubert says when I have handed him his cup. 'Do you like the people there?'

'Oh, they're nice enough,' I say then make a face, 'with one or two exceptions.'

'Oh, yes? And who are they?' Hubert takes the tongs and lifts a lump of sugar, letting it tumble down the side of his cup into his tea.

'Well … there's young Fred Johnston,' I begin. 'He's the same age as our Walter, more or less, but you'd never think it the way he acts. To be honest, he gets on my nerves sometimes, with all his silliness. And there's old Mr Arnold, of course – sour as a crab apple he is, though to be fair I suppose he's got to be strict, seeing as how he's got so many of us beneath him. Mostly the people there are all right,' I say. 'We have a laugh together, and that's what matters, especially Rose and me.'

'So you enjoy your work?'

'Enjoy it?' I look at him in surprise. 'Why, of course I do.'

'Yes, of course you do,' he repeats, then pauses. 'And what is it exactly that you like about it?' he continues, his spoon clinking against the side of his cup as he stirs.

'Oh, I don't know.'

Hubert smiles. 'You must know.'

Will it sound stupid if I tell him? I take a sip of tea before answering. 'Well … what I love best is the materials and the threads,' I say, looking down at my plate, then up again. 'I've always loved to stitch, and you wouldn't believe the colours you can get these days. Every shade of the rainbow, and more besides. It's them – the colours. Sometimes I think they're like words in a poem ….' I hear my voice tail away and risk a glance at him. He's staring back at me, his eyes dark with shadows in the failing light. I expect him to laugh. I know plenty as would. But he just says, 'More tea, Miss Timms?' and pulls my empty cup towards him.

'No, no!' Before I know what I'm doing, I've reached out and pulled it back. 'If we both pour from the same pot, there'll be ginger twins in the family!' Well, he throws back his head and laughs when I say that, so loud that people turn their heads to frown at us. But his laughing makes me laugh too, even though my cheeks are warm. 'Haven't you heard that afore?'

'No, indeed I have not!'

'My mother's always saying it. I suppose you think it's daft?'

He smiles at me. 'Very,' he says, and we laugh again.

A porter comes in and shovels more coal from the brass scuttle onto the fire, then he pulls a cord by the door and flat electric light floods us, making the shadows disappear, but I can't help wishing he'd switch it off again, for firelight's much more friendly for talking. I tell Mr Wells-Crofton how we had the electric installed at the Emporium last year, and he says they hope to get it in the factory before much longer, for it's a much superior light for his people to work by, he says, than the gas they have at present. I reach for the pot-holder and hinge back the lid of the teapot. Steam lifts in little swirls as I add hot water.

'Where is your home, Miss Timms?' he asks.

'Elmford,' I say, settling the pot back on its stand.

'Elmford! But, that's nearer Southampton than Portsmouth. Do you travel in each day by train?'

'It's not that far really, but actually I don't live at home any more. I'm in lodgings in Southsea – very respectable ones,' I assure him quickly. 'I've made friends with a girl there, Gertie. She has a room opposite mine. Actually, it was her as was with me at the Union Hall when you were speaking.' I drop my eyes to stare at the fancy blue band round the top of my cup. I hadn't meant to mention the Union Hall for fear of letting my tongue run away with me on the subject of women and rights. But I needn't have worried, for his reply takes us in a different direction altogether.

'You're lucky, being independent. I'm still living with the

parents.' I look at him in surprise. Him, envying me? And a grown man like him, living at home? 'I've tried to get away,' he smiles, 'but sometimes it feels as if I'm caught up in cobwebs. The more I struggle, the more bound-up I become.'

'Where do your parents live?' I ask after a while.

'Hilsea.'

I know Hilsea a little. It's on the outskirts of Portsmouth. There have been a lot of new houses built up there. I saw them when Gertie and I went for a walk one afternoon. Big, they are, and worth a mint, I shouldn't wonder. The sort of place I'd probably be working in, if I'd have done what Mother wanted and gone into service. If he lives in one of those, then the factory must be doing well, that's all I can say.

'Actually,' Hubert continues, 'Father would have preferred a house in the town, but Mother thinks a larger house on the outskirts is better. Says there's more room for her committee meetings.' He grimaces. 'Well, she's right from that point of view. There are always droves of people coming and going.' He pauses. 'My mother, you see, has … *aspirations*, Miss Timms.' He says the word in a stage whisper, and I know it's meant as a joke, but his words snag at me. Does she have aspirations for Hubert too? A girl perhaps? That's what happens in their class, isn't it?

'Oh dear,' is all I can think of to say, and for some reason it makes him laugh. I like it when he laughs, his even teeth gleaming in the brightness of the electric light. 'Do you work in the factory, or do you have an office?' I ask.

'Both. I have an office, but it's in the factory itself. I share it with my brother, Aylmer, though we each have our own desk, of course. It's on the factory floor, and there is a big window that separates us from the workers. We can see them – and they can see us, so any problems can quickly be sorted out. It's a good arrangement.'

'And do you like *your* work?' I ask after a pause, surprised at how easy it's becoming to talk to him.

'Do you want an honest answer, or the one I usually give?' His eyes hold my own.

'An honest one, of course. I've never seen much use for the other kind.'

'Well, honestly then.' He frowns. 'Let's just say that it wasn't my choice to go in with Father and Aylmer. Running the factory isn't at all what I'd envisioned doing with my life. But when Ralph left, the old man needed me … I couldn't let him down.' He looks beyond my shoulder in a faraway stare.

Well, I don't think I would stay, not if I didn't have to. 'Is Ralph your brother?' I ask.

'Yes.' His eyes focus on me again. 'Ralph's the eldest, then there's me, then Aylmer. Aylmer's the natural businessman in the family. Takes after Father.'

'And you don't?'

He hesitates. 'No,' he says abruptly. 'Not much.'

'What's your brother … Ralph, doing now?' Hubert raises his eyebrows at me, and I feel a blush rising to my cheeks. 'I'm sorry. I didn't mean to pry.'

'No, I don't mind. Ralph paints. Pictures. Very good pictures, as a matter of fact.' He shifts in his seat, glancing across his shoulder as if he's afraid he'll be overheard. 'I shouldn't tell you, we've only just met after all, but there was an incident. Unfortunately, Father has disowned him.'

I think of my own brothers, of Arthur at sea, of Walter a guard now down at the railway, and of little Horace who died. I can't imagine us disowning them, no matter what they'd done. No, no matter what. I'm quiet for a moment, for I don't know what to say.

Hubert picks up the tier of sandwiches and cakes, and holds it out to me. I take a tiny white triangle with thin green cucumber peeping out and put it carefully on my plate. Why it is that gentry always take off the crusts when they're the tastiest bits? And goodness, wherever in February have they managed to find cucumbers for sale?

I take a small bite, then place the sandwich back down on my plate, wiping an imaginary crumb from the corner of my mouth with my napkin as I see a lady on another table doing. 'What would you have done then?' I ask, 'if you hadn't had to go into the business with your father?'

He rubs his chin with his hand. 'What would I have done?' He smiles. 'Oh, I don't know … I used to want to go into politics, and I once had a fancy for the Royal Navy. Saw myself sailing the high seas.'

I feel a rush of pride. 'Our Arthur's in the Navy!'

'Arthur?'

'My brother.'

'Ah. Lucky cove.' He leans back in his chair.

'Lucky for him, perhaps. Not so lucky for us. It means we hardly get to see him any more. Once or twice a year maybe. He's always off around the world somewhere or other.'

Hubert sighs. 'Ah, but think what a time he must be having, seeing all those places one only usually reads of!' He frowns. 'Sometimes it feels as if I'll never get away from home. I think it will take a war to make them let go of me!'

'A war!'

'Yes, a war. Why not?' He shuffles his chair in closer. 'Actually, it's perfectly possible. Look at the situation in Ireland, there's plenty of conflict there.'

'Ireland? But that's all about Home Rule. Surely that's a different problem?'

'*Is* it? But, why? Conflict is conflict, after all, and there's unease everywhere, you know. Take the Balkans, for example. There are massive changes going on there.' He leans forwards to place his elbows between the cups and plates. 'The newspapers say that Germany's building up her armaments,' he continues. 'Did you know that?' I shake my head. 'Well, you can't tell me that's innocent!' His voice is excited. 'And what are we doing? Cutting down! It's utter madness! If we're not careful, we'll play right into Germany's hands.'

'*Will* we?'

'But, of course!' His blue eyes have paled in the light from the electric bulbs, and are now almost grey. I've never known eyes to change shade like his. 'Show them the slightest weakness, and they'll take advantage. Bound to.'

A waitress stops at our table. 'Can I get you more tea, sir? Madam?'

He sits back. 'Miss Timms?'

I shake my head. 'No, thank you.'

'Nor me.' He looks back at the girl. 'It seems we have enough, thank you.'

'Very good, sir.'

When she has left, Hubert leans forwards again. 'They're almost certainly training up more soldiers,' he continues. 'And what are we doing? Nothing. Not a thing! In fact, our own numbers are falling! Germany's thick as thieves with Austria, you know. Pretty chummy with Italy, too, come to that.'

I picture the map of the world that was on the wall at school, all the countries of Europe with their different colours, and our Empire marching across it all in a uniform shade of pink. It's unthinkable that it should change. 'Even if that's true,' I venture. 'Germany wouldn't dare to invade, surely?' Hubert's eyes burn into mine as he raises his dark eyebrows, his lips lifting in a smile.

'Ah, but that's my point precisely, Miss Timms. It's my opinion that she would! I think all the governments of Europe are getting worried. Even Belgium's introduced conscription, you know, and she's neutral!' Hubert leans back again. 'Yes, I'd say that war was very possible indeed!' I shudder, despite the warmth of the fire.

'I'm sorry. What am I thinking of, worrying you like this?' Hubert lifts the cake stand towards me again. 'You mustn't take too much notice of me. I'm always running on about things, and what does a clerk in a factory know about it, after all? Now, won't you have another?'

I take a cake. It's a little fancy thing, with a pink sugar confection in the shape of a flower on the top. I nibble at the edge, sweetness rushing over my tongue, as war and Hubert Wells-Crofton jostle for dominance in my thoughts.

Chapter 4

A chime strikes and the clock in the narrow hall of Solent View Lodging House tells me with its bent hands and faded roman numerals that it's a quarter to eleven already. I walk quickly towards the porch, passing through shafts of red, blue and yellow light that drop down from the stained-glass window above.

Hurrying down the shallow stone steps, I turn into the breeze that eddies down the treeless road from the seafront. When I reach the pleasure gardens, a sudden gust catches at the underbrim of my hat, lifting it against its pins, and I raise a hand to steady it, for it'll pull my hair out of shape if I'm not careful and I didn't spend a good twenty minutes this morning on it for nothing, that's for sure.

I think of Hubert as I walk, for we've met several times now, and we're even on first-name terms, despite the fact that he's from his world and I'm from mine. There are folk who might say it was wrong for us to be friends, and they could well be right, but the fact is I like being with him. He makes me feel *alive*, somehow. It's almost as if, when we're together, there are colours that weren't there before.

The sound of the waves surging into the shingle and the screaming of seagulls fades as I wind my way towards Portsmouth Town railway station, and soon I'm passing into the shadows of the draughty railway bridge where my footsteps echo until they're lost in the rumble of a train as it crosses the metal girders above me. The old woman who sells newspapers by the railings opposite the station entrance looks up at me as I stop.

'That's an 'alfpenny then, love,' she says. The wind ruffles the pages of the paper as I pick it up, and I drop a coin into the rusty tin she's set on the ground, tuck the paper under my arm and move towards the ticket office. My heart lifts as I cross the threshold into the station, for it always seems like I'm in a different country here, with the sounds mixing up and echoing in the high ceiling above me. They could be speaking Russian, for all I know. It makes me think of all the places Hubert's told me he's visited. He's even been to Italy, for a holiday with his grandparents. And there's me, never been further than the Isle of Wight, and that only once. The loudspeaker starts as I walk across the marble floor to take my place in the queue. Yes, I'd like to travel. Perhaps I will one day, when I've saved enough.

I wonder if Hubert will ever come home with me? The trouble is, every time I think of introducing him to Dad and Mother, my insides churn as if I'm making butter for an army, for I know what they'll think. I haven't even told them about him yet, and I should really, for we've been walking out for over a month, only ....

'Next!' An elderly clerk sticks his face against the wire grille and stares at me.

'Return to Elmford, please,' I say and place my money on the wooden shelf, watching as a silver sixpence separates itself from the rest of the coins and rolls beneath the grille. The clerk puts out an inky finger to silence it, then quickly counts the rest of my money before sweeping it into his till. He stamps a return ticket, pushes it back to me, and I walk towards the steps that lead up to the main platform.

The train's already in, and soon the shadows of the station are sliding away, transforming into the backs of sunlit offices and shops. As the train gradually picks up speed, the buildings slip by faster and faster, rushing past the way the water does in the millstream at home. I lean back against the hard slats of the carriage seat.

What would Hubert think of my family? Would he mind Mother and her sharp ways, her big, red hands? Or Dad's mill clothes, patched everywhere, and grey where the flour's worked itself into the weave? And would he expect china cups? He'd be disappointed if he did! Dad'd have more than a bit to say about *him*, I'm sure, for he'd know straight away that Hubert wasn't one of us, what with his nice clothes and his manners and all. And that's not counting his voice, neither. If there's one thing Dad can't abide, it's a posh voice like Hubert's. I sigh. Oh, yes, there'd be plenty said, all right.

The sun falls through the window and I close my eyes, let hedges and trees flicker their shadows across me. I turn my face to feel the warmth of the sun through the glass and imagine I'm walking up the path and round the back of the cottage.

There's washing boiling in the copper, as there always is, and I stop to breathe in the smell of it. Mother's there, of course, and I give her a kiss then introduce him, say something like 'This is Hubert, Mother, as I've told you about', though I haven't yet, of course. I cross to the living room and take off my hat. Then I show Hubert our Arthur's photograph and say would he like to go up to the churchyard after dinner and see Horace's grave, for I never like to leave our Horace out, even now. A pot's simmering on the range, rabbit I expect if Tom's been up, and I do the potatoes and make a cup of tea, persuade Mother to sit with us for a few minutes by the range. I don't suppose Hubert's ever eaten rabbit stew. He'd be more used to lamb cutlets and Dover sole, I should have thought. I make him take Dad's chair and I sit back at the table and mind my p's and q's, don't take off my boots as I usually do to push my feet into the bright rag rug by the stove. That rug's got all the shades of red you could imagine. There's even some from one of Horace's little shirts. Them bits are my favourites, though I never, ever, tread on them. I can't. I know every part of that rug, for didn't I help Mother make it after Horace died, to keep her mind off things? We used bits from old cast offs, and cuts Mrs Lawson gave me to take home from the ends of the rolls. Took us all winter, it did.

The train hoots like a banshee and I open my eyes with a start, feel myself pushed gently forwards as the train begins to brake. The wheels squeal against the track as we slide slowly towards our little village station.

'Mornin', Miss Timms.' The stationmaster acknowledges me with a nod, lifts his fingers towards his cap in that half-hearted gesture of his before striding past me down the platform. Whenever I see him, I can't help but remember the time he set his dog on me and Arthur, just for taking a couple of apples from his precious tree. I've never forgiven him, and I've often been tempted to show I've still got the scars, except it would mean lifting my petticoats which wouldn't be seemly.

'Mr Coggins,' I say curtly and nod at his retreating back, then glance towards the ticket office where I hope to see Walter. I always look forward to seeing him, even though we argue like cat and dog sometimes. A youth in a porter's uniform struggles with a large leather trunk, but I can tell from the stoop of his shoulders it's not him. Mr Coggins turns and strides back towards me. 'Is Walter not on this morning, then?' I ask.

He ignores me as he looks towards a group of young men who have stopped to chat by the open carriage doors.

'M-o-v-e along there, if you please!' he calls to them. Then he turns to me. 'No,' he says. 'I've put your Walter on afternoons. There's extra work with all them troop trains they be sendin' through.' He sniffs and looks up and down the carriages before glancing back at me. 'An' you can tell that brother of yours, miss, if you care to, that in future there'll be no excuses for being late.' He moves off and slams a door shut before blowing his whistle for the train to start again.

I lift my chin and turn to walk along the platform and through the white wicker gate that swings by the side of the station wall, shivering as the sun dips behind a cloud and passes its shadow over me. Then I'm walking down the lane between hazel trees that drip catkins, long and blousy with pollen. Beneath them, the grassy bank is brushed with primroses, soft yellow clots, looking like little drops of cream. I reach them and, drawing off my gloves, stoop down and begin to pick, run my fingers gently down the fragile stems into the cool green heart of each plant, moving along the bank until my hand is full. I select six large tongue-shaped leaves, fresh and darkly grooved, arranging them so they overlap around the edge of the flowers before I bend my head to breathe in the pale, delicate scent.

Mother stands at the sink in the scullery, her hands deep in cold water and looks at the flowers in my hand.

'They're for Horace,' I say quickly, then give her a kiss on her smooth cheek. 'I got them from the lane. You should see them, Mother. Such a sight, they are.' I bend my head to breathe their scent again, feel the petals brush, cool, on my skin. 'Do primroses make you think of things, Mother?' I ask.

'What sort of things?' She pushes a sheet beneath the water and pulls it up again, down and up, down and up.

'New things,' I say above the sound of the water as it races back into the sink. I think of Hubert, and the way his eyes crease when he smiles. 'Beginnings … you know, like everything's just waiting to happen, full of promise.'

'What nonsense you do talk, girl. Now put 'em in water, for goodness' sake. Primroses never lasts long at the best of times.' She nods to the high, deep shelf at the end of the kitchen, and a wisp of her hair, the colour of morning ashes, escapes from its pin to hang down the side of her face. She pushes it away with the back of her hand. 'You can have one of them old treacle tins.'

I stand on tiptoe and reach up, pulling the squat, empty tin towards me, then lean across Mother to drum water into it, liking the heavy coldness as it fills. 'I saw old Mr Coggins up at the station,' I say. 'He was on about our Walter being late.'

'That boy'll be late for 'is own buryin',' she says, pushing hard against the cloth.

'I heard that!' Walter's voice calls out cheerfully from the living room.

I walk through the open doorway, the flowers drooping against the rusty lip of the tin as I move. 'You all right then, Walter?'

''Course I am. You?'

I nod absently as I place the flowers beside the picture of Arthur in his sailor's uniform. I can't help wishing that we'd got a picture of Horace, too, for I can hardly remember his face any more. I don't think I'll ever forget that laugh of his, though. It was the sort that made you join in, whether you wanted to or not. Sometimes, when I'm here, I think I can hear it still.

Arthur's dark eyes stare at me across the space that separates us, past the invisible camera tripod with its heavy black cloth, into our small living room where I stand. He holds his head high, chin thrust out to challenge the world, the pale slash of his cap at a jaunty angle on his head. An ache settles in my chest as I realise how much I miss him.

'I've put them next to Arthur for a while,' I call to Mother, unpinning my hat and hanging it on the peg by the front door. I return to the scullery to stand and watch her for a moment. 'We can take them up to the churchyard after dinner if you like.'

'Flowers as means new beginnings, on a child's grave?' She throws my own words back at me and it's as if she's hit me, for it's not what I meant at all. 'Besides,' she continues, heaving the sheet from the wide stone sink onto the wooden board beside it, 'it depends whether I finishes this lot in time.' Water rushes back as she squeezes, her hands red as skinned rabbits against the length of twisted white cotton.

Dad pushes aside his dinner plate and scrapes back his chair, even though Walter and me are still eating. 'You goin' ter read me some of that paper you brought up then, or what?' he says, walking across the room to the window that overlooks the street. He picks up the paper from where I put it on the sill, and tosses it to me. I'm surprised he hasn't made me get up and get it for him, for it's usually, 'Get this', or, 'Do that', all the time with him. The newspaper flutters through the air and lands beside my plate as he sits down in the furthest of the two straight-backed armchairs at the far end of the range. He leans forward to swing open the tiny black door and stares into the remains of the morning's fire. Then he lifts the lid and pours in a shovel full of coal until the embers are dulled and barely red at all.

Next to me, at the table, Walter cuts a slice of bread and sops up the remains of the gravy that lines the edge of his plate. I narrow my eyes at him, remembering the stationmaster. 'Oh,' I say as I open the paper. 'I almost forgot. I've got a message for you.' Walter raises his eyebrows as he holds the sodden crust in mid-air and stares at me. 'From Mr Coggins.'

'What's he doin', sending messages?'

'Do you want it or not?' I say, slipping into the tone I use for the customers at the Emporium.

'Ooh, listen to her. 'Do you want it or not?" Walter says in an affected voice, mimicking me.

'You want ter watch that there voice o' yours, girl,' Mother joins in, coming through from the scullery. 'Folks'll think you're puttin' on airs. No-one likes a body who puts on airs. Not round here at any rate.'

'I'm not putting on airs!' Her words make me feel like crying. 'I'm no different now to how I ever was.'

'Except you are, my girl, sometimes. Walter's right. I expect it's that job o' yours that's done it. You'll be thinking you're too good for the likes of us before long.'

'No! I never would, Mother. Never!' I say, but I feel a small knot of shame somewhere deep inside me and think perhaps it's true what they say. A little.

'Well, you see as you don't. There's more important things than goin' up in the world.'

'Family, for one,' Dad chips in. I turn to look at him, but he's got his eyes shut.

'I know that,' I tell him.

'Well, just see as you do, girl.'

I look across at Walter and see he's enjoying the trouble he's caused, and my palm itches to slap the smile from his face.

'Well, d'you want it or not?' I say.

'What?'

'The message.'

'Not much.'

'You'll get it anyway.' I lean towards him. 'He says don't be late.'

33

'Bloody cheek! Bastard.'

Mother frowns and Dad raises his voice, and I'm glad that he's the one in trouble now and not me. 'That's enough of that language, boy,' he says. 'Just you remember that you comes from a decent home, not like some o' them lads you likes to mix with.' Walter shrugs and carries on eating. If only I could ignore Dad the way he does.

'I've a good mind to be late on purpose now,' he says, but he stuffs the last remaining piece of crust into his mouth and grabs the porter's uniform jacket he's hung carefully on the back of his chair, then smoothes back his tumble of dark curls from his forehead. At the door, he lifts the latch and pulls, pausing as he looks back at me, and I hear the soft clop of horses' hooves through the gap. For a moment, his face loses the cocky look it usually wears. 'You comin' up a bit early, then?' he asks me. I remember his taunts, and say nothing. 'I'll show you a redstart's nest if old Coggins ain't watchin',' he tempts, and he gives me that wonderful smile of his. Well, I never could resist his smile, so I nod, and he closes the door behind him, the clock pouring its ticks into the silence he leaves behind.

'What about that paper?' Dad growls at me. 'The hooter'll go before you even starts if you're not careful.' I pick up the newspaper and open it, rustling the pages to break the quiet that settles so easy on the early afternoon here in Elmford, and run my eyes down the front page.

'There's a bit about Mr Asquith,' I begin.

'What about 'im?'

'He's been made Secretary for War.'

Dad grunts and shifts in his seat. 'War! That's all everyone's on about these days. Secretary for this and secretary for that. Waste of the country's bloody money if you asks me.' He puts his head back and closes his eyes. I pause.

'Go on, girl. I'm listenin', even if he's not,' Mother says.

'I'm listenin'!'

I turn the page and lean my elbows on the table. 'It says that he left London yesterday for East Fife and that there's going to be a bye-election ....' I look over the top of the paper and watch as Dad's head begins to droop, let my eye drop to the next headline. 'Would you rather hear about Lloyd George then, Dad?'

'Eh?' His head jerks.

'Lloyd George.'

'What about him?'

'He's had a bad throat.'

''As 'e? 'E wants to try some real work, then. That'd soon cure 'is bleedin' sore throat.'

'Anyway, it says he's much better today and his voice is returning to normal, so that's all right.' I stop to look at the advertisement Crofton's have put in for their new corset design. Wouldn't mind one myself, especially the one with the lace trim, though not at that price. Suddenly, I have an image of Hubert handling such items in the factory, and I blush.

A soft snore escapes the chair and I let my eyes drift on down the page. 'Ah, this is more like it. Now, this is what I call news. Eighty per cent of women voted at a State election in Illinois.' I raise my voice. 'The sooner we get the vote here, the better, don't you think, Dad?'

Mother stands up and begins to stack the plates. 'Shh, for heavens' sake, girl,' she says to me. 'Can't you find nothin' else to read to 'im? You know how 'e takes on when you starts on about them suffragettes.' I avoid her eyes, for I still haven't told them that I'm a suffragette myself now. I sigh. Do other girls have such trouble telling their parents things, I wonder?

'He's asleep, Mother,' I say. 'Don't worry, you know when he sleeps, it's the sleep o' the dead.' Another snore makes me look across at him, slumped, his chin bent to his chest, and suddenly I see how his hair's beginning to thin and I have to push away the rush of tenderness I feel, for it's safer to hate my father than to love him. You know where you are then. It's when he's being affectionate that it's dangerous, for it makes you relax, and then he's in there with his sharp comments, quick as lightning, wounding you.

'Besides,' I say to Mother, pointing my chin in the air, 'he shouldn't take on. It's high time women had greater rights.' I pause, and my heart thumps as I dare myself to continue. 'We've even got men on our side now, you know.' Mother reaches for my plate and slips it beneath Dad's. 'I'll do that,' I say, rising to my feet and taking the plates from her. The knives and forks clink loudly together. 'It's going to happen, you know.' I watch her as she leaves the table and moves towards the scullery, reaching behind her to re-tie her drooping apron strings. 'You can see that it's right, can't you Mother? If we get the vote, we'll be equal won't we, and men'll *have* to listen to what we say. And if they'll only listen, things can change, can't they?' I hear myself sigh. 'Mother?'

She turns back then to face me and places her hands on her hips. 'An' who d'you think's goin' to run things in the homes if women 'as the vote and starts gettin' above themselves?' she says, keeping her voice low. 'If women starts actin' as menfolk an' gets out in the world, who'll cook the dinner an' wash the clothes then? An' if them things don't get done, nothin' else can get done neither, can it? No, it'll just be the start of a lot o' trouble, my girl, you wait an' see. It'll turn the world upside down, an' no mistake.' She pushes a hand across her forehead, and as I stack the rest of the plates together and follow her into the scullery, a shrill wail sounds from the Elmford Flour Mill and Dad starts to his feet.

'Remember how Florence put her wedding flowers on the grave?' I say to Mother. 'It don't seem a year ago since her and Tom got married, do it?' I bend back to sit on my heels. The sun has crept round the tower to slant across the churchyard and we kneel each side of the small grave, the headstone between us. *Born February 6th 1905, died November 17th 1912*, it says. Beneath the name *Horace George Timms,* are the words *In the Arms of Jesus.* That was Mother's choice and they chiselled the letters sharp and deep into the white granite like she wanted, 'So they'll last,' she'd said. No mention of what took him, of course, the diphtheria that choked him till no breath could get in, nor out. I bend my head and scissor the pair of shears I've taken from the shed, and the sweet green smell of grass lifts into the churchyard air.

Mother pulls at the weeds, but I see the brief shake of her grey head as I settle the treacle tin more firmly against the foot of the headstone. A movement catches at the corner of my eye and I look up to where an early swallow's looping round and round, the tower behind sliced across with the afternoon sun.

'So, how is she, Mother?' I ask, snipping again at the grass and moving the blades slowly and carefully up the sloping sides of the small grave.

'How's who?'

I'm never quite sure about Mother sometimes, whether she's deliberately slow or not, for at times she's sharp as an axe blade. 'Florrie,' I say.

'Better.'

'Good. Tell her I'll try to stop by and see her next time I come.'

Mother nods. 'You do that, my girl,' she says. 'Must be lonely over at that farm all day, without so much as a sight nor sound from anyone till Tom gets in. She's comin' home to 'ave the baby at any rate,' she says, tugging at a dandelion, easing its deep tap root with a broken knife. It gives suddenly and she starts backwards, its severed roots still held fast in the soil of the grave. I watch the gentle way she pushes back the dark, moist soil with her fingers and pats it down.

'Is she?' I say. 'What does Dad think?'

Mother snorts. 'You know your father,' she says, 'never happy unless he's complainin'. But it's like I tells 'im, for once it's not about 'im.'

I clip at the grass that grows thickly at the base of the grave. 'Yes, tell her I'll go and see her,' I repeat. 'And I thought ....' The words fail to come and Mother gives me one of her sharp looks. 'You thought what, girl?' she asks.

'There's someone ... a friend ...,' I begin, watching her out of the corner of my eye.

A robin lands beside me and bobs its head in a quick movement before flying up to a low holly branch. 'Someone from the Emporium, is it?'

'No, no-one from work.' I pause before I begin to wipe the blades clean of grass. 'It's someone I met at the Union Hall – where they have talks and things.'

'What sort of talks?'

'You know, politics and the like.'

'Hmph. I suppose you means them suffragettes. You don't want ter get mixed up in that lot, my girl.'

I close the shears and stand up to look at the neat green mound and at the primroses nestling in the shade of the headstone. 'Anyway, his name's Hubert Wells-Crofton, Mother,' I say quickly, pleased that I've said his name at last. I reach out to help her up. 'There, that looks much better, don't it?'

Chapter 5

Summer's come, and everywhere's hot as an oven. It's warming up in Europe too, only in a different sense, since that Archduke Franz-Ferdinand from Austria was assassinated over in Serbia. It's all the menfolk can talk about these days, how there's sure to be a war. It's all anyone can talk about. The worry of it buzzes around my head, like a fly caught in our shop window.

Normally, we're not allowed the door open, but Mr Arnold propped it ajar this morning, and it hasn't been closed all day. I heave the last of the stack of bales to the shelf above me, and feel a trickle of sweat run down my back between my shoulder blades. I hope against hope it won't mark, for sweat stains are hard to get out of a good dress like this. The sun's gone round, and I can tell without looking at the clock, that it's getting late. The inside of the haberdashery department on the ground floor of Mason's Emporium is dim as an underwater cave.

As I walk back across the floor, I wonder how much longer the hot weather can last. I've never known a summer like it, the air inside the shop not moving at all for weeks on end. I wish for the hundredth time I was down by the water's edge, with a fresh breeze fanning my face. I wish, too, that I was away from all the gossip. I don't mind the political workings of it, mind. In fact, I like to listen to the men talk about that, and I often wish that I could join in. No, it's the bragging and the boasting of the lads that I can't stand. It drives me to distraction, for it's as if they all *want* it to happen.

Fred Johnston's no exception, talking all the time of how he'll join up if war's declared, though anyone less likely to make a solider, I've yet to meet. There he is now, standing at the top of the steps that lead up to the Gentlemen's Department, being idle again, his normally doughy face flushed pink by all this heat. I'd like to give him a good talking to, for I can't abide people who leave all the work to others, but it's too hot and today I just can't be bothered, not even for a filthy look. I slip behind the counter and begin the last tasks of the day, drawing out the tiny narrow wooden drawers with their glass fronts, tidying the reels of cotton and packets of needles. I usually take my time when I'm sorting the embroidery silks into their colours, but today I just tuck a skein of 'midnight' next to the row of 'peacock blues', and fumble the drawers back into their slots. When I finally reach for the tin of polish and scoop up a blob of brown wax the size of a penny, it runs off my cloth onto the counter like melted toffee.

'Miss Timms!' Fred beckons me urgently and I can't help wishing he'd put that much energy into his work. I give him my best frown as I look across, but I have to feel a bit sorry for him when I see the perspiration that's started to run on his face. It can't be comfortable to be his size in this heat. 'I think it's your young man outside,' he calls in a stage whisper, then points through the open door. Through the display of hats in the window, I see Hubert dressed in his dark suit and bowler hat, pacing up and down on the pavement. I suppose Fred's right, he is my young man, for we've been out lots of times together, to music hall shows and talks and even to the dances on the pier, but he's never kissed me properly or anything like that so I'm not sure if we're really walking-out or not. 'You'll be in for it if Mr Arnold sees him,' he says, glancing over his shoulder as he speaks, and a look of delight comes on his face. 'You ought to tell him to be more careful, miss.'

'I'd say that was my business, Fred, wouldn't you?' I say, circling hard with my duster along the counter.

The bell begins the three shrill rings that means it's closing time, and I give the counter a final rub before tucking the tin and the duster on a shelf beneath. Then I scarper, quick as I can, to get my things from the cloakroom. I snatch my hat off my peg and position it on my head, slipping the pin out from the ribbon at the side and pushing it back through, catching just enough hair beneath to secure it. Rose comes in, wanting a chat, but I tell her that I can't stop, and walk quickly out of the back door. The heat hits me like a shovel, but then I'm turning down the alley to where Hubert's waiting.

'I thought you'd never finish. Come on,' he says, drawing my arm through his as we set off down Commercial Road. 'We're going to see the Fleet.' I have to almost run to keep up, and I bend my head so the brim of my hat can keep the sun off my face a bit. How is it he can wear a thick jacket like that and not break out in a single bead of sweat? The rumble of a tram makes me look up and I see from the sign at the front that it's heading down to the docks. It slides past us on the narrow lines that split Commercial Road from top to bottom, and Hubert pulls me into a run. 'Come on, we can just make it if we're quick!'

The tram stops outside Jacobs the grocers but there's not many as get off here at this time of day, and I know it won't stay for long. I'm laughing and puffing when I jump onto the tiny platform. Whatever would Mother say if she could see such unladylike behaviour? Hubert squeezes against the rail to let me climb the steep steps ahead of him, and we go round and round to the upper deck, though I know he'd pay extra to go downstairs if I asked. But, after the stuffiness of the Emporium, it's good to be in the air, even though all the seats are in the full glare of the sun. I make my way past the rows to my favourite place, the long seat at the front, and feel the pressure of Hubert's leg against mine as he sits down next to me. I lean over the rail to look at the street below, just so that I can move and press a little closer. The smell of dust and drains drifts upwards towards us as the bell rings and the tram begins to move. It whirrs, picking up speed, the wires above us fizzing and clicking as we cross the junction at the bottom of town.

A shadow falls across us. Hubert holds out a shilling and asks for the stop down by the Docks.

'Off to the Fleet?' The conductor takes it, and counts out his change, dropping the coins into Hubert's hand.

Hubert nods. 'Can't have the Navy put on a show on our doorstep and not have a look.'

'You and half the country, besides!' the conductor laughs. 'Bin ferryin' 'em there all day, we 'ave.' He shakes his head. 'Lookin' more an' more like war, don't you think?'

'Well, it all depends on Austria-Hungary. It might all be hot air but in my opinion, yes, it looks like war.'

I turn to look at Hubert when the conductor has disappeared downstairs again. His eyes are bright. 'What will happen if Austria-Hungary *does* declare war on Serbia?' I ask.

'It'll be like a game of ninepins. Germany will come in, and France. We'll knock against each other till we're all down. There's already talk of Russia mobilizing.'

The tram moves off again and I turn to watch as shop assistants pack up goods and push back blinds. Harsh sunshine reflects back from the windows as workers filter out onto the hot streets. I screw up my eyes against the glare, trying to imagine what this street would be like with all our young men gone off to fight. I can't picture it. It's unthinkable.

With each stop, the tram fills a little more, and the brakes suddenly squeal and grate as we pull to a halt at the junction by the Town Hall to let a cart pass. It's piled high with wilting fruit and vegetables, and lumbers across in front of us, the poor old horse dripping froth in big, dark stains to the road. Then we're off again, and at last cooler air begins to catch at us as we near the sea.

As the tram passes the main Dockyard Gate, Hubert rises and makes his way down the stairs. I follow close behind. We get off by the wide, cobbled jetty, close to where the fishing boats are moored, and we stand and watch for a minute as the bright hulls rock gently with the swell of the sea. I try to work out if the tide is ebbing or flowing, and turn to Hubert to tell him I reckon it's going out, when a voice calls out behind us.

'Hu, old chap,' it says. 'Wait up.' We turn and watch as a young man walks towards us. He's tall and dressed in flannels and a striped blazer, very smart, and his cane taps on the pavement as he walks. But he's an odd looking fellow, with his sandy-orange hair sticking out from beneath his straw boater. It looks a bit precarious, too, balanced on top the way it is. He tips the brim as he draws closer and I feel his eyes on me. I can't read what's in them because his lids half cover them, but it's not the sort of look as makes you feel comfortable, not at all.

'You old dog,' he says, speaking to Hubert, but looking at me all the while. Eventually, he turns his eyes to Hubert and holds out his hand. Now it's my turn to stare, for I've never seen such freckles. Thick they are, from the tips of his finger to where his arm disappears beneath his sleeve, and so close there can't be a pin's prick between them.

Hubert's cheeks have gone pink, as if he's embarrassed, but perhaps it's just the heat. When they've shaken hands, he turns quickly to me. 'This is an old school friend of mine,' he says, 'Archie McCudden.' He turns back. 'Archie, this is Miss Timms.' Archie lifts his hat fully off his head and his hair pops up as if it's on springs. It's all I can do not to laugh. He holds out his hand to me and I take it. His fingers are cool and soft, as if he's got a chill or something, and I immediately regret my strong grip as I watch his eyes widen. Perhaps he's not used to womenfolk showing their mettle? Well, perhaps it would do him good to come into my world for a bit, then. He might learn a thing or two. He turns back to Hubert.

'Off to see the bally old Fleet?' he says. 'I've got to join Father at a bash on the Royal Yacht. It's bound to be a bore. Doubt if there'll be anyone there under forty.' He yawns. 'Actually, old thing, you're just the chap I need.' As he speaks, he turns fully towards Hubert so that his back is firmly against me. 'We're short of an opening bat this weekend. What d'you say?' He leans towards Hubert in an exaggerated gesture. 'Clara's in charge of teas,' he says in a whisper so loud that I know he intends me to hear, and I watch as Hubert frowns. Who does he mean?

'I take it that's fixed, then?' Archie says. 'Luncheon first at the White Horse. Now, I'd better rush or I'll be in the soup good and proper.' He laughs. 'Bye-bye, Miss Timms.' He raises his hat, winking broadly at Hubert and we watch for a moment as he walks away, the silver top of his cane flashing in the sunlight.

Hubert tries to take my elbow as we turn to thread our way through the maze of tiny paths that weave an edge along this part of Old Portsmouth, but I shrug him away.

'Who's Clara?' I ask.

'Clara?'

'Yes. Your friend seems to think you'll be pleased she's going to be at the cricket.'

My stomach turns uncomfortably as I sneak a look at Hubert. 'It's Clara Fotherington, isn't it?' I say, suddenly wondering if perhaps he prefers tall girls with pale complexions to those like me, 'compact' as Mother says, with hazel eyes and skin that darkens at the very sight of the sun.

Hubert tries to distract my attention by pointing to where a boat is sailing into the harbour, screaming seagulls following it, but I won't be put off.

He sighs. 'Look, Maude,' he says, and he stops so that he can look into my eyes. 'Clara's my mother's choice of girl for me, not mine.'

My heart hammers against my chest. 'Your mother's choice?'

'I have no interest in Clara whatsoever, apart from the suffragette stuff and the debating society. She's a friend of the family, that's all.'

'Is she? A friend of the family, I mean. I never knew that.'

'But there's no reason why you should. There must be plenty we don't know about each other's lives. It doesn't mean anything.'

'I suppose not. But your mother'd like you to be interested in her?' What's got into me, to be so argumentative? Perhaps it's all the talk of war.

'Yes,' he says, sighing, 'she would,' and my stomach starts turning again as I search for the right words, but the only ones I can think of I know he won't want to hear, so in the end I say nothing. 'You can't expect me not to have friends, Maude. You've got friends, haven't you?' he adds, 'and I don't mind that.'

'Well, perhaps I wish you would!' I've snapped the words back at him before I can stop myself. We walk on in silence, Hubert choosing a route through the fish market where the remains of the day's catch is still being sold and the inky smell of fish innards and salt hangs heavily on the hot air.

We continue along the narrow streets beneath the wide bow windows that jut out above us, and join a straggling line of people heading our way, following them towards the sea. What I see when we emerge suddenly at the harbour edge makes me gasp. For a moment, I forget all about the trouble between us and stop and stare, lifting up my hand to shield my eyes from the glare that glances from the sea. There, before us, is row upon row of naval ships, sombre and dark, anchored in the Solent. How majestic they are, I think, but they frighten me too, stretching from the harbour mouth down past where we stand to the pier and beyond, for they look very menacing.

The sea ripples suddenly with the breeze. 'There must be hundreds …,' I say as I stare at the dark, broken lines that put me in mind of tacking stitches. I turn to Hubert. 'Does this mean war's definite?'

He's silent for a moment before he answers. 'Not definite, no ….'

'I don't see how anybody in their right mind would want to go to war.'

'It's not that simple,' Hubert says quietly. 'War's never simple.'

The nearer we get, the thicker the crowds become and we have to queue to pass through the tall, grey-stoned tower that guards the entrance to the harbour. But eventually we reach the wall that runs high along the water's edge, and climb the steps. The view from the top takes my breath away, for I can see more ships than ever from here. Hubert draws me close as we watch, and I forget all about Clara as I let his hand lay lightly on my waist, just where it curves out to my hip.

'Isn't that the most marvellous sight you've ever seen?' he says, and I can hear the excitement in his voice. 'The King's going to review them tomorrow, you know.' We stand and stare, till he says something that sends a shiver across me, despite the heat. 'My God,' he says, 'it's enough to make one join up.'

I change the subject then, for I don't want to encourage him to think like that. I've had enough of that sort of talk at the Emporium and from Walter at home, and the last thing I want is Hubert going off to sea and maybe never seeing him again.

'D'you think the *Good Hope* is here?' I ask, thinking of Arthur, and when we've stepped aside to let a family pass, I shade my eyes again to scan the ragged outlines of the ships, a rank, wet smell of seaweed rising on a drift of air.

'It should be towards the back,' Hubert replies, 'I saw a map in The Times. The whole blessed naval contingent's here, more or less.' We lean against the wall that lines the walkway, and the heat from the stone penetrates the skirt of my dress. 'Do you know that we've got twenty-four dreadnoughts, thirty-five battleships,' he recites, 'forty-nine cruisers, seventy-six submarines and seventy-eight destroyers?' I laugh at him then, and he smiles, our disagreement a thing of the past.

A rowing boat, trying for a closer look, moves out gently in a line from the shore. 'Will they be allowed off the ships, d'you think?'

'The sailors? Shouldn't think so.' He nods to the crowds that surge around us on the path, then below to all the people who have squeezed onto the narrow stretch of shore. 'Not with this lot,' he says, and he laughs. 'Portsea Island would sink.' He pulls me close again as a crowd of youths push their way past us. We watch them stumble their way down the steps to the water's edge, calling loudly to each other before bending low to skim stones across the still water.

A tall, middle-aged woman stops beside us. Despite carrying a parasol, tiny beads of perspiration dot her forehead. 'Young people nowadays,' she says haughtily, 'full of Brickwoods, I don't doubt.' She shakes her head and tuts, and Hubert and I smile at each other again. A couple at the front of the wall move away and we take their place, leaning across the warm stone to watch a family on the beach packing up their belongings. One of the men rolls his trouser legs back down before setting his bowler hat straight on his head, and a dog bounds out from the sea and shakes itself, sending sparkling spray cascading into the air.

We stay there looking at it all and enjoying the sights, taking our time as a soft sea breeze sweeps away the unbearable heat of the day. It isn't until the smell of frying onions drifts across from a booth on the grass behind us that my stomach gives a rumble, and I remember the lodging house and supper. As we start off again, a band in the stand by the bathing huts strikes up a tune. It's a music hall song, on everyone's lips these days, and the crowd, swept up perhaps in the feeling of holiday there is, takes up the chorus.

It's a long way to Tipperary, it's a long way to go.
It's a long way to Tipperary, to the sweetest girl I know.

Hubert's voice is deep and clear beside me and I think, not for the first time, how well I like it. I join in, and it seems as if everyone around us joins in, too.

Goodbye, Piccadilly, farewell Leicester Square,
It's a long, long way to Tipperary,
but my heart's right there! [1]

An aeroplane suddenly appears, dropping from the cloudless sky as if from nowhere, to swoop over our heads. Its engine drones as it tumbles like a large dragonfly, its high whine rising and falling in the blue above us. Children scream in delight at the rare sight and run to clutch their mothers' skirts before turning their sun-scorched faces to the sky. Another aeroplane appears, then another, and they seem to play together like the acrobats at the circus on the Common last year. Hubert stares from them to the Fleet and back again. 'What a sight, Maude,' he says to me, 'what a sight,' and he catches me more tightly to him. 'We won't forget this, heh?'

We pass a vending booth, and he pulls me into its shadow, pressing me to him, so close that I can feel the hardness of him against me. I look around, to see if anybody is watching us, but we're alone. My heart hammers. Is he going to kiss me? Here, in public? He gently lifts my chin until we are staring into each other's eyes. I can see dark flecks in his irises. Slowly, he bends his head until I feel the soft brush of his lips against my own. Then he catches me to him and his lips press harder, then harder still until I am keening against him.

We break apart, and step out of the shadows, stand breathless in the hot, still evening watching the spectacle before us for a moment longer. But it isn't the Fleet, spread out so magnificently before us that I know I will never forget, nor even the aeroplanes. It's the feel of Hubert's strong athletic body close to mine, the sense that the world is whole, and that the sun is where it should in the hot July sky.

Chapter 6

Can't you stay a bit longer?' Mother says as I reach over the table to kiss her goodbye. 'Our Florrie'll be up in a minute.'

I'd dearly like to linger inside our cool, thick-walled cottage and see my sister but I shake my head, looking at the clock on the dresser. 'I'll miss my train if I do.' I nudge past Walter to where Dad's sitting in his chair with his eyes closed and put my hand on his arm. He doesn't stir.

'She'll be wantin' to see you, with the baby so close to comin'.'

'I'm sorry, Mother, I can't. Tell her I'll see her next time,' I say. 'Besides, the baby might not come for weeks yet.'

'Hmph. That's all you know about it.' We turn as the scullery door opens. 'Well, speak of the devil,' Mother says to Florrie. 'Come and sit down, my girl. You've never walked all the way from the cottage on yer own?'

Dad opens one eye to watch as Florrie walks with slow, rolling steps through the scullery and into the living room. She makes her way towards the chair Mother's moved from the fireside to stand at the edge of the open window.

'That's the end of me shut-eye then,' Dad says. 'It'll be

nothin' but claptrap about babies now, I s'pose.'

'I'd forgotten what a charmer you was, Dad.' Florrie gives his forehead a kiss before sitting down heavily. She's only been there for a minute when she suddenly bends forwards and holds her hand to her lower back. 'Ruddy 'ell,' she moans.

'What's up, my duck?' Mother goes across to where she sits and begins to rub the base of Florrie's back, slowly and rhythmically.

'Must've been the walk up,' Florrie says. 'Ooh, that's better.'

'Tom not with you?' Mother straightens up and stands above Florrie, her arms folded beneath her bosom.

'He's down at the pond, talking to Alf Carter,' Florrie says. 'Tom reckons it's goin' to be war for certain. He can't stop talkin' about it.'

'Nothin's certain till it 'appens,' Mother says, moving to the table and rattling cups into saucers. She pours from our big, brown teapot then lifts the small replacement white lid before adding more steaming water. 'Do us a top up before you go, Maude,' she says, and holds out the big enamel kettle for me to take.

I turn into the scullery and drum water into the kettle, looking across at Florrie when I set it back on the range. There's something different about her today, something not quite right. Perhaps it's the beads of sweat that have formed on her forehead. Outside, a low rumble of thunder sounds. 'Listen to that,' Walter says. 'There's a storm brewin'.' He's dressed in his uniform and now lifts a foot to one of the wooden chairs by the table, ties one lace on a highly polished boot. 'An' I reckon it's not just the weather, neither,' he says. He twists the bow into a double knot and lifts his other foot to the chair.

'Hush now, lad.' Mother looks sternly at him.

'You don't really think there's goin' to be a war, do you?' Florrie says, reaching behind her to rub at her back again. 'I couldn't bear to bring a baby into a world that was at war.' She's cut short by a sharp intake of breath and rubs harder. 'That walk's fair done me in, it has an' all,' she says as she takes the cup Mother holds out to her. She blots her forehead again with her handkerchief. 'If only the weather'd break, it'd help.'

I see Mother give Florrie a long look as I turn to go. Another rumble, nearer than the first, sounds in the thick, heavy air.

Walter's waiting in the entrance lobby, by the ticket office, and I can tell by the look on his face that something's happened. His eyes are bright with excitement. 'You can't go, Maude,' he says. 'They've stopped all the passenger trains.' His words run together in his haste to tell me. 'Mr Coggins had a packet delivered about it, stamped 'secret' all over, it was.' He shook his head. 'You won't be gettin' back to Portsmouth tonight.'

'Slow down, Walter, for goodness' sake,' I say, 'and don't be silly. I've got to go. What will Mr Arnold say if I don't turn up?' I glance from the timetable on the wall to the clock above Walter's head. 'No, I must get back.'

'Well, you can't, an' that's that. All the trains've been given over to the military. Mr Coggins said you should've known better than to come visitin' today of all days.'

'But I always come on Mondays.'

'He means because of all the talk.' He steps closer and drops his voice. 'You know, the war an' that. Anyway,' he says, 'the next passenger train ain't till the three-ten tomorrow afternoon.'

'Tomorrow afternoon!'

He laughs. 'So, there you are. You'll just have to stay, won't you? I'll get the truckle bed out an' put it on the landin' for you, if you likes. Or you can have my bed an' I'll kip downstairs. It'll be a sight cooler, anyway.'

I stand there in the lobby, look again at the clock and feel my face crease into a frown. 'What about the bus?'

'You've missed the last one. Ain't one after four o'clock weekdays.'

''Course there ain't. I forgot. Damn, damn, damn.' I stamp my foot on the floor. 'I'll never get another job as good as that one.'

Walter snorts. 'You ain't goin' ter lose yer job, not just over missin' a day. It's not your fault. Besides, they'd be mad to get rid o' you.'

I smile, despite the way my stomach's churning at the thought of being absent from the Emporium without permission. 'You don't understand, Walter,' I tell him. 'There's hundreds of women who'd slip into my job given half the chance, quicker than you could say 'a yard o' ribbon', they would.' I watch as Mr Coggins walks past the open door of the station. 'Ah, well,' I say, 'that's it, then. What in heaven's name do they want with all them trains, anyway?'

Walter shrugs. 'All I know is that they've been requisitioned.'

'Oi, you there!' Mr Coggins comes back to stand in the doorway, looking at Walter. 'You don't get paid to stand around and chat to folks all day. Get a move on!'

There's nothing for it but to retrace my steps, and it's when I'm walking back up the path to the cottage that I hear a long, low moan coming from the open window of the living room. For once, I don't go round the back, but push open the front door. Florrie is still sitting where she was when I left, in the armchair by the window, but now her face is pale and squeezed up into itself.

'Whatever is it?' I ask as I go in. 'What's wrong?'

Mother has drawn up a chair beside her and I see Florrie grip it tightly. Tom's there too and stands to one side, towering tall above them both, turning his cap round and round in his hands. Mother doesn't ask why I've come back. She just says 'Florrie's pains've started,' then she looks up at Tom. 'You'd better be off out of it, lad,' she says, taking her hand away as Florrie's contraction eases and the grip on it slackens. 'T'ain't no place for men, now.' Tom looks uncertainly from Florrie to Mother and back again.

'Flo?' he questions.

'It's all right, Tom. I'm all right now I'm with Mother. You go.' But he still waits, until another pain starts its slow grip on her. 'Oooh ... go on,' she says, 'before I makes you stay for the whole bloomin' thing and you becomes the talk of Elmford.' Tom steps quickly backwards then, and as he reaches the scullery door, a fizz of lightning cuts into the room, followed some seconds later by a sharp clap of thunder. 'That's all I needs,' Florrie says, and groans. 'A ruddy storm. I 'ate storms.'

For what remains of the afternoon, thunder rolls round the surrounding fields and I sit with Florrie, telling her about the Emporium and even some things about Hubert I wouldn't normally say, trying to take her mind off what's happening. But it's not easy to keep her occupied for she can't concentrate for two minutes together, even between the pains, and Mother's bustling about the whole time getting things ready as if it's the most important thing that's ever happened, which I suppose for our Florrie, it is. When her waters break, we help her up the narrow stairs to the main bedroom and she starts crying. She says it's because her dress is all spoiled, but that's not it, for it'll wash out, and so I tell her. Then a clap of thunder overhead makes us all jump and she starts crying about the storm and when Mother pushes the windows open as far as they'll go, she cries because she wants them shut, but

54

the air is so thick and close we've got to have them open, Mother says, or she'll die of the heat and what would Florrie do then?

It isn't until the afternoon has slipped into evening that some coolness comes as, after a sharp stab of lightning that whitens the darkening room, rain begins to fall in heavy thunder-drops. The smell of wet earth drifts through to where Mother and I are getting things ready. She's brought the kettle upstairs and now pours steaming water onto a small pair of scissors that she's put at the bottom of a dish. The open blades glint, sharp and silver. I cut two lengths of strong twine under Mother's watchful eye and drop them into the water to float above the scissors. Florrie is lying on the iron bedstead covered only by a single white sheet and with each contraction she twists and turns, her moans becoming deep-throated groans, then quick panting breaths.

'You sure we don't need Mrs Watts?' I ask Mother in a whisper as I wipe the sweat from Florrie's face with a damp flannel.

''Course we don't,' she whispers back, but it's more like a hiss and she gives me one of her looks. 'I knows everythin' she knows, an' more, too, besides,' she says, pulling sharply at an old, clean sheet and tearing it into square cloths.

'But what if …?' My whisper trails away.

'There ain't goin' ter be no 'what-ifs'.' Mother's words are lost in the rough sound of cotton ripping. 'But even if there was ….' She pauses, looking at me across the bed then at Florrie again as she's gripped by another pain. 'We'd get Dr Samuel to come, that's what we'd do, and find the money after. Now, take that kettle downstairs and put it on the back of the range. Make sure you fill it first, mind, then it'll keep nice an' hot an' there'll be plenty for when the time comes.'

When I've run down and back, I bend over the bed and take the flannel from Florrie's forehead, reaching to rinse the small square in the cool water I've drawn into an enamel bowl and set on the little table by the bed.

'It's all right, my duck,' Mother says, crooning as another contraction grips Florrie. I can't remember the last time Mother crooned to me. I watch as Florrie heaves and twists. 'Hold on to Maudie's hand,' Mother tells her, and I sit on the bed and take Florrie's hot hand in mine. As I look down at her, I realise I don't want her to go through any more pains. I wish the baby was born and that it was all over.

A gust of wind blows a patter of rain against the window, and Mother moves across to pull it a couple of notches closer. Cool air is angled in and brushes against my face. I watch as she turns to lift the amber shade from the oil lamp on the chest of drawers, sets it down and strikes a match from the box beside it. As the flame flickers into life, she replaces the glass and carries the lamp to the washstand opposite the bed. The glow from it drops a dark yellow ring on the marbled surface.

I think of the light that floods every room at the Lodging House. 'I don't know why you didn't let the Mill put gas in when you had the chance,' I say, still holding Florrie's hand and watching Mother as she moves about the room. Her shadow dances on the walls as she turns to draw the thin curtains across the darkening windows.

Florrie groans again and I watch my fingers whiten as she grips them. I know Mother's trying to act as if everything's all right but I really think she ought to notice the way my hand is being squeezed. But her mind's still on what I said about the gas. 'Don't trust it, my girl,' she says. 'You never knows where you are with gas.'

Florrie's grip slowly slackens again. 'Maudie,' she says, tears slipping from her eyes to run across her temples to the pillow. 'Don't ever get in the family way. I'm never going to again. Never.'

'I ain't never getting married, Flo, you know that.' I reach across and kiss her flushed cheek, and she's suddenly unbearably dear to me and all our childish arguments over the years are forgotten. I look across at Mother, glad of the way she fills the room, her shadow falling across us.

'It'll soon be over,' I say to Florrie, smoothing her loose, fair hair back from her forehead. 'Remember how excited you was when you found out? And now you'll soon have a brand new baby all of your own and it'll all be worth it, won't it? Just think.' But my heart quickens, for I don't have a notion of how long it'll go on, nor what exactly it is that's going to happen, for I've only ever seen animals being born. Calves and lambs at the farm, and Blackie, our old cat, when she decided to have her kittens in the box beneath my bed. But, anyway, they were different, because my nerves weren't connected to them like they are now to Florrie, and me not able to do a thing to help her. One after the other the contractions come, Florrie resting as best she can between them. One time, she looks up at me and tries to smile, but soon she's gripped again and pants against the pain. I hear the latch on the front door and footsteps, the low murmurings of Walter's voice, and Dad answering. Backwards and forwards, distant rumbles, like the fading storm. Then Tom's voice, too. Then silence.

The evening deepens into night and shadows move about the room as Mother and I cross and re-cross it. Sometimes our dark shapes slip up the walls to flicker on the ceiling, or meet in strange, unearthly dances. Florrie's groans grow longer and closer and she writhes beneath the sheet while Mother and I sit on each side of the bed with her. Midnight blurs with the witching hours then, and it seems as if there's just Florrie, Mother and me in the whole world and there's never been anything else but what's happening here. Sometimes Florrie sleeps a bit between her pains, and we close our eyes too, but it's too hard to sleep on the wooden chairs we've brought upstairs, so mostly we talk, our voices humming low, stopping and starting, like bees on a patch of clover.

'I remembers when you was born, my girl,' Mother says to me in one of the times. I've never heard Mother tell of such things before, and I breathe as light as I can, listening. 'It was night then, too,' she says, 'like this, with the owls hootin' and the foxes barkin', except that it was a sight colder then, bein' March. But, thank the Lord, you was as quick out as if I was shellin' peas. It's first babies as always takes their time an' makes their poor young mothers wait an' suffer so.'

'What do it feel like then, Mother?' I ask, looking down at Florrie as she stirs, another pain beginning its hold on her.

She laughs, a short, snorting sound. 'Like nothin' as can be guessed at, my girl,' she says, 'but you'll find out one day, I've no doubt.'

'I'm not a bit sure as I want to,' I say, reaching out to replace the flannel on Florrie's forehead that's fallen aside with her tossings. 'Not if it's like this, I don't.'

'You'll want to,' Mother says, and laughs, this time a soft gentle sound and it makes me think of Hubert again, and what if he and I *did* get married and have a baby? But I push the thought away, for it's not something that's likely to happen, not with our different backgrounds it's not, even with the affection we feel for each other. Mother stands up suddenly and moves away towards the bedroom door.

'Where're you going?' I ask, starting up myself.

'Sit down, girl. I'm only going out to the privy. I can do that, can't I? You stay with our Florrie. I'm hardly goin' to be long, now, am I?' I do as I'm told, but fear whips around me like a draught all the time she's gone, and I don't take my eyes off that door till I hear Mother's slow footsteps coming up the stairs again, for what I'd have done if the baby was to come while she was away, I'm sure I don't know.

Dawn comes in slow, bringing with it a grey and overcast day, with still the occasional rumble of thunder. Mother keeps the lamp burning long after the room has filled with watery light, and Florrie's groans are continuous now. When I hear a soft tapping on the closed door, I get up from the bed.

'Dad's sent up some tea,' Walter's voice comes through the closed door. As I cross the room to open it, I can hear the sound of cups rattling in saucers. Walter hastily hands me two cups, and tips his head to glance past me into the room.

'What about our Florrie?' he asks. 'Do she want one?'

'She's past cups of tea, Walter,' I tell him and I hear my voice, full of myself. 'She'll have one later, when it's all over.'

'I'll be off then.' He turns to go. 'Tom's gone next door,' he calls over his shoulder, 'says he can't stand hearin' our Florrie no longer.' I go to shut the door but open it again as Mother calls out to him.

'You tell your father not to take all of that water, neither. We'll be needin' it soon.' I see Walter raise his hand through the open wedge of door before he disappears down the stairwell. 'An' you tell him he might have to get hisself his dinner,' she calls again. 'You an' all, lad.'

Behind me, Florrie's groans suddenly change, become more urgent, and I turn back into the room. She's drawn her knees up and is pushing against them. Her face is a bright, brick red, and a vein stands out in a bulging, crooked line on her forehead. Mother flings back the sheet and lifts Florrie's nightdress.

'Not long now, my duck,' she says gently. Then to me, 'Go an' fetch that 'ot water, girl.'

I put down the cups and rush downstairs. Walter has gone already and Dad's pulling on his work jacket. 'I need the water,

Dad,' I say, reaching to pull the kettle off the range. The handle burns into my hand and I start back, reaching for the holder. I pull the kettle up, expecting it to be heavy, but although steam wisps from the spout, it lifts too easily.

'You've used it!' I turn on him, my voice rising.

'I 'ad me shave, that's all, apart from the pot o' tea. I can't not 'ave me shave, an' I can't go to work on an empty stomach neither, girl.'

'Oh, for heavens' sake! It'll have to do. How can you think of yourself while our Florrie's upstairs in the state she is?'

'That were her choice,' he says as I pull open the door at the bottom of the stairs. 'She's made her bed an' now she's lyin' on it, good 'n' proper.' He walks towards the front door. 'You plants a blackberry, an' you gets a briar, girl,' he says across his shoulder.

'What sort of nonsense is that at a time like this?' I snap at him and turn up the stairs, taking the steps two at a time, spilling precious drops as I go.

The baby's head has appeared by the time I've returned with the big enamel kettle, and for a minute all I can do is stare at the dark, waxy ball between Florrie's legs till Mother shouts for me to hurry up. Florrie's panting like a dog that's run a mile in the heat as I pour what hot water there is from the long, curved spout into a clean bowl. Then I add some cold from the earthenware jug on the washstand. I hang back from the bed, rooted into the floorboards and just standing there, staring, not knowing what it is I'm supposed to do. I don't know why it is that I always notice little things when something big's happening, but I do, and this time I notice how the kettle holder I made for Mother has gone brown and crisp and some of the stitches have come undone.

'Put them cloths a bit nearer,' Mother says. 'And that towel, there, quick.' I lift the pile of torn cloths and put them on the foot of the bed. Florrie's still making terrible moaning sounds.

'One more push, my pet,' she croons to her.

'I can't.' Florrie lay back against the pillows, panting. 'I can't.' I feel my heart begin to pound.

'Yes, you can.' Mother's voice is sharper now. 'Come on now, for Mother.'

Florrie lifts her head from the pillow and puts her chin down into her chest, takes a deep breath and pushes. There's a long, low, animal groan, and it makes me think of the farm again, then Mother's guiding a tiny, wriggling form onto the waiting towel.

I'm not sure if I've spoken or not. I've meant to and I've opened my mouth, I know, for I can feel the air against my tongue, but I'm not sure any sounds have come out at all. Mother gestures urgently towards the tiny bowl and I hand her the twine, and she ties it tightly round the cord. She holds out her hand for the pair of sterilised scissors, and I lift them, dripping, from the cooled bowl, and pass them to her. Then the cord is cut, and Mother's wrapping the baby in the towel, wiping its face clear of blood and mucous. A thin, startled cry pierces the air and Florrie lifts her head as Mother hands the bundle into her open, shaking arms.

'It's a boy,' I whisper, moving as if in a dream towards the bed. The baby, held against Florrie's swollen breasts, is opening and shutting its eyes. 'A beautiful baby boy.' Then I'm crying, and Florrie is crying. Then the baby starts crying too.

Mother lifts the afterbirth onto an open sheet of newspaper and, with crimson fingers, wraps it and places it near the door to take downstairs. As she washes her hands in the basin, she glances across at us. 'You daft pair,' she says as she looks from us to the baby. His tiny fist has escaped the towel and now waves uncertainly in the sudden freedom of his new world. 'You daft pair,' she repeats, but I see her wipe the corner of her eye with the towel before she comes to the bed and rests her hand on my shoulder. She lets it stay there for a minute before she turns away.

When both Florrie and the baby have been cleaned up, I'm sent next door for Tom. Dad's long since gone to work and I make my way down the stairs and out into the garden, feeling the wet grass flick beneath my skirt onto my bare legs. I step over the low hedge that separates the two gardens and knock quietly on the scullery door. It opens immediately and Tom, white-faced, peers through the early morning gloom at me. I reach up on tiptoe to give him a reassuring kiss on his cheek, and feel his stubble rough against my lips.

'You've got a son, Tom,' I tell him. He looks at me blankly for a moment, before his face breaks into a smile.

'Is my Flo all right?' he asks, and I nod, then Tom brushes past me and jumps the hedge before disappearing into the house. I follow slowly back. As I pass into the living room, I can hear him clattering up the stairs and crossing the floorboards above. I lower myself into Dad's empty chair, suddenly tired to death, and lean back, feel my head sink into the shape his has left. I listen to the rattling from next door as the range is raked out, and across the field behind the Mill, comes the eerie call of a tawny owl, home from its night's hunting. Then the thin, new wail of the baby upstairs. Then quiet. I close my eyes.

Who's that shouting? Whoever it is, it's coming from outside. Men's voices. I open my eyes and listen. Perhaps something has happened at the Mill? Dad? The sounds grow louder as more people join in the rumpus. Women's voices now, too. Whatever is it? I sit upright and listen more closely. What is it they're saying?

The baby has made me forget.

'War!' I hear someone cry. 'It's war!'

Chapter 7

As I look down the stretch of Southsea seafront they call Ladies' Mile, it's a sea of tiny parasols and gentlemen's hats, a swell of black and white as folk stroll along. The evening sky is clear after yesterday's storm, and the sun is shining again, though there's something about the light that's different. Sharper perhaps.

It's hard to believe it's only the second day of the war, for already large areas of the Common have been roped off and hundreds of horses have appeared as if from nowhere, tied up to little wooden posts that have been hammered into the ground. The poor creatures are uneasy and I can't say as I blame them, for how do they know what's going on, or why they've come? They keep pinning back their ears and whinnying and snorting when folk get too close. I don't know why they can't just leave them alone.

Hubert and I walk slowly along a path that cuts the wide grass in two. The pale, scorched blades are already beginning to show green from the recent rain, and steam rises in patches, filling the air with a sweet smell, like wet straw. Behind us on the beach, huge coils of barbed wire, silhouetted and tumbling, have already been rolled above the tide-line and pinned into position. Put there against the threat of invading armies, Hubert says. Well, they must have been planning it then, mustn't they, I tell him back, for it to have happened this quick? Do they really think we'll be invaded? I ask, but he doesn't answer. He's too deep in his thoughts.

I look over again at the shore. They've had to take the rowing boats away, to make room for the wire, and that's a shame, for folk are still in need of a bit of fun, aren't they, war or no war? I miss the dark curved shapes on the pebbles, like a line of giant apple peelings.

The sun is hot again after the storm, and strikes me as I walk, making me wish I had bought one of the parasols that were going cheap at Mason's earlier in the year. I'm too fond of seeing my savings grow for my own good sometimes. I pull my old boater a little further down, then glance sideways at Hubert. He really is very quiet tonight. Perhaps he's cross with me for forgetting our arrangement, for to tell the truth, I didn't remember it until Mrs Packham knocked on my door to say he'd come. He had to wait while I put myself to rights and pinched my cheeks to get a bit of colour in them. How cross he looked when I went down, standing still as a statue in the hall by the grandfather clock, his hat in his hand. Wouldn't look me in the eyes, not even when I said I was sorry.

Our shadows drop long and thin across the grass as we walk, Hubert's legs making scissor shapes as they cross and cross again. I start on again about the baby. I can't help it, for my mind's full of it.

'You ought to have seen him, Hubert,' I say, pushing my arm a little further through his.

'Ought I?'

'Oh, I do wish you had. The way he curled his fingers into little fists, and his face so, well, so … crumpled.' My laugh leads immediately into a yawn.

'He's a baby, Maude. What do you expect?'

'*And* the trains were requisitioned, did you know?' I say. 'All of them. I couldn't get home.'

'Yes. You told me that too.'

'Oh.' I yawn again.

Hubert stops suddenly and turns to look at me. He sighs. 'Come on, you're tired. I'll walk you back.'

Any other night, I'd have been disappointed to have had our evening cut short, but now I can't say as I mind, for I'm looking forward to bed and a good sleep. We turn to retrace our steps and are silent again, each with our own thoughts until we reach the horses again. There's one on its own in a roped-off area by the path. A big black stallion. It dances around, pulling hard on its tether then, suddenly, it rears up, its hooves pawing the air. We stand and watch as a soldier rushes up to pull on its halter, trying to calm it. He steadies it, and strokes its neck, talking gently, his voice getting softer and softer as the horse calms. How smart the soldier looks in his uniform.

'Our Walter's talking of joining up.'

Hubert turns to look at me, then smiles a strange, secretive smile. 'There's a lot of that sort of talk, Maude. It's only natural, wouldn't you say, seeing that we're at war?'

'I didn't say it wasn't natural. I just thought you'd be interested, that's all.' The smile has irritated me, and we continue walking in silence.

'What does your father say?' he asks.

I look at him in surprise. 'My father?'

'Yes.'

'Not much, I don't think. Walter didn't say he did, anyway, and I haven't heard any grumbles. No, I don't think he objects, though he won't want him to go, of course. What father would? He didn't want our Arthur to join-up neither, and there wasn't even a war on or anything then. Not that Dad's a pacifist,' I add quickly, thinking of the cutting things he says, and the way he can wring an animal's neck with no thought or hesitation at all. No, there's not much of the pacifist in my father.

'Mine is totally against it. He says it'll take men from the factory and that it'll ruin the economy.' I try to picture Hubert's father, which is hard seeing as I've never met him. I imagine him as tall, with dark – no, grey – hair. And haughty. I look at Hubert, at his strong, regular features and the way he tips his chin in the air when he's thinking. Yes, definitely haughty.

'If the men go,' I say, just to provoke him, 'your father could always employ women in their places.'

'Women!'

'Yes! Women! You know – the section of society you joined the Federation to support?' I try to rein in my sarcasm, and fail. 'Women can do a lot of the things men can do, you know. Some things better!'

'I can't go into all that now, Maude!' There's a long silence. When he speaks again, his voice is lower, as if he's thinking aloud. 'Father's mad as a bull. Production's already falling, and it's only going to get worse. The men have done nothing but talk all day of which regiment they're going to join and the adventures they're all going to have. The trouble is, Father thinks I'm the same as them, that I'll go and join-up too.'

'And will you, Hubert?' I reach out and draw him to a stop, make him look at me. There's a strange look on his face, like he's got a fever or something, and what I see in his eyes suddenly makes me feel afraid. Despite the warmth of the evening, I shiver. What if it doesn't all peter out? What if Hubert and Walter *do* join-up like our Arthur, and are sent off to fight? I feel my heart thumping hard in my chest.

Hubert attempts a laugh. 'I want to do my bit, of course I do Maude, but the trouble is, how the devil can I leave Father?'

Despite my own thoughts, I have to be fair. 'It's your own conscience you've got to follow, Hubert, not your father's,' I say.

'It's hardly that simple.'

'I'm not saying it's simple ....'

'I don't blame Walter for wanting to do his bit,' Hubert says, removing my arm from where it's been resting on his. 'Any man worth his salt feels the same.' He presses his lips tightly together as we begin walking again.

'I'm not blaming him.' I sigh. 'I don't blame him in the slightest.' I am beginning to feel aggrieved at Hubert, but I'm too tired tonight to have the sense to leave it there. 'I never said so, not once. Though why there's a war at all,' I continue, 'I'm sure I don't know. Is it so difficult to find a peaceful solution? Perhaps if men refused to go and fight, the governments would be *forced* to find an answer.' I feel Hubert tense beside me and I know I've said the wrong thing again, but suddenly I don't care. Nothing seems right at all between us tonight.

'Just why is it,' he mutters, 'that women can't grasp the complexities of politics?' He says it more to himself than to me, and as I feel the annoyance rising in him, so it rises in me, too.

'I thought you were on the side of women, you being in the Federation and everything?' Ah, yes, he was quick enough to join the men's movement for women's rights when it suited him, wasn't he? Where's all his fine talk about women being equal now, eh?

'What if the Germans come across here and invade us? It's perfectly likely, you know. They've already invaded Belgium. Would you want them to walk straight in and take our country, our women ... you? Would you honestly expect our men not to fight to protect what is ours?'

'But ....'

'But, what?'

'That'd be different.'

'How? How would it be different?' We've reached the road that runs along the seafront and are waiting to cross back into Stansted Road. I sigh. I hadn't meant for this argument to start. Hubert reaches out and turns me towards him.

'How would it be different, Maude?' he says, and I see that feverish light in his eyes again. I tug myself free and look away to where the breeze is eddying a piece of greasy paper, round and round, by the edge of some railings.

'I don't know how.' I stamp my foot at him. 'I'm too tired to think.'

'This isn't an academic exercise any more. What people don't seem to realise is the consequences of it. The war's for real now.'

'You've changed your tune. I thought you were all for it? And in any case, you don't have to treat me like a child, you know. You think that you know it all, don't you, just because you've had a fine education?' The words are out before I can stop them, and I make it worse by pulling a childish face. 'Well, you don't! People like you can never understand. You have to be in touch with real life to do that.' We walk apart after that, quick angry steps, and we only slow as we approach the lodging house. I turn silently to the gate.

'Look,' he says, reaching out and touching my arm. 'Maude, I'm sorry.'

I hesitate. I should apologise too, I know I should, but the differences between us tonight are like a wedge separating us. Besides, I've always found it hard to say sorry. 'It's a stupid argument,' I manage instead.

'What you said about my education – I can't deny it was a good one, but that doesn't necessarily mean I was happy.' He pauses. 'I sometimes think that perhaps you're the lucky one.' I stop and look up at him. What does he mean, I'm the lucky one? What's lucky about not having the chance to learn, not ever being given the opportunity of studying at a ladies' college, or at a university? He doesn't know what he's talking about. 'Come on, don't let's argue,' he continues. 'It's not as if we're on opposite sides, is it?' He smiles. 'It's the War. It's unsettled everyone.' The evening is closing and the shadows have begun to thicken. We both look up as a lamp flares in Gertie's room above us.

Hubert reaches out for my hand, and we stand close together for a moment. I'm hoping he'll say something more to make it right between us again, when I hear a sound that takes my mind off everything. Wrenching sobs are coming from the room, dropping down on us from the open window.

I say goodbye to Hubert all in a rush then, and go in, for I know if Gertie is crying it must be something serious. I've never known her to cry.

I should open the window a bit further, for it's hot again, as if the storm has never been. It's strange how that long spell of weather we had broke the very day war was declared. Mrs Packham reckoned it was God showing His displeasure at the turn of events, but I said to her did He think anyone was taking any notice, then?

Hubert's right, the war's upset everyone. Our Walter's talking of joining up and Hubert's in a peculiar mood, and now there's poor old Gertrude. What a surprise I had when she told me she was German. She always seemed so English somehow. How upset she was. She doesn't know what to do, what with having no mother and her father somewhere in London, she doesn't know where. London's not the place to go anyway, not now, I told her. She reckons she'll have to go back to Germany, then, although she said she'll probably feel more like a foreigner there than she ever has done here. Let me push back the blanket a bit. Yes, that's better. How red Gertie's eyelids were; she must have been crying for hours. And she's normally so pretty with her big blue eyes and fair hair. Felt like a criminal, that's what she said. But you'd never know she was German. Speaks English better than a lot of us naturals do, me, for one. She's got an aunt over there, somewhere near Frankfurt. Wonder what she'll say when Gertie turns up on her doorstep?

Poor Gertie, I wouldn't be in her shoes for anything. Big burly policeman coming round here. No, thank you very much. I'm glad it wasn't me, for I don't know what I'd have done. Four days he told her she had, to leave! The new Defence of the Realm Regulations or something. Reckoned Portsmouth's a sensitive area, although I do understand that much, when I think about it, what with the docks and everything. I suppose I can see that someone might think she was, what was it? Oh yes, an alien. But you wouldn't think that if you knew her. Oh, no. Twenty-seven years she's been here, since she was two, though not all of it down here. She should have changed her name. I would have. Though they'd have found her eventually, I suppose. I wonder if she'll come back when it's all blown over? I wouldn't like to think I'll never see her again, for good friends don't grow on trees. And what Mrs Packham will have to say about it all, I dread to think.

What about our Walter? Just what would you want to go and do a fool thing like that for? I asked him in no uncertain terms when he said he was joining up, but he was too darned excited to listen to reason and I just know he'll go and do it. That's our Walter all over. Always up for a bit of excitement. Besides, Hubert's right what he says, all the young men are talking like that; it's not just him. Strange that Hubert asked what our Dad thought about it. It's because his father doesn't want him to go I suppose, what with the business and everything. Yes, that's what's making him miserable.

How dark it is without the street lamp outside. They were a bit quick off the mark stopping the lights like that. Wire on the beaches and lamps off, sooner than you could say 'The Germans are coming'. Not that I reckon they will. Not with all this water around us. Their ships would just be a sitting target for our Navy, wouldn't they? No, they'll have more sense than that.

Oh, dear. I did go on a bit about the baby tonight. But I couldn't help myself. Fancy me having helped deliver a baby! Wouldn't have thought I'd have had the stomach for it, not that I actually did much, for Mother did most of it. But I was there, wasn't I, and that's the main thing. Just goes to show what you can cope with when you have to. Like our Arthur, being sent up to the North Sea, and putting up with all those storms, and learning to fire the big guns. They've got torpedoes, horrid things that they shoot under water. What if German ships have got them, too? I suppose they will have. What if they shoot them into the *Good Hope* and get our Arthur? My stomach turns. I won't let myself think like that, I won't.

What they need is women running the country. We'd jolly well soon put an end to the war and no mistake. I wonder if the WSPU will ever campaign for that? Women in parliament! Ha, ha. Not in my lifetime, I shouldn't think.

I'll just turn over and try my other side. I'm over-tired, that's the trouble, but if I don't drop off soon, I'll never get up for work on time, and that'll be another black mark against me in Mr Arnold's blessed book.

Chapter 8

The interval's over and we gradually settle in our seats, voices around us quieting amidst a rush of rustlings as the lights dim. A few lingering coughs then they, too, fade to silence.

It's the first time we've met since we had our argument, and Hubert and I are sitting at the back of the stalls of the Theatre Royal, trying not to lean against each other, as things are still a bit frosty between us. I crane my head to the other side in order to see round the burly figure in front of me. Normally Hubert would offer to change places so I could see better, for he's got lovely manners, but tonight he hasn't said a word.

I glance quickly at his profile, at his long straight nose and sensitive, finely-etched lips, and I feel a surge of tenderness. I don't pretend to understand the workings of why we're together, but I'm glad we are, despite our differences. The world is a different place when I'm with him.

I glance up at him again. He's deep in thought, too. But then, he always seems to be these days. He's fiddling with the programme sheet, curling it up, uncurling it then curling it up again. I look back and glance around the theatre, do a double-take when I see someone who looks like Gertie, but it isn't her, of course. I suppose she must be back in Germany by now. Funny to think of her as the enemy. I let my eyes sweep down to the front to where Rose from Ladies' Wear is larking about with her young man. A lively spark he looks and no mistake. I'll be able to rib her at work about him in the morning. I catch her eye as she turns, and we wave.

The pianist comes back into the auditorium but for some reason he doesn't start playing like he normally does. He just sits on his stool with his hands in his lap looking back at us. Whatever's going on? We wait there for several minutes, then the crowd begins to boo. Hubert looks at his wrist watch. It's a lovely time-piece, silver, with a big white face and black Roman numerals. He frowns as he tugs his jacket sleeve back down.

'Why don't we go?' he says, turning to me. 'It's obvious something's gone wrong backstage.' I feel a surge of disappointment. It's the highlight of my week coming here, or to the Astoria, on a Saturday night. 'Besides,' he continues, 'I'm not really in the right mood for this tonight.' I bite back the retort that he hasn't been in the right mood for much at all lately, and reach down instead for my handbag.

'They're bound to get going again in a minute,' I mutter as I go to stand up, and it's as if my words are a cue, for suddenly the auditorium dims and the lights come on over the stage. I pull Hubert back down and we settle, the audience quieting again, but still the long red drapes stay shut. What *is* going on? The silence lengthens till someone breaks it with a whistle, and it's taken up all around us, shrill calls of impatience filling the air. Finally, the gold fringe at the bottom of the curtains shivers and they draw slowly back. Everyone's quiet again, expecting the show to start again.

But it's not the Brown Brothers, tumbling and balancing, as our programme has promised. No. It's a screen that's been erected in the interval when we were having a glass of stout. Suddenly, the white square flashes with big, black letters.

YOUR KING AND COUNTRY NEED YOU!
LORD KITCHENER WANTS YOU!
COME AND ENLIST.

A uniformed Army officer appears from behind it. He makes me jump as he suddenly stands stiff, as if to attention, clicking his heels together. He squints against the brightness of the lights as he looks towards us. I raise my eyebrows at Hubert, but he just shrugs and turns back, his eyes wide now and fixed on the stage. There's a lot of fidgeting and whispering, and a girl in front of me begins to giggle. Then the officer holds up his hand.

'Ladies and gentlemen,' he says. His voice is the sort that doesn't need a megaphone, and it echoes round the theatre. 'My name is Sergeant-Major Roberts. I have been assigned as your local Recruiting Officer.' He pauses and sniffs, twitching his nose so I want to laugh, thinking it's going to be a skit on the war.

'Look at these words, gentlemen.' He turns to point with his baton at the screen. 'Our king, our beloved King George … needs YOU.' He turns back suddenly to point at the audience, and a woman in the front gasps. 'Yes, Madam,' he goes on, bringing the baton to rest pointing directly at her, 'he needs your man. And yours.' He points elsewhere in the darkness. 'And you, there at the back. Yes, YOU.' When I see his baton aimed directly at me and feel Hubert tense beside me, I realise it's no skit after all. I glance quickly up at Hubert, my heart beating fast. He's staring, unblinking, at this sergeant-major whoever he said he was, and his eyes don't move from him as he struts up and down, up and down, first tucking his baton beneath his arm, then pointing it somewhere different, until all the theatre's been covered, including the boxes and the balcony.

'Yes, your country needs you,' he booms out, as if he's still on the parade ground. When I hear Hubert's slow intake of breath, I shift uneasily in my seat. Don't be taken in, Hubert, I plead silently. Oh, don't be taken in. 'Ask yourselves,' the officer continues, 'what does this wonderful country of ours mean to you, this great island with its magnificent Empire?'

Before I've got time to think what it means to me, the sergeant-major strides to the centre of the stage. He slowly lifts his arm and points a finger straight down the middle of the theatre, and in that moment, he looks exactly like the new posters of Lord Kitchener. He even has the same drooping moustache that curves down like the handlebars of a bicycle. There are posters like that everywhere these days, on hoardings, sides of carts, in windows – why, even on pillar boxes like the one at the end of Stansted Road, and it's true what they say, Kitchener's finger follows you everywhere you go, same as his eyes. Whatever position you look at those posters from, there's no escaping him.

'That's right, lads,' the sergeant-major continues. 'It's YOU I'm pointing at. Who's going to protect the little woman by your side from the marauding enemy, if *you* don't, eh? Your dear old folks sitting by the fireside at home, too old to fight for themselves, don't they deserve your protection, too?' He brings his arm smartly down to his side and begins to march up and down the stage.

'And what about you young lads who haven't got a girlie by your side, I can hear you thinking?' He reaches the end of the footlights, and turns to march back. 'Well, let me tell you.' He sniffs again, but by now it doesn't seem funny and I don't want to laugh at him at all. He waits for a few whistles to silence before continuing. 'This uniform'll get you the girl of your *dreams*, lads.' His voice is thick with suggestion and a cheer goes up from beside me as a skinny youth stands up.

'I'll join, mister,' he shouts.

'An' me, if it'll get me some o' that.'

The audience laughs then, and some young people at the back stamp their feet.

'That's the way, lad,' he says to the boy, beckoning him down, and walking to the side of the stage where he makes his way down the steps. He tucks his baton under his arm again, and marches along in front of the seats, his free arm swinging stiffly in time with his stride.

'All those who want to save their country and fight like men ....' He pauses, dramatic as you like, as he turns up the aisle towards where we're sitting. 'Follow me! Come and enlist!' His voice rises, loud, on the last word. 'All it takes is a signature. It's quite painless. And there's a car waiting outside to take you to the Town Hall, right now. Come with me, if you've courage enough! Protect your country, and take the King's Shilling!'

The sergeant-major is almost level with us now, and his voice has grown to a bellow. I shrink back in my seat. All around me, men and boys are standing up and leaving their seats, Rose's young man among them, stumbling across knees and feet to walk behind the officer in a straggling row to shouts of encouragement from the women.

'Kitchener's Army is a place for men, real men,' he shouts from the back of the hall. I turn to watch over my shoulder as he smoothes his thick, dark moustache between his fingers. 'Who's got it in them, then?' Everyone's looking back at him now and Hubert shuffles his feet, as if he's going to stand up, and I quickly put out a hand to rest it on his arm, for it all feels like a trick to me. If he has to go, surely it's better to do it in the cold light of day when he's in his senses, and not caught up in some kind of trickery? I feel his muscles tensing beneath the fabric of his coat as I squeeze my fingers. Then, the swing doors close behind the last volunteers, to the cheers of the crowd left behind, and I breathe out a long sigh of relief.

The Brown Brothers come on stage then and start their act, but those of us who are left are restless and, after a brief word with the pianist, they start some communal singing instead. Everyone likes singing, me as much as the next one, and my voice lifts high to the ceiling for chorus after chorus of patriotic songs.

But, for once, Hubert doesn't sing, and he hardly speaks as he walks me home. He leaves me standing by the gate of the lodging house, not even waiting for me to push open the door and turn to wave at him. He just spins on his heel in the darkness, and walks away. I expect he's angry with me for stopping him, but he could have volunteered, couldn't he, if he'd really wanted to?

I wait by the open door, listening to his footsteps echo on the pavement, and a deep foreboding fills my heart.

I stand there in the dark, listening, till I can't hear him any more.

Chapter 9

A couple of days later, when I get back to the lodging house after a day at the Emporium, there's a letter waiting for me. I take it quickly upstairs to my room, crossing to the window to read it better.

The Gables
Laburnham Grove
North End

September 19th, 1914

Dearest Maude

You will be surprised to receive this, I think, but I have important news. I don't know what you will think of it (or rather, I'm afraid I do). I have joined up! There. I have confessed. The push for volunteers at the theatre felt like the final straw, and when an enlistment parade passed me on its way to Guildhall Square today, before I knew it I had joined them. I am to be a soldier! I tried for the Navy, fancied riding the waves like your Arthur, but so many men wanted the same that they've had to close their lists. So I'm to be in khaki.

I have to stay living at home for the time being, and wait for my papers. Then they'll find a camp to send me to for training. The word is that it'll be somewhere in Surrey, although there's talk, too, of Dublin. Some chaps have apparently been sent there already, but in the meantime, we're to drill on the Garrison Parade Ground at Old Portsmouth. So you see – I'll only have to look up and see the harbour walls to be reminded of you!

I've already met a lot of the other men, all shapes and sizes and all classes mixed in together, but they seem very decent chaps for all that. I broke the news at home this evening and, after the initial shock, Father actually seemed resigned to the fact that I've joined up, although Mother immediately went down with one of her headaches, of course, but I'm sure she'll soon get used to the idea. I do feel some pangs of guilt about Father - the business and all that – and I had dreaded the moment of confession. But, in spite of everything he had said previously on the subject, in the end all he did was shake my hand, and there we were, men standing together on equal terms, so I need not have worried. It was most affecting, especially when I consider how he is set to lose so many men from the factory, and what with sales falling sharply since war was declared, well, it is understandable that he is worried, I think.

Finally, please accept my apologies for my bad temper of late. I've been as growly as a bear, I know. But I really do feel much more cheerful now I've made the decision, and I hope you'll understand, even though I know you disapprove of the war. But, like you said the other day, I have to follow my conscience, and there are bigger things to think of now than making corsets! I feel sure that when you have had time to think about it, you *will* understand.

Yours affectionately,

Hubert

Chapter 10

I'm walking down the seafront to where the pier begins, for I mean to sit for a while on the seat there. But I can see, from where I cross the Common, that it's taken. A man. Young, by the look of him. The sea beyond the barbed wire is pricked with autumn sunlight and the waves break and crash. Break and crash.

And there's a girl — she's young, too. I can tell by the way she carries herself, standing looking down at him. The boy hasn't noticed her, mind, he's that hunched into himself. I'm closer now. I can see the auburn of his moustache and the shadow of the seat, dark lines on the grass behind, like a five-barred gate. Beyond the swirls of wire, the waves break and crash. Break and crash. Whatever is it she's got in her hand? Something white, curling from her fingers like a tiny sickle moon.

The boy doesn't see her until she moves, and her shadow falls across him. He starts then, lifts his fingers to the brim of his hat. 'Can I help you, Miss?' His voice, faint, carried by the wind towards me.

My steps bring me closer. 'Oh, yes. You can help all right,' the girl says. 'You can help your country by getting off your arse and fighting. Why is it you're not in uniform, then? Shame on you!' She thrusts the white sickle into his hand, and he holds it up to look at it, clutches it and it flutters in the breeze. I watch as his eyes widen. He looks at the

White Feather of Cowardice that now belongs to him, and bows his head to his hands.

Then his words, '... It's my heart ... they won't have me ...,' but she just snorts. 'It's true,' he insists. 'It was the rheumatic fever as did it.'

'Coward!' she spits, and I see the word splinter above him, and fall like ice.

I shake my head, trying to get the scene out of my mind. It replays itself at will, like the chorus of a music hall song; when I'm walking or eating, trying to sleep or simply climbing up to sit on a tram. The sink of the boy's head, the way he shrinks with the shame of it until, by the cast of his form, he could have been seventy. It unrolls in my memory, like the moving pictures at the Astoria on Tuesday nights.

'Mr Arnold, I'm sorry,' I hear myself say, 'but I can't sell these things.'

The box sits on the counter between us, its upturned lid at an angle beside it. Inside the narrow container, feathers are packed, and they lift in the gentle movement of air as I bring my hand down to rest it on the counter beside them.

'Miss Timms.' Mr Arnold's voice sounds tired, and he sighs. 'It's not for you to say what is and what is not to be sold in the Emporium.' He looks across at me. He's a short, slight man, and his eyes, which I've never trusted, are level now with mine. It reminds me of the stand-offs I've had with Dad at home, and I determine not to be the first to look away.

'I'll ask you again, Miss Timms,' he continues. 'Are you prepared to sell these feathers, or not?' I can tell by the look on his face that he's not best pleased. He tries another tack, puts a wheedle in his voice. 'Look, these are difficult times. Profits are down everywhere, and Mr Mason, the same as all the other retailers, is having to diversify, take advantage of any small opportunity he can.'

'Well, I'm sorry about that, Mr Arnold, I'm sure, but I can't … and I won't … sell them. You can say what you like, it's not right.' I continue to stare at him. 'How would you like it if someone gave one to you?'

'Ah, but there's the difference, Miss Timms. I'm not one for shirking my duty. No, if I were a younger man, I'd have been first in the queue to enlist, don't you think for a moment that I wouldn't.' He puffs himself up then as best he can for a small man, and rolls back his shoulders. I just look at him.

'You really leave me with no choice, Miss Timms,' he says, the wheedling tone gone now.

'What exactly are you saying, Mr Arnold? That I'm to lose my job over a box of feathers?' I try not to let my voice rise.

'Not over a box of feathers, Miss Timms,' he says. 'No, no, not at all. But rules are rules as you very well know, and refusing to sell shop goods when you are specifically employed for that purpose, is going against one of them.' He stares at me. 'You've put me in a very difficult situation. However ….' He pauses, replacing the lid on the box and pushing it across the counter towards me. 'I like to think I'm a fair man. I'll let you think it over and we'll speak about it again in a day or two. I'm sure I don't have to remind you, Miss Timms, that despite the war, good jobs are still hard to come by?'

I feel my fingers curl into my hand. 'No, Mr Arnold, you don't have to remind me of that,' I say.

Chapter 11

'Walter. What are you doin' here? You changed your shifts again?'

I've been to visit Florrie and have come now to have tea with Mother and Dad. I look at Walter's face as he sits hunched over the table, and reckon he must be going down with something, he's that white. Then I look across to the fireside where Mother and Dad are sitting. For once Mother's not busy with some chore or other, and there's no sign of the tea things yet. She's staring into space and Dad's slumped in his chair, his head down. I was going to tell them about the feathers, ask Mother what she thought of it, but now they go right from my mind.

'What is it? What's wrong?' I let my basket slip from my arm and I notice, next to where I put it on the table, a small buff envelope. It's stamped with 'His Majesty's Service' but Arthur's already in the services, so I wonder if Walter has gone and done what he's been on about for so long.

'You gone an' joined up, then?' I ask him.

He nods. 'I have, but it's not that.' He looks away.

'Surely they don't want an old codger like you, Dad, do

they?' I laugh, trying to cheer them up as I reach for the envelope. 'Don't you worry, Mother,' I say. 'It's sure to be a mistake.'

'It's no mistake, Maude,' Mother says, turning now to look at me. 'Walter, son, tell her.'

'Tell me what?' I've a feeling then, like cold water, trickling down my spine. 'Walter?'

Walter reaches out to take the envelope from my hand, and slowly draws out the folded paper from inside it. He looks older, no longer a boy. 'It's Arthur,' he says, holding out the single sheet. It quivers gently, as if caught by a breeze, except there is no breeze.

'What d'you mean, it's Arthur? What's Arthur? What is it?'

'He's gone. Don't you understand, girl?' Dad's eyes blaze at me as if whatever it is that's wrong, is my fault. 'They've all gone. Every single one of 'em. The *Good Hope*'s been sunk. No-one's survived. None of 'em. He's never comin' back.' He bends his head to his hands, and begins to rock gently. 'Two sons I've lost, Walter, boy,' he says. 'And now you've enlisted an' all,' and he starts to cry, harsh racking sobs that I've never heard before, not from him nor from any man. Bile burns my throat. I've never heard my father cry. Why, even when we buried Horace, he didn't.

Mother slips from her chair to kneel at Dad's feet. She puts her head on his lap, and clasps his knees like I used to hers when I was small. 'Don't, my duck,' she says. I've never heard her use endearments to him, and it shocks me. 'Don't,' she says, and I look back to the sheet in my hand. It's perfectly and sharply creased with a single fold across the middle. But I don't want to read what it says, and I put it on the table next to the envelope. It looks so innocent lying there, I wonder how it is that such a thing can contain the force to shatter worlds.

I glance across at Arthur's photograph that stands on the dresser. His eyes still stare back at me. They haven't changed. They still make that same journey they always did; the same dark look, the same suggestion of a smile, the same proud tilt of his head.

Only things *have* changed. Because he's never coming back. Never … ever. Ever.

I reach out and pick up the kettle. Its heaviness stills my shaking hand as I turn towards the scullery.

It's evening. I open the door of my room and prop it ajar, wedge my hairbrush into the jamb so the draught won't pull it shut. The wind always sucks through the top of the window frame when it blows off the sea. I can't stop thinking about Arthur, and it's all mixed up in my mind with that blessed box of white feathers.

From the end of the landing, faint splashes come from beneath the bathroom door. They mingle with the deep drone of Mr Beavis's tuneless singing. Mr Beavis is the oldest of the tenants, and not my cup of tea at all. His voice drifts across the coconut matting to my room. I'm trying to ignore him and concentrate on what I'm going to tell Mr Arnold in the morning about the white feathers, when a picture of Gertie comes into my mind. There she is, standing there, arms akimbo, just like she used to when she was here. 'What's the use of principles, Maude, if you don't live them?' She was always saying that, and she's right, of course. No, I won't sell those damned things. I don't care what anyone says, and what's more I don't even care if the men *are* cowards. No-one deserves to be treated like that.

I pick up the small enamel jug from the washstand, put it with my towel on the bed, then add a bar of soap and a small bottle of vinegar, testing the stopper for secureness, for the last thing I want on top of everything is Mrs Packham giving me what-for for spoiling the counterpane. I'd probably give her some back tonight if she did, and then where would I be? Out on my ear, most like. Truth be told, I don't feel like bothering with my hair, but like Mother always says, there's nothing to be gained by moping, is there? So, when the splashing stops and the old, loose pipes rattle and knock against the walls, I collect up my things.

Standing by the bathroom door, waiting, my thoughts drift off again. I remember the last time Arthur came home, all his talking about the sea and the ships, all the ports and places he'd been. He'd brought silk shawls for Florrie and me, and some baccy for Dad, and gave Mother a wooden heart he'd carved for her with her name on it.

Then I can't bear to think of it any more and I count the slow, solemn ticks of the clock in the hall below till the singing stops, and the key grates in the bathroom lock. The china doorknob with its tiny roses turns and Mr Beavis comes out, his face pink and bashful as if he's been doing something he shouldn't.

'All yours, Miss Timms,' he says, and gives me one of his smiles that always seem so full of his teeth. 'I've tried to keep some hot water back for you, seeing as how it's your night for washing your hair.'

Well, I know he won't have, but I nod, and manage a smile as I pass into the bathroom. I make sure I well and truly lock the door in case he comes back in, like he did the time before. Thin, lingering wafts of steam wisp around me as I make my way past the bath, but for once I don't care about the water, nor the state he's left the bathroom in, no, not even the ring of grey scum round the top of the bath. My heart's too heavy.

The water from the hot tap in the basin's cold as I knew it would be, but I hold a finger to it as it trickles, letting it run, just in case. I wait, my mind full of Arthur, for I can't believe he's gone. I think of him in the garden at home, his back against the sun, digging; then he's walking up the hill with Gracie Pavey, her as wouldn't wait for him and went and married Tommy Burden, though our Arthur didn't mind much in the end. And now none of it matters, for he's never coming back.

The water changes from cold to lukewarm which I know is the best it's going to get, so I lift the plug from where it hangs on its chain around the tap at the corner of the basin, and place it in the central draining hole. I press it down firmly and the water begins to pool. Suddenly, it occurs to me that there *is* something I can do. I can't help our Arthur any more, but perhaps I can help those men as do make it back? That'd be a bit like helping him, wouldn't it? It all begins to become clear in my head. They're always on about the Red Cross down at the Union Hall these days, about how we should be doing our bit. Miss Fotherington reckons we've got to put aside our political aims and come to the aid of our country. 'It's a chance for us to show those in power just what we women are capable of,' she'd said. 'They think us weak? We are not weak!' She'd raised her voice then. How wonderful to be able to speak like that. 'Let us show them. We must all take action and join the fight. The WSPU might have suspended militancy, but we can fight in other ways. Perhaps you would like to join the Red Cross? Become a nurse, or perhaps a Voluntary Aid Detachment driver, a cook or a kitchen maid, a clerk, house-maid, laundress, ward-maid?' She had ticked the list off on her fingers. 'You may even be able to serve overseas. You name your skill, my friends, and the war will find a use for it. Occupations are as diverse as you are yourselves, but there's one thing you can be assured of – each and every one of you is needed.'

The level of the water has risen to within an inch of the top of the basin, and I quickly turn the handle of the tap. The flow slows, then stops, and I place my towel on the chair that Mrs Packham always has standing by the end of the bath, before setting the soap and the vinegar bottle between the taps. As I unpin my hair, I take each of the long, curved hairpins, and range them along the edge of the bath, then unbutton my blouse and hang it carefully over the back of the chair. Mr Beavis's steam from all that hot water he took has blurred the mirror, and I have to circle away the condensation. I look at my reflection, but I have to glance away, for it's not my face that is staring back, but Arthur's. Two peas in a pod people always used to say when we were children.

I scoop up my hair, and bend forwards so it falls in the bowl. The water feels cold against the warmth of my scalp and I shiver, reach for the soap and twist it round and round between my fingers before smearing it across my hair. I work it to a lather, rubbing deeper and deeper till my nails catch against my skin.

Squeezing out the soapy bubbles from the thick twist of hair, I pull the plug, refilling the basin as I feel for the jug and pour fresh water over my head. I can see the long strands as they float in the basin. It reminds me of the seaweed in the rock pools by the Round Tower at Portsmouth. Is there seaweed, I wonder, where Arthur is? I push the thought away, swish water through my hair, then empty the bowl and fill it again, but this time I add the vinegar, and I can feel the clean hair resisting against my fingers, and the thin squeak that tells me the suds have gone. I squeeze out as much water as I can from the wet coil, and reach for the towel.

My eyes smart. What would Arthur have thought of me joining the Voluntary Aid Detachment? What was it he said when I practised my bandaging on him for my First Aid Certificate? 'Whatever you do, don't become a nurse, Maude.' Yes, that's what he said, pretending to flinch from my impatient fingers as I wound the long white ribbons round his head, round and round, but liking it all the same, I could tell by the way he laughed. They need nurses, and I've got a strong stomach, for I helped to deliver little Horace, didn't I? I wouldn't be a regular nurse, of course; a VAD, just till the war finishes. I'll catch the train to Southampton, go to the Red Cross Office in Carlton Crescent, and if they let me choose where, I'll ask for the big hospital over at Netley, the Royal Victoria. I won't be too far from Mother and Dad then, if they need me. Some VADs get paid, don't they, even if it isn't much? I rub my hair with the towel, and look in the mirror again. My eyes, large at the best of times, are like saucers tonight, and there are dark scoops of shadow beneath them. Nothing's ever going to be the same again, our Arthur going has made sure of that. But, if I do my bit to look after those as make it back, I'll be helping him in a way, won't I? I watch myself nod, and it's as if Arthur himself is nodding too. Yes, that's what I'll do, and in the morning I'll tell Mr Arnold so, and I'll let him know, too, just what it is he can do with his feathers.

Chapter 12

Military Training Camp
Portsdown

November 3rd, 1914

My Dearest Maude

How sad I felt for you all when I read the dreadful news in the newspaper about the 'Good Hope' going down at Coronel. All hands it said and, sadly, I think it must be right or they wouldn't have printed it.

And the Monmouth, too - a combined total of nearly sixteen hundred lives lost. What a dreadful defeat. It really is quite unthinkable. In the report it says that the Germans ambushed the Fleet, waiting until nightfall before opening fire on them in the port. I cannot help thinking that there will be the devil to pay now.

I do so wish I had met Arthur. From what you have told me about him, he was a brother worth the name. I wish, too, that I could think of something I could write that would ease your pain, but I cannot think of anything that you will not have heard, by now, a hundred times. Suffice to say that my thoughts are with you at this time, dear. I will write a few lines to your mother and father, if you think they will not mind?

I hear there is to be a memorial service in Kingston Church soon. I will speak to the powers that be to see if I might be given leave to attend. I will try my best, but do not be looking for me, in case I cannot be there.

With sincere and deepest sympathy,

Hubert

Chapter 13

Mother's steps slow as we approach the church, and I slip my arm through hers so that we can cross the threshold together. My eyes don't need to adjust much from the grey of the day outside, for it's almost as dark outside the church as it is in. I try not to breathe in the musty church smell as I look around, and I can't help wishing that I was anywhere but here. Walking on the beach, perhaps, my boots crunching on empty shells, or in the woods at Elmford, moisture dropping in little dull thuds upon the fallen leaves.

There's a low murmuring of voices and the shuffle and scrape of feet as people take their places. Candles flicker on the altar at the end of the aisle. 'I wish Dad had come,' I whisper as I pause in the nave to look for a place to sit.

'It's not everyone as can,' Mother says, stopping beside me.

'Hiding from the truth only makes things harder though.'

'Your father knows the truth, girl, but he's still got to get up in the mornin' and find a way through till bedtime, ain't 'e? You'll realise things as you gets older. You leave 'im be.' Her harsh words add to the grief in my throat, a tightness that no amount of swallowing seems to ease.

'Excuse me.' A gentle voice comes out of the gloom. 'Are you the bereaved?' We look up at the tall, gaunt man beside us, who is clasping a prayer book in his hand. 'Only, if you are, there are seats reserved for you,' he explains. I nod, and he points a long, bony finger down the aisle, gesturing for us to continue. Mother follows close behind, our heels clicking on the stone floor and soft, restrained notes from the organ begin to seep into the air, slowly swelling till they seem to fill my whole head.

The reserved seats are half full already, and we ease our way along a row to the centre where a woman is kneeling, her head pressed to her hands like she's praying. Her shoulders are bent low, and the elderly man by her side wipes his eyes, his white handkerchief still folded. When he lays a large, calloused hand on her shoulder, the woman rises silently to sit beside me.

The church behind us continues to fill. A bell begins to toll, a dark solemn sound, as local dignitaries and officials walk slowly up the aisle to take their seats. I turn my head to watch them, anger stabbing at me when I see a large woman with silver hair near the front smiling and looking around. How can she do that? Does she think it's an Easter parade or something?

There are so many people now, that after the vicar has made his way to the altar, those who are standing at the back shuffle forwards into the aisle. We begin with the Burial Service, and I find it in my prayer book, holding it out for Mother to share. The vicar's words echo in the stillness as he begins, and I wonder if he's lost someone, too, for the newspaper said that hardly anyone hereabouts has been untouched by the going down of the *Good Hope*.

We all stand to sing. There are the usual rustles and coughs as we stand, and it takes us a while to get going, but bit by bit our voices grow together in strength. Then a lesson is read, the words echoing in the space above us. I close my eyes, trying to understand the meaning of it, but the voice doesn't wait for me. It races on, telling me how the good will be saved, and the evil damned.

I shift in my seat. What does it mean? Isn't everyone a mixture of both? They've got to be, surely? And why is it that people only like to think good of them as are dead? Take our Arthur. I'd rather remember him as he really was; the shouting matches with Dad, his chin thrust out, his eyes blazing; and on Friday nights, stumbling up the stairs after a skinful, swearing and cursing, waking us all up. But then I think, too, about the long evenings downstairs, just him and me, after the others had gone to bed, talking-talking-talking, and a picture comes into my head of him when we were little, racing through Bent Meadow down by the farm, poppies and cornflowers as high as our waists, the August sun on his hair.

A hand squeezes my heart as the force of what's happened hits me. He's gone, hasn't he? First Horace, now Arthur.

The choir stands to its feet in a whisper of robes, and a beautiful blend of voices gradually calms the beat of my heart. The vicar moves slowly and solemnly to the desk in the nave, and asks us all to pray. We stoop to kneel as one, heads bowed. This time the prayers are for everybody taking part in the war, for the wounded – and for us, too, the bereaved, but I can't think about it all any more. Instead, I stare blankly at the swirl of dust beneath the pew in front as it sways gently backwards and forwards, caught in a draught.

Before I know it, we're coming to the end of the service, and singing *Abide with Me*. I hear Mother's voice mingling with mine, hers a tone above as it always is, and slightly off-key. We stand up tall, don't miss nor stumble on a single word, and we hold our heads up high. But my heart? That's somewhere over the heaving waters off the coast of Chile, searching the green-lit water for him. *The darkness deepens; Lord with me abide.* I reach out, slip my hand beneath Mother's arm, step closer so that she can feel my arm against hers. I have to force my mind away from the words so that I can sing them. *Heaven's morning breaks, and earth's vain shadows flee; In life, in death, O Lord. Abide with me.*(2)

'Maude!' I turn quickly, recognising Hubert's voice. He's still in the temporary blue uniform he was given when he enrolled. I would have thought they'd have issued them with khaki by now.

'I didn't see you inside,' I say.

'I was at the back.' He gives me a little smile before joining me beneath the dark branches of the yew tree. I watch Mother talking to Mrs Ashby, her as lives up by Elmford Station and has the sweet shop in the Square. Her eyes are rimmed with red. For once, I don't know what to say to Hubert. I look down instead at the fallen yew berries with their strange, seductive holes. They glisten scarlet on the bare, poisoned earth.

'Oh, there's Mary Stacey, from the factory,' he says suddenly. 'She lost her husband, you know. I wonder if I should ....' I follow his gaze to where a young woman is walking down the path toward the gate, a single file of children behind her, dark little shadows like silent ghosts. They go slowly out of the gate, and disappear into the mist.

Hubert sighs. 'Never mind,' he says, 'I'll speak to her later.' He pauses. 'Archie's here somewhere.' He turns round, as if looking for him. 'You remember Archie McFadden, don't you? We met him when we went to the Fleet Review.' Oh yes, I remember him, with his damp hands and his condescending looks. 'He lost a cousin, you know.'

I feel a flush of shame. 'I'm sorry for him, then,' I say, and mean it.

He continues to look around. It's as if he's avoiding my eye.

'My mother's here, too,' he says. It sounds more like a warning than a statement. 'She's on the committee. Helped arrange things.'

Crowds are still pouring out of church and a large, red-faced gentleman in a top hat, bumps into us. As we move to make room for him, we have to step away from the shelter of the tree. The mist has become a fine drizzle, and it falls onto my face as I look up at Hubert.

'I'm afraid I've got to get back this evening,' he says. 'I promised Father I'd join them for dinner.'

'It's all right, Hubert,' I say. 'It was good of you to come. I have to get Mother home anyway.'

'I'm really very sorry about Arthur, Maude.'

I hesitate, searching for the right words but don't find them, so I just say, 'Thank you,' as if he were a stranger. Mother starts to make her way through the crowds toward us, pulling Mrs Ashby behind her, and I am just stepping forwards to meet them when a loud, high voice behind me makes me jump.

'Hu, darling! *There* you are.' I watch as the large, silver-haired woman I saw in church bustles up the path towards us. She flicks the briefest of glances at me before fixing her eyes on Hubert.

'Mother! I thought you must have gone.' How easily Hubert blushes. I do wish he wouldn't.

'So I see.'

'May I introduce Miss Timms to you, Mother?' Ah, she's got to look at me now, hasn't she?

'I'm pleased to meet you, Mrs Wells-Crofton, I'm sure,' I say, and it's all I can do to stop myself from curtseying.

She's a good four inches taller than me, though perhaps it's her heels, but she uses the extra height to look right down her nose at me. I'm glad I didn't hold out my hand, for she doesn't offer hers.

'Indeed?' she says instead, turning back to Hubert. 'I have to get on, darling. There's a reception at the Town Hall and I must be there. Don't be late for dinner now. Clara's coming.'

We stand and look at her retreating back. Clara.

'You don't want to take any notice of Mother,' he says. 'She can be a bit frosty at first. She'll be all right once she gets to know you.' A small snort escapes me. There's little chance of that happening.

'Well, perhaps I don't want her to,' I say, finally finding my voice, and lifting my chin. Mother comes up with Mrs Ashby, and it's my turn for introductions. My stomach flutters. I so want her to like Hubert. 'This is my friend, Mr Wells-Crofton, as I've told you about, Mother.'

He immediately gives her his full attention. It's as if he's trying to make up for his own mother's poor manners towards me. He reaches towards her with his hand. 'Mrs Timms,' I hear him say, 'please accept my sincere condolences.'

She nods, clasping his hand in hers. 'Thank you, lad,' she says, giving him one of her long, measuring looks, 'but we ain't the only family grievin'.'

She glances at Mrs Ashby, and I introduce her, too. 'Lettie's comin' back on the train with us,' Mother says, 'so we'd best be gettin' off, if you don't mind?'

'Of course, of course. I perfectly understand. Indeed, I must get off myself.' As I step forward to follow Mother, Hubert puts out his hand and stops me. 'I'm up for some leave soon, Maude,' he says. 'We could go out somewhere for the day. Would you like that?'

I shake my head. 'I don't know. I'm sorry, I can't think of such things at the moment, Hubert.'

'No, no, of course not.' He pauses. 'I'll write then,' he adds, as I turn away.

Chapter 14

The sun is bright on the chalky surface of the lane as I walk, and I lift my head to look towards the distant row of farm cottages. The crop in Bent Meadow beside me has long been cut and the stubble burnt, but a faint smell of scorching still lingers, and patches of gold glisten here and there amongst the swathes of black, like sunny islands.

The day is hung with the end of autumn. Not the dismal grey we've been having of late, but the glut of bright warmth that often comes late in the year, like a last reminder of summer. The baring trees are a mix of yellows and browns, and the sky above the slate cottage roofs is uncluttered by cloud. I slow my steps, enjoying the feel of the sun on me, and my thoughts slip back as they've been doing so much lately to the times when Arthur and I were children. How we loved to play in the lane, and race across the stubble.

The remains of the year's wild flowers are bent and brown now beneath the hedges, but the hawthorn berries in the hedge beside me are full and blood-red. Pain strikes through me like a hammer blow as I think how Arthur will never see this hedge again, nor watch the flowers come up, nor ever get off the train at Elmford Station to wander home through the village. I aim a kick at a flint stone in my path, watch as it scores a path in the dust, before bouncing to a stop in the verge.

The cottages grow steadily larger. I reach the five-barred-gate on the other side of the lane and stop, running my fingers across the roughness of the warm wood. It can't be long before Hubert is sent off to fight. The thought that I might lose him, too, makes me shiver despite the warmth of the day. They say the war will be over before Christmas, but I don't see how it can be when there's fresh trouble brewing up and battles being fought everywhere. That big one down at Mons for instance. Belgium's occupied, and now the Russians are joining in and there's talk of Portugal too. Heaven only knows where it's all going to end. And all because of the Germans. I can't help thinking that Hubert was right after all, we've got to fight them. We can't just sit back and let such things happen. I don't know how I could ever have thought we could. No, he was right and I was wrong, and I'll write and tell him so, too.

So many are being killed and wounded. They'll need a separate newspaper to put all the names in soon, if it goes on at this rate. Ron Cox was killed last week, Mrs Cox's son, her as runs the butcher's shop down by the forge. Died at Ligny. I remember Ron from school. In our Arthur's class he was, two years above me. Tall, strong lad, clever Mother said, but always acting the fool. Well, he won't be acting the fool any more, will he?

I reach the row of cottages and cross over the lane to Tom and Florrie's. Theirs is the one on the end. I pull up the latch of the gate, and push against the nest of honeysuckle that hangs in a tangle behind it. Tom'll have to sort that out before much longer. There'll be no getting through it at all soon. There are a few last roses, their heads thrust bravely against the cottage wall, a sweet reminder of the summer gone.

The corner of the cottage is in shadow, and the air is sharper there, but I'm soon out and passing by rows of onions and parsnips in the back garden. I pause by the last straggle of runner beans, and look in through the open door. Florrie is at the scullery sink, draining carrots in a colander. The autumn sun slants through, and I watch her as she sweeps a strand of hair back from her face, pink with the heat of cooking. A billow of steam rises up from the colander as she lets the water run through the carrots and, as I stand for a moment, I take in her creased brow and the unaccustomed stoop of her shoulders. Behind her, the baby lies, kicking, in its cradle. I can see his little toes peeping above the sides. He's whimpering.

The steam clears and suddenly Florrie looks up.

'Christ Almighty, Maude!' she says, balancing the colander on the empty saucepan, and putting a hand to her throat. 'You made me jump. I was miles away.'

'I can see that!' I step through the open door to give her a kiss on her hot cheek. A delicious smell of cooking fills the small room. 'Sorry,' I say, as I laugh at the look on her face.

'Well, you're just in time, anyway. Tom'll be in in a minute. I was beginnin' to wonder where you was.' The baby's whine kicks into a full-throated cry. Florrie looks across to where the crib stands in the shadow of the living room door. 'Oh, dear,' she says, and hesitates. 'He's not due a feed yet, not for another hour at least.' She turns back to spoon carrots onto three plates she has balanced on the draining board. I walk across to the crib, and stand looking down at little Horace. His face screws up, and another determined yell pierces the air.

'Is he hungry?'

'He's always hungry.'

'Well, if he was my baby, I'd feed him. I wouldn't take no notice of whether he's due, or not.' I look back at Florrie. 'I'll hold him till you finish dishing up if you like. See if I can take his mind off it till you're ready.'

Florrie looks at me for a moment, then smiles. 'Would you? That'd be a big help. I don't like it when he cries, poor lamb, an' he's been doin' a mite of that recently, what with him gettin' his first teeth early.' Florrie turns to lay knives, forks and spoons on the tiny kitchen table, and I reach into the crib to lift the baby up. The crying stops immediately.

'See?' I say. 'He likes his Auntie Maudie, don't you, my pet?' I rock him gently backwards and forwards as I walk towards the kitchen window. Dappled sunlight from the branches of the old apple tree plays across us and Horace kicks his little legs in response as he follows the shifting patterns with his eyes.

'He smiled!' I cry out.

'He's been doin' that for weeks.'

'Well, I haven't seen it before.' I turn him round to face Florrie, and Horace obediently repeats his gummy grin. Florrie comes towards us and pats his tummy.

'There weren't any smiles in the middle of the night, were there, you young tinker? Just wait till I tell your daddy you were savin' them all up for your Auntie Maudie.' A shadow crosses Florrie's face and she turns away, returns to lift the heavy enamel saucepan from the tiny range to the sink.

'What is it, Flo? What's wrong? Are you sad because of Arthur?' I ask. 'It's only natural, you know. I am, too. Sometimes I can hardly concentrate at all, for thinking of him.'

She holds the saucepan lid close against the pan of potatoes and slowly drains the steaming water away. 'That's part of it, Maude.'

'Then what's the rest?' I ask, gently rocking the baby backwards and forwards.

'Nothin'. It's nothin'.' Florrie is silent again as the shadow slides back onto her face.

'Flo? What *is* it?'

She turns to look at me. 'Well, it is summat, then. There! But it's no different for me than it is for anyone else,' she replies.

'What d'you mean? What isn't? Good God, Flo, it's like getting milk out of old Daisy, getting information out o' you.' I glance down at Horace as he begins to squirm in my arms. She sighs.

'It's Tom,' she says at last. 'He's talkin' of joinin' up. He wasn't goin' to, 'cos of me an' Horace. He said it wasn't fair, which it ain't, but he's been gettin' more an' more restless, an' I know it's because the others from the farm are all goin', an' he's not. But, someone's got to stay, or where would the country be, I told him, but he said it's not like that an' that I don't understand, an' maybe I don't.' She turns to look me full in the face. 'But I'm thinkin' he might as well go, Maude, 'cos he ain't no good to man nor beast the way he is, an' a man's not a man if he's not true to himself, is he, when all's said an' done? No, I've come round to thinkin' that it's no good him bein' here when he wishes he wasn't. That sort o' thing only creates a cart load o' trouble.'

'Most of the men are feeling like it, Flo,' I tell her. 'Everywhere you look there's an advertisement asking them to volunteer.' I think of Hubert and the trouble he had coming to a decision. 'It's hard for them.'

'I'm not sayin' it's not hard. An' I'm not sayin' that the Army don't need him, neither. The thing is, so do we.' The baby starts to cry again and I lift him so he lies across my shoulder. I rock his warm little body to me, supporting the back of his head with my hand. He turns his mouth to my neck and nuzzles against me.

'Here,' Florrie says suddenly, reaching out for him. 'You're right. If he's hungry, he should be fed, shouldn't you my darlin'? Do you mind carryin' on servin', Maudie?'

''Course not.' I carefully hold the baby out to her, and Florrie goes through to the living room, sits down with him in the low wooden chair in the corner of the room. She leans back to nurse him and I stand a moment in the doorway watching her.

'I don't know why there ever had to be a war in the first place but, there, that's as may be. I still never should've made him promise, I knows that now,' she says, gently stroking the baby's soft down. ''Tweren't fair. I were only thinkin' of myself, after all.'

'And Horace,' I remind her, watching as the baby suckles against the pale fullness of Florrie's breast, his eyes never leaving her face for a second as he sucks.

'Yes, an' the baby,' she says quietly, and traces the outline of his plump cheek with her finger. 'But it's been killin' Tom, Maude. One night last week he up an' told me he felt only half a man, because any man worth the title was enlistin'.' She looks up. 'His face has been that troubled at times, Maudie,' she says. 'It's worse than anythin'.' The baby suddenly releases its grip on Florrie's nipple, and smiles at her, milky bubbles at the corners of his tiny mouth. I wish for a moment that he was my baby, and that I was the one dropping a kiss onto the soft silky down of his head.

'But he still won't go and do it,' Florrie continues, 'not unless I says it's all right.' She pauses. 'He's promised, you see, an' my Tom's a man of his word. He won't go back on it, no, not even though his heart is breakin'.' She guides her dark nipple back into the baby's mouth and, with a fierce little shake of his head, he nuzzles against her again, and resumes his sucking. 'So I'm goin' to return his promise,' she says. 'I love that man well enough to want what's best for him, Maude, an' never mind the rest. Besides, he's just miserable bein' shackled to that promise I made him give.'

I hear a sound in the scullery behind me, and turn round.

Tom is standing behind me, looking down across my shoulder at Florrie. Tom's the best sort of husband, I always reckon; steady and strong. He's dressed in his work shirt and trousers, his sleeves rolled up to the elbow and open at the neck. He fills the little cottage with his presence.

'An' I'll never forget it, neither,' he says, his eyes holding Florrie's for a long moment. 'Now,' he says, rubbing his hands together and smiling. 'Enough of that there talk. Where's my dinner, woman?'

Chapter 15

I wait outside the lodging house for Hubert. The good weather has held and the day, for late November, is bright, the sunshine surprisingly warm as it seeps through my coat.

Mr Arnold didn't like it when I gave him my letter of notice, said hadn't I heard of such a thing as loyalty? I told him loyalty was something as couldn't be given but had to be deserved, and he called me ungrateful. I didn't give him the satisfaction of knowing he'd upset me for I'm not ungrateful, and never have been. Then he said that, what with so many of the men leaving, I was to give two weeks' notice, not one. But that's all right with me. I haven't gone across to Southampton yet, and don't even know if the Red Cross will have me, though Clara Fotherington reckons they're crying out for VADs and I shouldn't have any trouble at all. Anyway, I'm bound to find *something* to do to help with the war effort, surely, and if I have to draw on my savings for a week or two, well it's not the end of the world, even though I'll hate doing it. I'll miss the Emporium, mind. All those beautiful materials and threads. I'll miss the gossip of the place, too, and all the customers I've got to know. But then again, already it's not the same as it was, what with so many of the men joined-up, and people not buying like they did.

I step to the back of the pavement to let old Mr Simpson from Number forty-nine pass, and stay for a moment in the lee of the hedge. Opposite me, above the line of houses, gulls circle and scream in the clear blue sky, lifting lazily on the currents of air. I used to like seeing them, for Arthur told me that the sailors always knew when the ships were near land because they'd see the seagulls coming out from shore. Horrid, white harbingers of death, they seem to me now.

The horn, when it sounds, startles me. I look down the road in the direction of the seafront, trying not to gawp at the large maroon vehicle that is approaching. It's Hubert driving it! He didn't tell me he'd be arriving in a motor car! It slides to a halt beside me, and the engine stops. When the door opens, I see that Hubert's wearing a proper khaki uniform at last. He looks very handsome.

'What d'you think?' he asks, stepping onto the pavement to stand beside me and gesturing with his head. 'Beautiful isn't she?'

I can't help smiling, because it sounds as if he's talking about a woman. 'Yes,' I say, and I walk round, admiring the brass trimmings and the hood stretched over the top. 'She is.'

Hubert inserts the starting handle, and the engine catches at the third turn. He stows the handle away, and soon we're easing away from the pavement. I feel like royalty as I direct him along the narrow streets, and it's all I can do not to wave to the people who turn to look at us. We overtake horse-drawn carts and bicycles, and weave around stationary vehicles and waiting drays until we're on the road heading out of the city.

Hubert accelerates, breathing out a long sigh and leaning one hand lightly on the steering wheel. 'So,' he says, 'where shall we go?' The scenery is flashing by and I'm starting to feel quite giddy. As we leave Portsea Island behind, it suddenly feels as if I'm free.

'I don't care,' I laugh. Air sweeps into the car and buffets against him, ruffling his hair. 'You choose.'

'All right,' he says, smiling. He reaches out to cover my hand with his own, and I let my hand rest in his, enjoying the feel of his skin against mine, as we drive along the coastal road. The sea runs along parallel to us. It sparkles with sunshine. A flock of geese, come for the winter, glides across the road in front of us and lands on its grassy edge, and I turn my head to watch them as they waddle together, shaking their wings and waggling their tails before beginning to graze.

'It's hard to believe there's a war on. Everything looks so normal.'

'No war-talk today, Maude,' Hubert says with mock sternness. He traces my hand with his own and I link my fingers with his. 'By the way, we've got a picnic,' he says after a while.

'A picnic? At this time of year?' Despite my protest, excitement surges through me.

'Why not this time of year?' he laughs. 'Look at the day, it's as good as summer. There's a hamper under the blanket on the back seat. Cook's packed everything up for us. Ham, a bottle of wine, bread, cheese … lots of things. She's even done us one of her apple pies.' I grow quiet, thinking of the picnics we had on our Sunday School outings to Hayling, Arthur and I racing across the sand, Walter in tow, the wind in our hair, exhilarated by a childish sense of limitless space and time.

'Hubert?'

'Hmm?'

'Do you think it's wrong to feel happy after someone's died?'

'Are you thinking of Arthur?' I nod. 'I should think he

would want you to take every bit of happiness while you can,' he says gently.

'There's a part of me that I feel will never be happy again.'

'Perhaps we have to try even harder when that happens.' I lift Hubert's hand to my lips and kiss it gently when he says that, for it's just what I needed to hear. A feeling catches deep in me as my lips touch his skin. I let them linger on each of his fingers in turn, slide my tongue against his thumb.

He clears his throat, shifting his position, and lets his hand run down my thigh. I feel the warm pressure of his fingers through the thick serge of my skirt, and my breathing quickens.

He takes away his hand, and I turn to watch the countryside again. We're travelling northwards and we pass through Waterlooville and the little villages of Cowplain and Horndean, before entering a wood. I shiver, for it's much colder beneath the trees. The sunlight drops in patches, flickering on us as we pass slowly through it. Eventually, we emerge just south of Petersfield, and the sun streams through the windscreen again.

'What about the Downs?' Hubert says. 'The view's always glorious up there, and it might even be warm enough to sit out on the rug.'

'I've never been to the Downs before.'

'Well, let's go there, then.' He turns the car and I have a glimpse of hills, high, green and rolling. Excitement surges up in me. It feels as if we're in a different country.

We follow a sign for South Harting Village, and soon we're motoring past cottages with timbered frames and thatched roofs, then up a steep hill where Hubert has to change gear several times, and the car slows to a crawl so that I begin to think I'll have to get out and push. But, eventually we reach the top, and turn into a clearing. Hubert brings the car to a halt, and puts on the brake.

'Come on,' he says, 'let's walk first. Work up an appetite.'

The slopes are steep here, and they roll sharply down to the valley below. The sunshine picks out the tiny village of South Harting, nestling amongst the trees. We stand together, looking across the miles that lay between us and the horizon beyond. Everywhere, there is space and quietness.

We're all alone except for two tiny specks far away on the top of the highest fold of the Downs. The smallest of them races down the slope, back up then down again waiting for its owner who's walking behind it. The dog's excited bark comes faintly across the still air.

We've been walking for ten minutes or so when Hubert stops and points down the slope to a tiny glade surrounded by a rough circle of fir trees. 'There,' he says, 'the perfect place. We'll be sheltered there.' He turns. 'Come on, let's get the picnic. Race you to the car!' I begin to run, laughing and holding my hat, and I sprint the last fifty yards. My skirt catches at my ankles, and I reach down to lift it with my other hand so that I can run more easily. Hubert's close behind me. I know he's letting me stay just in front on purpose, for he's far fitter than me with all that training he's been doing. At the last minute, he accelerates past me as I knew he would, and he's not even out of breath as he touches the bonnet.

I'm laughing and panting at the same time. I lean back against the car and look up. The sun's past its highest point now, but it's still warm, and though I notice a purple-black cloud at the far edge of the valley, it's far off and with a bit of luck, it'll pass us by. Hubert reaches into the car, and hands me a red tartan rug. Then he lifts out a wicker picnic basket, and we start back along the small path that leads up into the Downs.

'Come on.'

With our burdens, we're slower than we were before, but eventually we reach the spot where the tiny path leads downwards. It's no more than a rabbit track really, and we have to walk carefully, Hubert bending back the snapping branch ends for me. When we get to the clearing, I feel the grass before I open the rug to spread it on the ground.

'It's all right,' I tell him, patting it down now over a stubborn tuft, a thrill running through me as I think of being here with him, secluded from the world. 'It's quite dry.'

Hubert places the basket on a corner of the rug then flings himself down in the centre, leaning his head back against his folded hands. I sit beside him, watching as he reaches out and breaks off a stem of dry grass, slips it between his lips. I laugh at him as I unpin my hat and lay it carefully beside me, tell him how he looks like one of the lads at Elmford at haymaking time. A chill breeze reminds us every now and then that it's late November as it catches at the branches at the edge of the clearing, but mostly it stops there, and inside our little hollow there's warmth and sunshine. It could still be September, if you didn't know.

'Let's eat.' Hubert sits up suddenly, and unbuckles the straps fastening the basket. The leather hinges creak against the wickerwork as he swings it open. He passes me plates and knives and forks then the packets of food, and I arrange it all carefully between us. He produces a thick tea towel, unwraps it to reveal two wine glasses, then reaches into a side section of the basket to draw out the bottle of wine. He twists a corkscrew down into the neck of the bottle and draws the cork with a practised movement. It slides out with a soft popping sound.

The sun catches at the pale yellow liquid as he pours. 'Why, it's like sunshine,' I say, and he laughs, lifts his glass to clink against the rim of mine.

'Here's to sunshine, then,' he says, and I let the cold wine slip across my tongue. The taste of it surprises me, for I've never had wine before. I let it linger in my mouth before I swallow. There's a burst of sharpness before it softens to a taste that reminds me of honeysuckle.

Hubert cuts a slice of ham, places it on a plate and passes it to me before taking some for himself. As we eat, I listen to the stillness of the day, broken only by the cries of passing birds and the slow buzz of a late bee. Hubert pours more wine into our glasses.

'Oh,' he says, patting the breast pocket of his coat. 'I almost forgot.'

I feel myself sway a little as I watch him pull a red, cloth-bound book from his pocket, and I put my wine glass at the edge of the blanket, wedging it down firmly, before taking the slim volume in my hand.

'I hope you'll like it,' he says. 'It's to say sorry for having been such a boor before I joined up.' We hold the book between us for a second, and he looks deep into my eyes. 'It's not a goodbye gift, Maude, but ….'

My voice sounds fierce when it comes. 'Don't say it!' I place the book in my lap, and bend my head low so my shadow falls across its cover. I rock gently, for his words have touched the conviction growing deep inside me, the certainty that the world is changing and I cannot stop it. All I can do, and it's the most awful thing of all, is to let it happen.

He reaches out his hand to me, lifts my chin so I have to look at him again, and I see the sunlight catch the darkness of his hair, so that it shimmers like the sheen of a rook's feather. Love wells up in me, but panic does too. I am afraid. Afraid of what I have already lost, afraid that he will leave and never return, afraid I will lose Walter, and Tom, too.

Afraid of this war.

'Listen,' he says, taking the book from me, and flicking through its pages till he finds what he's looking for. He leans back on one hand, holding the pages open with the other. Above us, the branches of the fir tree lift in the breeze and send a dappled pattern of sunshine and shade across his face. 'Come here for a minute,' he says, patting the space beside him. 'I'll read you some.'

I stand up and step across the food to sit next to him. 'Lay your head on me,' he commands, and I do what he says, adjusting my position till my head is resting against his legs. I can feel the hardness of his muscles beneath my neck. We have never been so free with each other before. It's wonderful. 'Now ....' He rests back again and lifts the open book high above him, the pages white against the blue sky. 'What about this one? We can dedicate it to your young nephew, if you like. It's called *A Clasp of Hands*.'

I think of baby Horace, the way he's grown so already. Hubert's voice is deep and soft as he reads.

> *'Soft, small, and sweet as sunniest flowers,*
> *That bask in heavenly heat*
> *When bud by bud breaks, breathes, and cowers,*
> *Soft, small, and sweet.*
>
> *A babe's hands open as to greet*
> *The tender touch of ours*
> *And mock with motion faint and fleet*
>
> *The minutes of the new strange hours*
> *That earth, not heaven, must mete;*
> *Buds fragrant still from heaven's own bowers,*
> *Soft, small, and sweet.*
>
> *A velvet vice with springs of steel*
> *That fasten in a trice*
> *And clench the fingers fast that feel*
> *A velvet vice.'* (3)

The air seems to absorb the words and keep them within the bower with us. My heart beats fast. What if it were possible that I might one day feel such things for a child of my own?

He puts the book down, and folds his arms behind his head. We lie together, my head pressed against his thigh, watching the sky through the lifting branches of the pine. My voice when I speak is almost a whisper.

'Today is so beautiful,' I hear myself say. 'I don't want it to end.'

'Everything ends, Maude.' I don't answer, because I don't know how. 'But, we can have other days like this.'

'Can we?' The wine must have loosened my emotions for hot, unexpected tears run across my temples.

'Of course we can. I'm jolly well going to do my best not to get killed over there, you know.' He dislodges me gently, sits up and bends over me so that his face is near to mine. 'Come on, cheer up. None of us know the future. Look, I've written something in the book for you,' he says. He turns to the fly-leaf and holds it open above me.

'To Maude.' I read the words silently. 'So you may keep me in your heart when I am away. Affectionately yours, Hubert.'

'You read one to me now,' he says, rolling on his back again. Come close, where I can see you.'

I ease nearer till I'm lying beside him, as you would with someone in bed, my body almost touching his. As I turn the pages, I sense Hubert watching me. I feel a blush start at my throat and rise to warm my cheeks.

'What is it? What have you found?' He takes the book from me, looks at the page and smiles. 'It's one of my favourites,' he says. 'Read it!' I hesitate. 'Please?'

I begin.

> *Lying asleep between the strokes of night*
> *I saw my love lean over my sad bed,*
> *Pale as the duskiest lily's leaf or head,*
> *Smooth-skinned and dark, with bare throat made to bite,*
> *Too wan for blushing and too warm for white,*
> *But perfect-coloured without white or red.*
> *And her lips opened amorously, and said-*
> *I wist not what, saving one word - Delight.*
> *And all her face was honey to my mouth,*
> *And all her body pasture to mine eyes;*
> *The long lithe arms and hotter hands than fire,*
> *The quivering flanks, hair smelling of the south,*
> *The bright light feet, the splendid supple thighs*
> *And glittering eyelids of my soul's desire.'* (4)

I turn to look at Hubert's face. His eyes, always such a deep blue in shadow, are almost colourless in the sunlight that touches them now. I lift a finger and gently trace his mouth. His lips quiver beneath my touch.

'Take your hair down for me, Maude.' Hubert's voice is low. I know I shouldn't. It isn't a seemly thing to do. But, it's private here, so who's to know? I sit up, slowly lift my hands to unpin my coils, and my hair falls to my shoulders. I hear Hubert's breathing change. 'I've waited so long to see you do that,' he whispers, raising himself up so that we're both kneeling, then he bends towards me to touch my lips with his own. I feel my breath catch, and I press into him, part my lips to taste him with my tongue. He tastes me back. So different this kiss from the kisses that have gone before.

'*The long lithe arms and hotter hands than fire*', he quotes, smoothing back my hair. He runs his lips along the length of my neck, *'with bare throat made to bite'*. He smiles as he slips an arm round me, and gently eases me, as if I weigh nothing at all, to lie on the blanket. I arch towards him, his face above me now, so close I can feel his breath on me.

'I didn't know there could be times like this,' I whisper, and feel the sunshine flick across my skin as the pine trees dip and creak their branches in the wind. We kiss, and each kiss seems to last an eternity. They follow, one upon the other, until their urgency leaves me breathless. But, when I feel his fingers begin to unbutton my blouse, I pull away, for I am afraid of what might follow. He does not pursue it and we lay together, breathless, silent and still, wrapped in each other's arms, until a shadow passes across us, and I look up to see that the large purple-black cloud has edged our way. Spots of rain splodge onto the picnic things, clinking into our empty glasses.

We get up quickly, laughing as we brush down our clothes. I haven't time to do up my hair, and I flick the long coils back across my shoulders. Then we begin to pick up the food, wrapping the remnants hurriedly in their greaseproof wrappers, and returning them to the hamper. Scooping everything up, we hasten up the slope and run to the car, the hamper bumping between us as icy rain begins to fall, cutting down on us in long, wintry needles.

Chapter 16

Carlton Crescent. I walk against the flow of people, looking along the terraced buildings for the VAD recruiting office. The weather turned with the month end, and a raw December wind cuts at me. It seems that winter has set in at last. I feel my hat lift, and slow down. It's hardly going to create the right impression if I arrive for my interview all blown about, is it?

The interview. I try to calm the butterflies in my stomach. What sort of questions will I be asked? I only hope they won't be too difficult, for they'll be sure not to want me if I just sit there opening and shutting my mouth like a fish on dry land, with nothing coming out at all. I feel for my handbag, unclasp it and, for the tenth time that morning, peer in. It's still there, of course. My First Aid Certificate. My stomach flutters again. What will I do if I don't get accepted? I've only got three days left at the Emporium. What a fool I was to hand in my notice first, but those blessed feathers got me so riled up, I just couldn't help it.

I look up again, glance along the street, and breathe a sigh of relief. There it is, a large red cross on the wall, several doors down. I hurry on, turn up the wide shallow steps and push open the door. Just in time, too, for at that very moment a downpour starts, heavy raindrops spattering the window panes. An elderly woman looks at me from behind her desk, and raises her eyebrows in disapproval as I stand there, leaves swirling about my ankles. I quickly push the door shut, and step towards her.

'I've come to see the recruiting officer, please. I have an appointment.' I unclip my handbag and take out the letter I have received.

'I don't need to see that,' she says curtly. She looks down at a list on her desk. 'Name?'

'Timms – Miss Maude Timms.'

'You're rather early.' She writes something down by my name. 'Wait over there,' she says, and points to a row of chairs by the window. 'You'll be called when we're ready.' I can't help but narrow my eyes at her. Hasn't she heard that manners cost nothing?

I'm the only one in the waiting area so I sit down opposite the window, and watch the people outside as they hurry up and down the pavement, their umbrellas bumping against each other. A woman with white hair emerges from a corridor and walks up the room towards me. I get up, but she only smiles at me as she passes, then disappears through a door behind me. I sit down again, listening to the rain on the window, watching the drops grow slowly larger until they fall, one by one, in zig-zag paths onto the frame.

What dreadful weather it is. I'm glad I dodged the worst of it. I wonder what Hubert is doing. Do they send them out when it's like this? I dismiss the thought as soon as it comes. Of course they do. They don't molly-coddle men who are going to be sent to war.

A girl hurries along the railings outside. I see her pass the window before turning up the steps, holding onto her hat against a sudden gust of wind. The door opens and she reports, breathless, to the desk, waiting impatiently, her hands on her hips. She's small, like me, a little bit taller perhaps but dark, more Hubert's colouring, and has on a lovely green coat, almost black, with a fur trim. The same fur is picked out on her hat and her cheeks are rosy, whipped up by the weather outside. She's very pretty. At last the receptionist looks up from her writing and asks her for her name. The girl bends forwards over the desk to give it, but even though I strain, I can't hear what she says from here. Then she's sent to sit with me, and I'm glad. At least I'll have someone to talk to.

She comes across, and holds out her hand. Our gloves slip together. 'Anastasia Pemberton,' she says. 'Call me Ana, everybody does.'

'Maude,' I reply. 'Maude Timms.'

'Are you volunteering?'

I nod. 'I want to become a VAD nurse.'

'Good show! Me too.' She sits down and leans against the hard upright chair. 'I say, what do your family think of you becoming a VAD?' she asks me immediately, but doesn't wait for a reply. 'When I told Mummy and Daddy that I was going to be a nurse, they said I wouldn't last more than a day.' She laughs and I join in, for even though I don't know her, it's hard for me to imagine her emptying bedpans and suchlike. She seems too ladylike for that. 'I told them they were in for a big surprise, then,' she said, 'for I'm quite *determined* to be a success.'

'Well, at least you're trying, and nobody knows anything till they try, do they?' I pause. 'I'm not really the Florence Nightingale type myself either to tell the truth, but I want to help, so I thought I'd give nursing a go.'

'Good for you, Maude,' she says. 'I may call you Maude, mayn't I?' I nod and we sit, talking quietly, the only other sounds the tapping of the branches of the tree outside on the window pane and the clink of the receptionist's cup in her saucer.

'I'm going to ask to be sent abroad. That's where the real action is. Are you?'

I have a sudden vision of myself working in a tented hospital, surrounded by wounded men needing my help. 'I can't,' I say. 'We … we had some trouble at home. It's my brother – he was killed last month.' I say it quickly, so the words don't have time to settle. She smiles her sympathy, and I rush on. 'I want to stay close for a while in case Mother and Dad need me. Besides, we'll have to do our training first before we think of things like that, won't we?'

'Yes, you're probably right,' Ana replies. 'I say, you're not the sensible type are you? I can't *bear* being sensible.' She pauses. 'Wouldn't it be grand if we trained at the same hospital?'

I'm about to answer that yes, it would, when the door opens and the lady with the white hair appears again, trotting towards us. 'Miss Timms?' she says to both of us, her eyebrows raised.

'That's me,' I say. My knees suddenly feel weak as I stand up.

'Well, this way then, dear.'

'Good luck,' Ana whispers.

'Thanks. You too.'

I follow her down a corridor, and we turn left into a small office. She goes inside, and I hesitate on the threshold, not sure if I should enter or not. 'Come along in,' she calls. I step into the room. 'This is Mrs Talbot,' she says with a gesture of her hand to a woman sitting behind a desk. 'She's in charge of recruitment, and will be interviewing you.' She takes a seat by the side of the desk, and motions me to close the door. I feel Mrs Talbot's clear grey eyes take in every aspect of me, from my best felt hat and woollen gloves to my long winter coat, and I draw myself up as tall as I can.

'Sit down,' she orders. I move forwards to sit on the edge of the chair in front of the desk, and look across to where she sits on the other side. Mrs Talbot's in her late forties I reckon. She has on a navy-blue uniform, and has pulled her hair back tightly in a coil. She sits there, straight as a ramrod, looking at me, and I think how the single electric light bulb hanging down above the desk makes her skin look very pale. If she's trying deliberately to scare me, she's doing a very good job.

'So, you want to be a nurse?' she says, resting her hands on the desk in front of her as she looks at me. My heart bumps uncomfortably.

'Yes, Madam. A VAD.'

'Why?'

'*Why*, Madam?'

'Are you deaf, girl? Why do you want to be a nurse?'

I take a deep breath. 'Well, because of the war.' It seems such an obvious thing to say, but I can only tell the truth, after all, even if it does seem lame. I lurch on. 'All our men dying and being injured. I want to help, if I can.'

'Everyone wants to help,' she says, linking her fingers together. 'Just what is it that makes you think you've got what it takes for nursing? You young girls have such a romanticised view of it, but what it comes down to is a great deal of hard work. It's not a game, you know,' she adds, frowning at me.

'I understand that. I never thought it was a game.' I feel the hairs on my neck bristle. 'And I'm not afraid of hard work, Madam, neither.'

A half smile forms on her lips. 'Well, I'm glad to hear that, for you'll certainly get plenty as a nurse.' Her eyes stay fixed on me. 'You'll need to have certain attributes if you're to be any use to us,' she continues. 'It's my job to ascertain whether you have them or not.' She pushes a sheet of paper towards me. 'Please read the list from that section there.' I look to where her finger is pointing. 'Aloud, Miss Timms.'

'These words here?' She nods.

'*Courage, patience, humility, determination to overcome difficulties ….*'

'There will be many of those, make no mistake,' she interrupts. 'You'll also need to be courteous, unselfish and kind. Do you think you have any of those qualities, Miss Timms?'

I straighten my back. 'I'd like to think I have them all, Madam, but I suppose I won't know until I'm put to the test. But I *am* strong, even if I don't look it.'

She smiles then, a proper smile. It melts the frost from her face. 'I know from experience that appearances in that department can be deceptive,' she says.

I look at her own slight frame. 'I don't tire easily,' I continue. 'My dad always says ....'

'Ah yes, your family. What sort of background do you have?' I return her look, stare for stare. If this is about class, I'm not going to get in. 'I have to establish your financial position if you're to be a VAD,' she says gently. 'I gather you have no independent means?'

'No.'

'It's not the end of the world, Miss Timms,' she says. 'Don't sit there looking as if you've lost a crown and found a farthing. There are funds available for girls like you.'

Girls like me? There she goes again. What does she mean, girls like me? 'I've got some savings,' I say, lifting my chin. I think of my trips to the Post Office each Friday, and the slow way the pennies have grown into pounds. The last thing I want to do is spend them, but then, what's the use of savings when there's a war on?

'Good, then you'll be able to buy some of your uniform. If you can't afford everything, we can arrange it so that you pay a monthly amount against the cost. Your salary will be twenty pounds per annum to start, and you'll have seven days' leave for the first six months, fourteen for the second.'

Mrs Talbot draws the form back towards her and begins to fill it in, writing my answers to the questions she now fires at me. I give her my address and my date of birth, Dad as my next of kin. She asks me about my present job and how long I've been there and what it is that I do, exactly. I tell her I'm a senior drapery assistant, but I don't say I've already handed in my notice, for there's no point courting trouble, is there? Eventually, she puts down her pen.

'Well, I think I can safely say we can take you – subject to one month's probation period, of course,' she says, and I feel a smile begin. I can't help it. It just spills out across my face. 'If it all goes well, and should you wish it, of course, you'll be able to sign an agreement after that for a further six months.'

'Thank you, Madam,' I say.

'Now, I just need the name of a referee.'

Oh dear. Dare I give Mr Arnold's name after that bother with the feathers? But who else can I give? I suppose I could say Mrs Lawson who I worked for when I'd finished being a helper at school, but that seems too long ago now. I swallow hard. 'Mr Graham Arnold,' I say. 'Mason's Emporium, Commercial Road in Portsmouth.'

Mrs Talbot dips her pen in the ink again and writes down the details. 'Assuming that's all in order,' she says, 'your application will go off to be approved by the War Office. You'll be required to start in approximately two weeks' time.' She lifts her eyebrows to look at me. 'Any questions?'

I feel a flutter of excitement as I shake my head. 'No, Madam.'

'You will be undertaking your training in one of our local hospitals, but after that you will be sent anywhere the authorities have need of you.'

I feel my stomach sink. 'Oh.'

'Do you have a problem with that, Miss Timms?'

'I hope not,' I begin, watching as her eyebrows rise. 'But ....' The pause seems to fill the little room.

'But ...?'

'Could I possibly stay at a hospital nearby? If it's not too much trouble,' I add in a small voice.

She slowly places her fingertips together and stares at me.

'And why is that?' she asks.

'To be near my parents, Madam.'

'Perhaps if you are still tied to your mother's apron strings, you should ask yourself if nursing is quite the thing for you?'

'It's because of my brother, Madam. He was killed last month, at sea. My parents have taken it hard. It'd only be for a little while, I'm sure.'

She looks at me for a second, then makes a note on my form. 'I'll recommend that you serve at The Royal Victoria Hospital at Netley for the time being,' she says. 'I'm sure they'll be pleased enough to have a nurse who doesn't want to keep moving on.'

'Yes, Madam. Thank you.'

'That's all. You'll receive a letter with details of what to do next. Thank you for attending, Miss Timms. Send the next girl in, please.'

'Yes, Madam.' I stand, my chair scraping on the brown linoleum floor.

Reception has filled while I was being interviewed. I pick Ana out, and she smiles at me as I walk across to her, my steps light as my mood.

'What's she like then?'

I glance behind me. 'She's all right,' I say in a low voice, and my eyes sweep the girls' anxious faces, thinking that's how mine must have looked ten minutes ago. 'She says the next one's to go in.' Ana jumps up.

'That's me, then,' she says. I stand aside and watch as she moves quickly across the room, and turns down the corridor.

Mother looks at the piles laid out on my bed, and at the sheet of paper she's picked up headed 'List of Required Clothing and Equipment.' 'Good Lord, child,' she says, 'this lot must've cost you a fortune.'

'I haven't paid for it all yet, Mother,' I explain to her. 'I bought my dresses and underwear, but I'm allowed to pay for the rest monthly, out of my wages.' We stand together, looking down, and a slant of winter sun slices through the window to lie across the items spread out. It catches, too, on the opened trunk that stands against the wall by the door, and excitement and nervousness twine together inside me.

On the bed, collars lay next to aprons and undershirts, corsets and petticoats next to dust-skirts and stockings. There's a night jacket, too, and galoshes and handkerchiefs, a hand-towel, mirror, clothes brush and shoe cleaning equipment; then there's my sewing kit, New Testament, a pack of stearine candles, a lantern and a lighter. I shiver, pulling my cardigan close around me. The temperature is dropping quickly. The sky outside my bedroom window is already growing pink with the lowering sun.

'Can't think what you'll need it all for,' Mother says. 'But there, rules is rules I suppose, an' if they says you've got to have it, then you've got to have it.'

'I have, Mother.' I look across the room at the chair in the corner where I've draped my uniform, feel a thrill at the thought of putting it on tomorrow, and walking through the village to the station. I'll walk right past the shops, leave early and go slow so folks can see me.

The following morning when I wake, I tug aside the thin floral curtains. There's frost on the inside of the darkened windows. I hold my finger against the pane, like I used to as a child, and melt a dark circle in the white leafy pattern. Despite the way my skin shivers into tiny pimples in the cold air, I dress slowly, relishing each garment. My excitement grows with the layers until I'm not Maude Timms, senior drapery assistant, any more but Nurse Timms, VAD probationer. And I'll be the best they've ever had at the Royal Victoria, too, I tell myself.

I pack the rest of my things, and buckle up the straps on my trunk. I'm the first up so, once downstairs, I light the fire in the range, then put the kettle on to boil for tea before washing my face in the scullery sink. I move around, trying to get used to the heaviness of my uniform, and hang my new coat with its flannel lining, on the peg by the front door. That weighs a ton too. I'll feel as if I'm carrying a sack of potatoes with everything on, though I won't be cold, that's one good thing. Mother comes down the stairs, and through to where I'm spooning tea into the pot on the living room table.

'You're up then?'

'Have to be if I'm to catch the seven-ten Southampton train, Mother. You know I can't bear being late, unlike our Walter,' I add, walking across to the range to take the holder and lift the kettle that's wisping curls of steam from its spout. 'I've been meaning to say, Mother ....' I hold the kettle steady as I pour, and try to make out that what I'm about to say doesn't matter much, though it does. 'If you need me for anything urgent, don't forget you can use Mrs Spinks's telephone at the Post Office. The hospital will always get a message to me, providin' it's urgent o' course.'

'I ain't usin' no blessed telephone,' Mother replies, bustling through to the scullery. 'I've managed without telephones all me life, and I ain't startin' now. Modern, new fangled things.' I watch her through the open door as she lifts cups and saucers from the draining board, wipes the rims with a cloth. She comes back to place them on the table in the living room, and I pull forward the breadboard with its half-loaf upon it wrapped in a cloth.

'Anyone would think I was suggesting throwing yourself under a train, Mother, not making a telephone call,' but I soften my words by moving towards her and putting an arm around her. I feel her tense, for normally we don't touch

125

much. 'Anyway,' I say, releasing her, 'like as not you won't need to anyway. It's only just in case.' Mother nods then and turns towards the little door that blocks off the stairway, opens it and shouts up the stairs.

'You gettin' up, George?'

'I'm already up, woman,' comes the reply, and as she turns back into the room, I suddenly notice how stooped she's becoming. Her shoulders, usually so strong and straight, have developed a hunched look. How is it that I haven't noticed that before?

We don't start breakfast till Dad comes down. Then we have bread and a bit of left-over cold meat. We're half-way through when, suddenly, Mother gets up and puts out butter and some of her plum jam. I smile, for normally we only have jam for Sunday tea. It makes me think of Walter. He loves jam. I wonder if they have it at training camp? I feel a sudden stab of longing for him to be here, clumping about upstairs and Mother shouting to him to hurry up.

When we've finished and I've helped clear away, I remember the book Hubert gave me. I'm sure I've left it on the chair by the side of my bed, for I was reading it last night before I went to sleep. I run quickly upstairs to get it. Yes, there it is. I pick it up, stroke the coarse red cover and stand for a moment, looking around the tiny room. My eyes travel across my narrow bed, pushed hard against the wall, to my trunk, then to the tallboy with its collection of stones and shells. I walk across to the window, and release the latch. In the growing light, the garden looks grey and untidy, desolate apart from two shadowy rows of sprouts and some curly kale.

'You want an 'and with that there thing, then?' I turn round. It's Dad. He points to the tin trunk I've closed and strapped, and I nod as I pull the window closed. He stoops and picks up the trunk with a grunt, for though it's not large, nor full, it's heavy enough with my things inside. I hear his slow footsteps on the stairs as he makes his way down. The silence is empty with his leaving, and the cold air in the room feels stopped somehow. I think of Horace and Arthur, and Florrie away at the farm. Now, with Walter joined up, it seems a part of my life is over for ever. It's our going that's suffocating the room, taking the life from it. I look down again at the garden, and at the gardens beyond, and those beyond them, too, to the edge of the village square. With the winter sun drawing long morning shadows over everything, it feels like I'm saying goodbye. Memories of us as children come towards me like a wave, then break over me in one heart-squeezing moment and are gone, draining away as they recede into the past.

I square my shoulders, turn and walk out of the room, down the narrow stairs. Dad's in the scullery, shaving. The steam rises from the enamel bowl that stands in the sink, and he peers into the tiny mirror that's propped up on the window sill. I watch as he scrapes the razor over his cheeks, taking care near his thick moustache so as not to spoil it. I often think it's Dad's only vanity, that moustache. He dips his flannel into the hot water, wipes the cloth over his face.

He senses my presence and turns, reaches for the towel on the peg and returns my gaze. I'm dressed and ready to go, my nurse's apron already tied on over my dress. Only my head square is left, folded neatly in my pocket, to do later at the hospital.

Dad and I stand there for a minute looking at each other. Then he tips the water from the bowl into the sink, and slowly wipes his hands on the towel before hanging it back on its nail. He walks towards me and as I step back to let him through, he pauses.

'You look the part, girl, I'll say that for yer.' He puts out a hand and rests it on my shoulder for a moment before passing through to the living room, and it's all I can do not to let go the choke of tears inside me.

I can still feel the pressure of his fingers as I wait for young Jimmy Wheldon from up the road to come and help me to the station. I feel them as I sit on the train, chugging along the coast to Southampton, and I feel them now as I step onto the platform at Netley.

'You go on, love,' the porter says to me. 'This'll come up later with the others.'

He lifts Dad's old tin trunk as if it were a bundle of twigs, places it onto a trolley, and drags it away into the shadows of the platform.

Chapter 17

'Stop!'

I'm so deep in thought about Mother and Dad and the home I've just left, that I jump an inch off the ground when the guard shouts at me. He comes out of his hut by the hospital gate and marches towards me, a clipboard in his hand.

'Here on business, are you?' he asks.

'Yes.' I point to my uniform, for I should have thought that was obvious. The wind is icy, and cuts at my face as he looks down at his list.

'Anyone can dress up, miss,' he sniffs. 'That don't mean a thing. You're expected, then?'

I nod, looking up at him. 'My name's Timms.'

'You should be on the list, then.' He runs a finger down the page. 'Fact is,' he says, flicking over his sheet of paper, 'I'd lose my job if I was just to take people's word for it. Never know who might get in. You could be a German in disguise, for all I know.' A picture of Gertie comes into my mind. 'You can smile, miss, but it's more than possible. Trained to look out for it, we are. Here it is,' he continues, 'Miss Maude Timms. That you, is it?' I nod. 'In you come then.' He lifts the barrier and smiles at me. Ah, yes, nice as pie he is now. A German indeed! I put my chin up as I pass into the hospital grounds, taking the path that runs along beside Southampton Water.

The wind whips off the sea, slicing into my face as the sky clouds over. I was right about this coat being warm at any rate. Yes, warm as toast, it is. I watch the sea as I walk, for I like the way the wind ruffles the surface and pushes the waves across the shingle, making that shushing sound. I settle my feet into a steady stride. How grey the water is. Yes, grey as our old zinc bath.

On my left, I catch glimpses between the trees of the long, long building that is the Royal Victoria Military Hospital. It stretches down to a dome in the middle, and then away again beyond. I've heard say it's a quarter of a mile long. A quarter of a mile! But I can't say as I ever really believed it till now. How grand it looks with its red and white bricks, and its lawns that go down to the sea; more like a big hotel than a hospital I'd say. However many patients can there be here? Hundreds, I should have thought. Thousands, perhaps.

I walk along until I reach the pier that juts out into the sea opposite the dome. The cloud is low on the water, and I can only just make out the landing stage at the end, shaped like the top of the letter 'T'. There are little pockets of ice here and there, looking like ghostly footprints.

Despite the cold and the early hour, there are a good number of people about, especially on the pier, patients with bandages and walking aids, some in invalid carriages being pushed along. I can hear them talking and laughing as I approach. There are nurses, too, their short capes splashes of red, welcome colour in the late December day.

I glance quickly at the clock on the chapel tower that rises behind the main entrance. Nearly a quarter to ten. I still have fifteen minutes before I'm expected. Good. I can collect my thoughts before I go in. I turn, walk onto the wooden slats of the pier, and make my way to one of the benches that have been placed there. A man is leaning against the trellised balustrade, wearing an overcoat that looks far too big for him. He looks as if he's been very ill, for his face is pale and hollowed out. He stands up and lifts his fingers to his cap as I pass, then turns back to lean across the rail again, the line from his fishing rod pulled taut by the swell of the dark water below.

Another man comes from behind me, and I smile at him as we sit down together on a bench. I know by his blue suit and red tie that he's a patient here. Why ever hasn't he got a coat on in this weather? He sits at the end of the bench, pressed close to the wrought-iron edge, and stares at me. No, not at me, more through me, as if I'm not here at all. I watch him in alarm as, suddenly, his mouth begins to twitch uncontrollably.

'No place for a lady, this, miss,' he says, lifting a shaking hand towards me. I shrink back, even though I try not to, until I feel the hard edge of the bench against my arm. 'They're blowing them all up.'

'Are they?' I watch his face as it grows animated, his mouth working and his head shaking from side to side. His eyes stare, wide open, not blinking.

'You make sure you stay well back in the communication trenches. Don't go up to the front line, whatever you do. They're blowing them all up. All of them. All of them, I tell you.' Suddenly, he makes the sound of a loud explosion and aims a pointed finger towards the sea, spraying invisible bullets as he rat-a-tats. I feel my sharp intake of breath, my heart pounding, and watch as tiny gobs of spit arc from his mouth.

The thin man at the edge of the railings now limps quickly towards us, leaning heavily on his walking stick. He nods in my direction before crossing to the man beside me.

'Easy, Colin, mate.' He places a hand on his shoulder and looks closely into his face, trying to catch his gaze. 'Easy, mate,' he repeats. 'You're all right now. You're back in Blighty, remember?' He glances across at me. 'Shell blast,' he explains. 'He was at Ypres.' He looks back at Colin. 'Weren't you, old chap?' Colin has stopped firing, but now sits, shaking from head to foot. 'Only one in the trench who survived,' he tells me. 'Dug the others out with his bare hands. Not that it was any use, they were all dead anyway.' He points towards the hospital. 'They call it shell-shock in there, but I know what I'd like to bloody well call it, begging your pardon, miss.'

A nurse must have seen what was happening, for she hurries towards us now and puts out her hand to touch Colin's arm. 'Come on, my dear,' she says. Her voice is soft and low. 'Let's go back inside and have some tea, shall we?'

Colin looks at her with wild eyes and pulls away. He shakes his head, and frowns as if he's trying to understand who she is and what she's doing there. The nurse gently puts her hand on his arm again, and Colin looks at her. This time, there's recognition in his eyes, and the frown disappears.

'Come along,' the nurse repeats, and he allows himself to be led away. The thin man tips his cap at me once more, and returns to his fishing rod. I listen to the uneven, retreating footsteps and I wonder, as my heart continues to thump in my chest, whether I have done the right thing, after all, in coming here.

It's too late for thoughts like that, I tell myself firmly. I turn round to glance at the clock behind me, then stand up and make my way up the avenue to the main entrance. But, what if they put me on a ward full of men like Colin? My stomach turns over at the thought. Would I be able to be like that nurse, the way she treated him with such patience and kindness? I hurry up the avenue. Or would I be heartless? Worse still, would I be afraid? And, what if Hubert got sent to war, and came back like that? Would I still feel the same way about him? The frost, melting from the branches above, falls with little pattering sounds onto pools of blackened leaves beneath the trees.

Despite the rawness of the day, the large doors of the entrance to the hospital are open. Inside the lofty hall, it's not the wide stone staircase sweeping upwards that takes my eye, though that's grand enough. It's the skeleton of an elephant that stands in the centre. An elephant! It towers above me. I drag my eyes away, and look around. There are glass cases, each containing strange exhibits. The most gruesome of all is one that has shelf upon shelf of human skulls. But, everywhere there's something odd; a display of curling antlers rising high above me; a shoal of fossilized fish that seem to be swimming upwards beside the staircase; there's even a stuffed crocodile that looks as if it's making its way down to snap me up. I stand there, staring, mesmerised. It's as if I'm in a museum rather than a hospital.

'Don't worry, miss,' a voice behind me breaks into my thoughts, 'everyone gets a surprise when they come here for the first time. They're South African, brought across in the last war.' I turn to where an elderly man sits behind a high desk. 'Now,' he says. 'How may I help you?'

'I've come to work here as a VAD.'

'Have you now? Well, well. Down the corridor, then, and Lecture Room Eleven. Sister Tompkinson's doing the new intake this week.' He comes out from behind the desk, and gestures towards another set of swing doors. He holds them open for me, and I look down a long corridor. It seems to stretch on and on forever. The wall on my left, the one that faces the sea, has windows that drop from the ceiling almost down to the floor, and though the day is overcast, they still fill the corridor with light. The floor gleams, and dotted here and there are chairs and tables with potted plants. There's even a bird cage with a pair of canaries in it. The atmosphere reminds me of the conservatory at Elmford Manor House that I saw once when I went with Mother to deliver the washing, only this is bigger. Much, much bigger. Oh, I do wish Mother could see it. Perhaps one day, if they let us have visitors, she'll come and I can show it to her.

'Now then,' the clerk behind me says, 'straight down till you get to the group of chairs. See?' Half-way down is a wicker table with seats ranged round it. I nod. 'The lecture room's there on the right, next to G. Eight. You'd better make sure you don't go in there, miss. G. Eight's Sister Browning's ward. No-one's allowed in there as shouldn't be.' He laughs. 'Look for the door marked Number Eleven. Good luck, now.'

'Thank you,' I say uncertainly.

'You'll be all right, miss.'

I hear the swing doors close behind me as I begin walking. I don't feel as if I'll be all right. A patient, one leg heavily bandaged, lurches towards me on his crutches. He's laughing, and a man beside him whose head is swathed with bandages, is laughing too. How is it that they can be so cheerful with injuries like that? Perhaps it's just that they're glad to be away from the war. A nurse emerges from a door, and walks briskly by, nodding to me. I draw myself up and nod back.

The empty wicker seats have filled with patients by the time I reach them, and I have to endure their frank looks of appraisal as I turn towards the lecture room. My cheeks are still burning from their stares as I make my way past Sister Browning's ward. I stop at a door painted brown on which a small brass plaque is fixed. 'G. Eleven Lecture Room', it says.

'Go on. She won't bite.' I turn to look behind me. It's the man I saw on the pier, minus his fishing rod, leaning on his walking stick. 'Well, not enough to draw blood, anyway.' He smiles then limps past me and I listen to the tap, tap of his walking stick as he passes through the swing doors to the ward. I turn back and knock softly on the door and listen. Nothing. I hesitate, then knock again, this time more loudly.

'Come!' A deep female voice booms from within the room. I turn the handle of the door and push. It swings open easily. I hesitate on the threshold. 'Well, don't just stand there, girl. Find yourself a seat.'

I move forwards, closing the door behind me. Upwards of twenty girls turn to stare at me as I sit down, and a surge of annoyance rises in me. If I'd have known they were going to start early, I'd have come in sooner. I choose a chair next to a plump, dark-haired girl at the back. The room is laid out with chairs in rows, like a classroom, and it makes me feel as if I am back in school. My eyes focus on the woman who has called out to me. She's standing next to a blackboard and easel, looking at me. I take in the starched white cap pinned on top of her greying hair, the cleanliness of her uniform that falls to her ankles without a single crease, the whiteness of her cuffs. My heart bumps uncomfortably, and I drop my eyes. How fierce she looks.

When I come out of the lecture room, my brain is spinning. There seem so many things to remember, all the do's and don't's. The golden rule, it seems, is not to run, either inside the hospital or out. And never report late for duty. What else was it she said? Oh, yes, we must always speak with civility, to our patients, our superiors, and to each other. 'And I'm sure,' she'd said, 'I don't need to tell you that you must exhibit clean hands and uniforms *at all times*. You are to treat the patients with the compassion fitting your profession, and show a cheerful manner – whether you are feeling it or not.' She'd looked sternly at each of us then. 'And as for your rooms, it is your duty to keep them neat and tidy. Be warned, there will be inspections to ensure that you do!' And so on and so on and so on. How we're supposed to remember it all, I'm sure I don't know.

'What a dragon!' The girl I was sitting next to in the lecture room, slips into step beside me. She nods towards Sister Tompkinson who is in front of us, leading the way out of the swing doors and up the wide pathway at the back of the hospital. 'Kitty Brown, by the way.'

'Maude Timms.' I turn to look at Kitty. She's what Mother would call well-built and she has fine, dark eyebrows that go up and up without turning down at all. It makes them seem as if they want to fly off her face.

'What made you become a VAD, then?' she asks. I hesitate, then tell her about Arthur. There's no point hiding it, after all. 'He was on the *Good Hope*,' I say.

'You poor thing! How awful.'

'I didn't have much time for the war before, but our Arthur going seems to have changed everything.' I'm quiet for a moment. 'What about you?'

'Me?' She laughs. 'I just wanted to wear a uniform. I say, Maude,' she says, after a pause. 'Can you keep a secret?'

''Course I can.'

'Actually, I'm engaged.'

'What? To be married?'

'Of course to be married. His name's Conrad. He's a pilot,' she says, tossing her head. 'You know, aeroplanes. It's wonderfully exciting, isn't it? He's waiting to be sent overseas. Look.' She turns round to make sure Sister Tompkinson's not looking, then slips open the top button of her dress and eases up a red velvet ribbon. It has a gold ring threaded onto it, a band with two blue stones set in it, sapphires I suppose, with a diamond in the centre. She shields it with her hand. 'No-one knows about it yet.'

'What? Not even your parents?'

'Pooh! Especially them. They've got someone very different

in mind for me. Someone who works in my father's office at the Town Hall. You ought to see him. Ugh!' She gives a mock shudder and I laugh.

'Well, the ring's lovely,' I say and as she slips it back beneath her dress, I feel a sudden stab of envy. I wonder if Hubert will ever give me a ring? If our worlds weren't so different, he might, for I know he cares about me. But there's never even been a whisper of such a thing, not even after our day on the Downs.

We step aside as a trolley rattles towards us, and I look at the man lying on it. I can't help staring. His face is pale and he's clutching a grey blanket close up beneath his chin. He's shivering. The porter is only a lad, younger even than our Walter, I'd say. He's still got pimples on his cheeks. He doesn't seem at all worried about his patient, and gives us a cheeky grin as he turns off the path towards one of the huts by a tall flag pole. As we walk, the wind suddenly takes the flag and stretches it out, revealing a Welsh dragon.

'That'll be where the *she* lives, then!' Kitty says, pointing to Sister Tompkinson, and we giggle as if we are children rather than probationary nurses with responsibilities.

'Come along, look lively. We haven't got all day.' Sister Tompkinson hurries us along, stopping at one of the huts halfway up. We all gather round her as she reads from the list in her hand.

'Tremayne, Morris, Smith and Owen,' she says. Four girls move towards the front. 'You'll be billeted here. You'll find your trunks inside. The rest of you come with me.' She turns and walks quickly along another path that runs parallel to the hospital. We stop at another grey hut, exactly the same as the first, and a wave of homesickness suddenly washes over me. Everything here is so strange and different.

'Barrington, Hesslop, Jarrard and Walker, in here.' We carry on in this way, our numbers depleting till there are only four of us left. Our hut, when we get to it, is the best one I reckon, for it's tucked right up against some woods, and although the branches are bare now, I can easily see how lovely it will be when spring comes.

'Brown, Timms, Pemberton, Houseman and Roberts in here. Rather a squeeze for you, I'm afraid,' she says. 'We've had to put an extra bed in your room, but I'm sure you'll be perfectly comfortable.' She turns to look at me, and I feel myself frown. Am I the one who's being squeezed in, then? As if she picks up my thoughts, Sister Tompkinson looks away. 'Unfortunately, Miss Pemberton is a little delayed. I had a telephone call from Lord Pemberton to say she's on her way. She'll join you as soon as she can.' Good heavens, I think, *Lord* Pemberton? 'Well, in you go, all of you,' she continues. 'Get your bearings then go down to the refectory for luncheon. You've got the afternoon to unpack and settle in. Supper is at six-fifteen, lecture at seven. Do not be late for either events.'

'No, Sister,' we chorus.

'A lecture? Tonight? On our first night?' the girl called Houseman says beside me when Sister Tompkinson's out of earshot. Houseman is taller than me by a good head, and I have to look up to see her properly. Her nose is pinched white by the cold, and she's shivering. We stand together, staring at Sister Tompkinson's back as she hurries away, her grey cape with its red trim blowing open as a gust of wind catches it.

'They're not wasting any time in getting us started, are they?' she complains.

'Well, I don't mind,' I say, thinking that if I'm busy I won't have time for any more homesickness. 'I'm glad, actually. It's what we're here for, isn't it?'

'I didn't say it wasn't,' Houseman replies as we file round to the door at the back of the hut. Her voice has got a whine in it, like she's opened her mouth and a mosquito's come out.

We walk along the little path by the hedge, then step up into the tiny porch of the hut. Two more strides and I'm in a small living area, with armchairs and a big sofa. There's a table, with writing things on and a bookcase full of books, and a black stove in the middle of the room. There's a smell of yesterday's ashes on the air, but someone's put some holly in a jug on a small table and, with the bright red curtains, it feels homely even without the stove lit.

'Ooh, I didn't realise we'd have our own sitting room,' a voice calls out. It's Roberts.

'There'll be a lot of us sharin' it, though,' Houseman chips in. 'There's four other girls as well, don't forget.'

'Still ....'

I rub my hands together to warm them. However Hubert is managing to live under canvas at this time of the year, I really don't know. I don't think I could do it, but then, I don't suppose they have any choice, do they?

Roberts comes to stand beside me, taking off her hat, and pushing back a strand of fair hair that has escaped its pins. 'Drat it,' she says. 'Why can't my hair ever behave itself?' I unpin my own hat and lift it from my head. 'I wish I had hair like yours,' she says, looking at me, and I smile to remember the pains I took this morning with it, brushing and rolling and patting it till it curved round as I wanted, just so. 'I'm going to cut mine all off while I'm here,' she says.

'Cut off your hair?' I look at her, aghast.

'You can't do that,' Houseman says, looking across the sofa at us.

'Oh, can't I, indeed? You just watch me. It'll be much more comfortable under those caps we've got to wear.'

'But cut it all off? No! You simply can't. Women don't *have* short hair.' I feel a sudden delight in the awfulness of the idea.

'I will! Then perhaps I'll become a man and join the Army, go off and fight and not have to become a nurse, just because my mother wants me to.' I look at her trim figure, her pretty features and smooth complexion, and she must see the astonishment on my face, for suddenly she laughs, and I feel my spirits rise as I join in. 'Well, perhaps I wouldn't get away with going as far as that, then.' The curl drops down again and she pushes ineffectually at it. 'Oh, hang it,' she says and leaves it where it is.

'What about the stove?' I bend down and a puff of ash rises on the disturbed air. 'Are we allowed to light it?' I move across to look at the pile of coal in a bucket behind the fender. The ashes haven't even been cleared from the grate beneath yet.

'Actually, I really don't think we should,' Houseman says. 'It might be against the rules. I think we should wait and ask the others when they come in. I don't want a black mark by *my* name on our first day.'

'Quite right,' I say. 'A black mark would not be a good way to begin.'

Houseman seems impervious to my sarcasm, but I leave the stove anyway, and go across to a door in the corner of the room. Inside is a tiny kitchen with a gas cooker and a sink. There's a cupboard beneath and some shelves above, a green canister marked 'TEA' and a shiny brown teapot beside it. It's the very spit of our teapot at home, except this one's got its proper lid. For a moment I have a vision of Dad in his chair, his head nodding, and Mother pouring tea into the cups. I feel my eyes smart, and I'm glad when the others come and poke their heads round the door, for it's not going to do me any good to get all maudlin. When we've seen all there is to see, we troop back and go through a door at the rear of the sitting room into a narrow corridor. 'No sign of the other girls. They must be still on duty,' Ana says.

The first door off the corridor opens onto a bedroom. It's obviously occupied, for clothes and other personal items are strewn around. '*They* haven't taken any notice of the tidiness rule!' I mutter. Then there's a bathroom with a small bath and a basin, and another door with a water-closet. The last room is ours.

My bed, it seems, is the one by the window, for that's where my trunk has been placed. My eyes trace its familiar, battered edges and suddenly I'm having to blink back the tears again as I remember how Dad carried it downstairs for me. I cross to stand beside it. What is the matter with me? I'm acting like a baby, for it's not as if I hadn't already lived away from home, is it? Outside the window, the wind gusts and I feel a draught come through the frame. I glance at the bed that doesn't have a trunk beside it yet, then drag mine towards it. First-come-first-served, seems fair enough to me.

'I say, Timms, should you do that?'

'Too late, I've done it now.' I avoid Houseman's eyes as I bend down to unbuckle the straps. As I begin to unpack, Kitty falls onto her bed beside me, and bounces up and down.

'I've slept on worse,' she says. I'm just thinking that she'll break it if she's not careful, with her weight on a small frame like that, when she gets up to squeak open a door at the end of the room. 'Only one wardrobe,' she groans, 'and it's tiny. We'll have to share!'

'Well, that's not going to be a problem,' Roberts calls. 'The amount we were allowed to bring wouldn't fill a broom cupboard anyway.' I can't help but think of how I've had to buy more than I've ever owned before, and am just opening my mouth to say so, when the door opens and a pretty, dark girl pushes her way in. It's Ana, the girl I met at Southampton Red Cross. She glances at each of us in turn, then gives a squeal.

'It's you!' she calls, coming quickly over to me. I step back, but she's already put her arms around me. I feel myself blush. 'How marvellous to see a friendly face,' she says as if she's known me all her life. 'I just *knew* we'd end up together.' A porter, the young one we saw earlier, now enters the room, dragging Ana's trunk.

'Where shall I put it then, miss?' he asks. I drag my eyes away from his pimples, for they've turned purple with the cold. Ana looks round, then waves her hand towards the window.

'Over there I suppose. Only bed left. Thank you, Austen.'

'I say, what are your names?' Ana asks as she goes back to sit down on her bed. She puts up her hand to feel the draught and shivers, and I feel a surge of shame. I'll get hold of some newspaper from somewhere later, and stop it up for her. If I'd have known it was her as would end up with it, I wouldn't have swapped. She turns to look at me. 'I know you're Maude,' she says. Now I'm over the surprise of seeing her, I realise how glad I am she's here, and I smile. 'I'm Ana, short for Anastasia,' she says.

'I'm Lilac,' the fair-haired girl says, removing her hat and laying down on her bed with a sigh.

Houseman sniggers, and I turn to face her.

'What's wrong with that?'

'Nothing. Mine's Susan,' she adds hurriedly.

'Don't worry,' Lilac says to me. 'I'm used to it. Blessed parents have called all us girls after flowers. There's Rose and Marigold, then there's Daisy,' she counts them off on her fingers, 'Foxglove ... no, I'm just pulling your leg ... Pansy, and me. Could be worse. We could be called after vegetables, couldn't we?' I wonder how many times she must have said that, but she laughs, a loud peal that's infectious and has us laughing too. It breaks the ice. 'Anyway, everyone who knows me calls me Lil,' she says.

'And I'm Kitty,' my friend from the lecture room says. 'Do let's use Christian names. I can't bear being called by my surname, can you?'

I watch as Ana places a pair of bedroom slippers beneath

her bed, and a picture of Sister Tompkinson comes into my mind. She'll confiscate them if she sees them, I'll bet sixpence she will. I'm sure we were only meant to bring the things on the list. I look at the slippers enviously. They're made of blue velvet and are trimmed with fur.

'Oh, bother it all,' Ana says suddenly, standing up. 'I'm going to unpack later. Come on, let's go and have something to eat. I'm absolutely *famished*.'

Chapter 18

Hut 49
Royal Victoria Military Hospital
Netley
Hampshire

December 28th, 1914

Dear Hubert

I hope this letter finds you well. It's quiet here for a few minutes, as the girls in my hut are getting ready for bed. I stole a march on them and used the facilities first as I wanted to have enough time to write you a few lines, and I know what it was like at Mrs Packham's with everyone wanting the bathroom at the same time. We've been told it's lights out in a quarter of an hour, and that as soon as we hear the bugle blowing at nine o'clock, that's it!

I have to tell you that it's very exciting to finally be here. I have been put in a hut right at the back of the hospital, so it's nice and quiet. There are rows and rows of huts, and the trouble is they all look the same from the outside. I'm sure if ours wasn't so easy to spot, I would end up walking into the wrong one! We have two bedrooms, five beds in one room, which is ours, and four in the other. It's a bit tight, but comfortable enough and, like Kitty keeps saying, there is a war on, so we mustn't complain! The girls I am sharing with are:- Ana (which is short for Anastasia), Kitty, Lilac (Lil) and Susan. Ana is the girl I met at the Red Cross place in Southampton, and she's very well spoken. Kitty is dark, and very clever, I think. Lil is fair, and she laughs a lot – you should hear her. Susan Houseman I'm not sure about yet. She's local – her family live in a village just outside Netley, but she seems rather moody, although maybe she's just one of those people who take a little while to get to know. Time will tell, I suppose. I do hope I can like her, for it will make life difficult, don't you think, to have to share with someone you don't get on with? I shall do my best, anyway.

The hospital itself is enormous. There are three hospitals here really, the main building (which is a quarter of a mile long – it's true, it really is!) and two hutted hospitals behind, the Welsh Hospital and the Red Cross. We've been warned there's a lot of competition between us all! I'm to be in the main block, which is very grand, but I'm not sure I like the corridors very much, for they seem to go on forever and footsteps echo so.

We had our first lecture tonight. It was just a talk explaining where things are and all that and what our training will consist of. Earlier on, we were told about all the rules and regulations we will have to keep. I'm sure I'll never remember them all and that by the time I write my next letter to you, I'll have got myself into trouble! I've been placed on G.8, by the way, which is a surgical ward, under Sister Browning. I haven't met her yet, but everyone says she's very strict, so I'll have to watch my p's and q's. I have to report there at eight o'clock tomorrow morning <u>ON</u> <u>THE</u> <u>DOT</u>, Sister Tompkinson says.

I thought you might be interested to know the sort of things I will have to do as a probationer. They are: taking the men their breakfasts (nearly all of them stay in bed for that), preparing the table for the doctors with hot water etc, tidying up and dusting the ward, helping the men get up and dressed, making the beds, taking round the milk, and for what time is left (!), we'll be at the beck and call of the nurse who's over us. If we're lucky, later on, we might get to do some bandaging. It sounds as if we're going to be kept hard at it, doesn't it, so there won't be much time for larking (though Kitty has said she'll jolly well find some).

The wind is blowing a howler round our hut as I write and I wonder if it's the same where you are, for we're not so very far apart are we, not as the crow flies? It seems to blow right off the sea here, just as it did at Southsea, and as the hospital is only set back a little bit, it's whistling round us good and proper, and trying to get down the chimney. But for all that we are quite cosy here, and I can't help but think of you in your cold tent, for there's a lovely big stove here in the sitting room. In fact, I have my feet upon the fender now, warming my toes. But, perhaps it's a little mean to tell you that?

The girls are making a proper racket and it's almost nine o'clock already, so I must finish. But, before I go – nearly everyone has brought their knitting things from home and are making 'socks for soldiers'. Would you like it if I knitted something for you? Some socks or a scarf, or a balaclava perhaps? We get three hours off every afternoon and I shall have to find something to do, so it had just as well be knitting, and I'll enjoy it all the more to know it's for you.

Ana has just said Sister Tompkinson's coming up the path, though it's just to frighten me into finishing, I think. Now she's thrown her towel at me, and they're all laughing, and there's the bugle, so I must go.

Good Night, Hubert dear. I do think of you, greatly. It seems such a long time since I last saw you.

With fond affection,

Maude

Chapter 19

January 3rd, 1915

My Dearest Maude

A happy New Year to you! It seems rather strange to be wishing such a thing with our country at war, but we must make the best of things, after all.

It was good to receive your letter and to know that you arrived 'safe and sound' at the Royal Victoria. The hospital sounds terribly grand, and I understand how excited you must be feeling. A little nervous too, I expect?

I have heard from my brother, Ralph. He is training somewhere on Salisbury Plain and seems to be enjoying army life, which I wouldn't have thought at all likely with his fine sentiments, but there it is.

A group of us – Will, Roger, Charles, Randolph and I were granted forty-eight hours' leave, quite unexpectedly, over the New Year and we all thought it would be rather jolly if we stayed together somewhere. My home (The Gables) was chosen as being the most convenient place, so I telephoned Mother to warn her we were on our way. Good old Cook put on a fine spread and, afterwards, we visited several hostelries on our way into town and had a most enjoyable evening. We were going to attend one of the watch-night services, but thought when it came to it that we were rather too inebriated, so went straight on to the Square. Even though the weather was not too grand – it was rather cold and blustery – it seemed as if the whole town had turned out. After the old clock on the Town Hall had tolled the old year out and the new one in, pandemonium broke out with bells ringing and the railway whistles blowing and hooters from somewhere (the Docks I should think) joining in. We sang Auld Lang Syne and there were rifle shots, then someone began to play the fiddle and we all capered about like mad things. One would have thought there had never been a New Year before! I wish you had been there, Maude dear. You would have so enjoyed the jollity of it all.

Yes, I agree that it seems an age since we last saw each other, though it cannot be more than six weeks. But even so I am growing impatient for sight of you! I do not know when it will be, for we are now in the midst of intense training. I'm beginning to think you may not recognise your best boy when you see him, I am grown so fit and strong! We are still sent out for route marches every day, fifteen or sixteen miles at a time, sometimes more, and we have to go whatever the weather, as they think it will toughen us up, as indeed it does seem to be doing. After that we have to dig trenches and practise bayoneting old Fritz and his chums (sacks filled with straw in actual fact), and what with that and inspections, not to mention manoeuvres, drilling and physical fitness exercises, you can imagine that, like you, my time is pretty well filled.

Now, I have a request – I am going to have a photograph taken of myself now that we have at last been kitted out in khaki. Sanders' Photographic Studio in Wells Street. Do you know it? I am wondering if you have thought of doing the same so that I could have a photograph of you to keep by me, perhaps in your VAD uniform? It would be very warming of nights to look at your smiling face before I settled down to sleep. Will you do that for me, dear? I will send one of mine to you. How about it?

I have just re-read your letter and, yes, the wind does howl around our tents, and is doing a good impression of a banshee as I write this, and it is turning colder, I think, and is very damp altogether. One poor chap here was sent down by field ambulance to a hospital in Southsea, Charlotte Avenue – isn't that near where you used to lodge with Mrs Packham? They suspect pneumonia, but what can you expect from living under canvas? I can't begin to imagine what it must be like out in the trenches, open to all the elements (though the sooner I get to find out, the better I will like it, of course). I think I must be very fortunate in my constitution, for the worst I've had since I've been here is a head cold, and even then I was only laid up for a day.

I see your Walter, and Fred Johnston from the Emporium, too, quite often. Although they're not in my platoon, there are only so many square yards available to us all here, so we bump into one another from time to time. Walter is always cheerful and seems to be enjoying military life. Fred, without fail, asks after you. Do try to think, dearest, of some kind message I could pass to him from you. It would bring him such delight, I know, for he told me the other day that his mother is not at all well and, apart from her, it seems he is quite alone in the world.

I think constantly of my commission, and am hopeful that I will soon be recommended but of course no-one knows when, or even if, so I am having to sit it out as best I can. Alas that patience has never been my strongest point!

A chap called Cradock has been transferred here and has been put in our tent. Wants to be a signaller and is very good at the physical stuff, but I'm not sure about his character at all. He doesn't seem to be the sort one needs on one's side in a War. He has a talent for putting chaps' backs up but, there, he's been put in with us, so – just like you and your chum, Susan – I'll just have to make the best of it. I have been thinking I might be interested in signalling myself, so perhaps he can teach me something, who knows?

Well, Maude, I will have to stop now for I am overcome with tiredness. Goodnight and God bless you dearest.

Affectionately,

Hubert

Chapter 20

'Hey, Nurse!' a soldier calls to me when I'm walking through the ward on my way to the sluice room. I look round to make sure a nurse has heard him, and it takes a minute for me to realise it's me he's calling. Will I ever get used to being addressed like that, I wonder? Two months I've been here, and still it catches me by surprise. I smile as I move towards the bed.

The boy is Private Willis. He lifts his head from the pillows, his face pale, his eyes a little too bright. I look at the cage beneath the blankets where his wound is, on his upper leg. He had half his thigh shot away. I know, because I saw it when Nurse James changed the dressing. I thought I was going to faint. Red raw, it is. You could easily put your fist in the space it left, if you wanted to. Both fists, in fact. And I know they're afraid of gangrene, because I heard the doctor say so to Sister, and if that happens, he'll lose his leg, no question. He smiles up at me now.

'Listen, Nurse,' he says, 'I need to know what your name is.'

'You know very well it's Timms,' I tell him, folding my hands against my apron. I can smell tobacco smoke on his breath and wonder how on earth he could have had a smoke in here, what with Sister Browning in and out every few minutes, and us nurses too, but I'll not be one to squeal on him for that, no, not with everything he has to put up with.

'I know that,' he says. He pauses and turns his head to look up and down the ward. 'What none of us know is your *Christian* name.' His voice drops to a whisper. 'It's just that we've got bets on. I've laid a shilling that you're Elizabeth, but Rodgers over there,' he points to the bed opposite, and a hand lifts in greeting, 'he's convinced you're more of a Rose. He's so sure, he's put half a crown on. The English Rose, he calls you.'

'A shilling? Half a crown? You must all've got more money than sense!' I bend over to smooth down the rumpled blue and cream counterpane, taking care not to jog the bed. 'Anyway, I'd have said I was the complete opposite to an English rose!' I bend closer. 'It's Maude,' I whisper to him. 'Plain Maude. But don't you go calling me that in here or I'll be in trouble again.'

'Maude it might be, but plain it definitely ain't. No, there's nothing plain about you, Nurse,' he says, 'and I don't care about the money. It was worth it just to know.' He grins at me then, a boyish grin that suddenly puts me in mind of Walter, and I wonder what he's doing. Does he ever think of me, like I do him? I shrug. I wouldn't have thought so, not if his lack of letters are anything to go by.

'Hey, Rodgers,' Private Willis shouts across the ward, 'we were all wrong, it's Maude.' He grins as cheers go up from the men. They fade to silence as Sister Browning appears and walks quickly to where I'm standing. Now the cat's amongst the pigeons! I make a show of pushing the stool back beneath the bed, my heart in my boots.

'And why aren't you at your duties, Nurse?' she asks, lifting her chin to look down her nose at me. 'Do you really think you are here to stand in idle chatter with the patients?'

'No, Sister.' I look at a spot on the floor, between my shoes, determined to keep my temper down, and my lip buttoned.

'I suppose you *do* want to pass your probation?' I fight the surge of annoyance, for she knows full well that I do. Aren't I always the first to volunteer for everything?

'Yes, Sister.' I lift my gaze to look her straight in the eye then, so she's in no doubt that I mean it. 'More than anything.'

'Well, I can assure you that you won't if you carry on in this manner. And I won't have idleness on my ward.'

'No, Sister.'

'Aw, don't be hard on her, Sister,' Private Willis says. 'It's my fault. I was just being friendly, like. No harm done, eh?'

'I'll be the judge of what is harmful and what is not, Private Willis, and I'll thank you not to interfere with my staff while they're on duty.' She turns to me. 'Now, get on with your work, Nurse.'

'Yes, Sister,' I say.

Still smarting from my telling off, I go to the sluice room. I wish I could tell her what I really think, that he's just a lad, and needs a bit of fun. I put on a coarse over-apron, and thread my arms through the long cuffs that I keep on the shelf. Why *is* it the laundry girls have to put so much starch in them, that they chafe so? I ease them up a little and begin to empty the pile of bedpans that has been stacked ready, trying to push thoughts of Sister Browning from my mind.

The cold, wet weather of late has turned worse, and icy rain blusters against the windows as I work, making them rattle in their frames. The papers say we've got snow on the way. Just when March is about to begin, if you please, and all our thoughts are turning to spring. I empty and rinse, the enamel pans clanking against the sides of the sluice. What if Hubert was sent off to fight and came back with a wound like Private Willis's? What if he was sent here, to my ward? What if I could see him every day, take him his breakfast tray and make up his bed for him? I think of seeing him in his pyjamas, then of seeing him without them, and I feel desire stir inside me.

I push the thoughts away, try to concentrate on what I'm doing. I hardly notice the smell in here any more, that mix of antiseptic and excretion that always hangs on the air, no matter if the window's open or not. I didn't think I would ever be able to stand it, not at first. I even take normal breaths when I breathe now, and don't cover my nose every chance I have. Funny what you can get used to.

'Timms! There you are.' Nurse James pokes her head round the door. She's older than me by a long chalk and already has grey hairs mixed in with her dark. I saw her with her cap off in the cloakroom once, so I know. 'Sister Browning says when you've finished those, you're to scrub up then come and help me with the washes. Oh, and she says have you finished dusting?'

'Yes, and yes I have, Nurse James,' I reply.

'There's no need to get sarky, Timms. Just come when you've finished.'

'Yes, Nurse James.' I empty and rinse, disinfect and wipe as quickly as I can until the stack of pans has been shifted to the shelves ranged along the wall. My spirits lift as I think about the washes. I haven't been allowed to help with them before. The more different jobs I do, the better I like it, for I can't wait to pass all the tests and have a red cross to sew onto my apron. When I've finished the bedpans, I scrub my hands, brushing hard with the nailbrush that stands next to the lump of carbolic soap on its dish. Then I peel off my over-apron and cuffs, and hurry into the ward. A whistle from Private Willis makes me look round anxiously for Sister Browning, but her tall form is bent over a patient, so I shake my fist and pull a face at him, and he grins.

Surgical Eight hasn't got curtains for pulling round each bed like some of the wards, so we use screens that we keep piled at the far end of the ward for personal procedures. Two of the screens have been pulled together round a bed at the end of the room, so I know how far she's got. I make my way there now, slip between the two open ends, and pull them shut after me. A patient is lying in his pyjama bottoms on the bed, and Nurse James is running a soapy flannel across his face.

'It's all right, Nurse, I *can* wash myself, you know,' the man says and reaches up with his good arm to take the flannel. His other arm is bandaged and motionless beside him.

'Now, now, Sergeant Webb,' she answers. 'How many times do I have to tell you? I'll be shot at dawn if you don't let me do my job, and I'm sure you don't want that to happen, now do you? Just let me get on and do it.' She tweaks the flannel out of his reach, then motions to me to go round the other side of the bed to help her, and we lift our patient gently an inch or so from the pillow.

'Not too high, Nurse,' she says sharply. 'Doctor says he doesn't want him to sit up yet.'

'However will we do his back, then?'

'We'll roll him on his side in a minute. Now, rinse the flannel out, please. It's all right, you can let go, I've got him.' I let go, and somewhere in the corridor outside the ward, a man's voice begins to sing *The Rose of Tralee*. I hum the tune under my breath as I rinse the flannel. The water trickles back into the bowl as I dip and squeeze, then I hold it out for Nurse James to take. 'You do it, Nurse,' she says to me. 'Quickly now! And for heavens' sake stop humming. Sister will have a fit if she hears you. Come along, now, we haven't got all day.'

I rinse the back of his neck, then the front, and as I do, I realise with a sudden surprise, that I like doing this. Yes, I like making him clean. Perhaps it's because it reminds me of when I used to help Mother with Horace when he was little. I towel Sergeant Webb dry, and Nurse James lowers his head gently back against the pillows, then quickly soaps his chest and beneath his arms, and I rinse again. We roll him gently onto his side and wash his back. Soon we're easing him into a clean pyjama top.

'That feels better girls,' Sergeant Webb says. He's smiling, but a look of apprehension flickers across his face as he looks first at Nurse James, then at me.

'Now, undo your pyjamas, there's a good man.'

I can feel a blush begin at her words, and I turn away to take a pair of clean pyjamas from the pile on the trolley shelf. Sergeant Webb unties the cord at his waist, and Nurse James eases his pyjama bottoms down and off in a practised sweep, then hands them to me. I'm glad of having to place his garments in the laundry bag that's attached to the side of the trolley, for my face is red hot. Even though I'm not attracted to Sergeant Webb in that way, his manliness makes me think of the things that happen between men and women. I stay there for a minute before turning back.

There's a large dressing across his stomach, and a dark yellow circle stains it. Nurse James wipes carefully round it then begins to wash the man's genitals and between his buttocks. A stale smell wafts up.

'Usually we let the men wash their own private areas if they can,' Nurse James says to me, 'but this patient is not allowed to bend or he'll disturb his wound.' Sergeant Webb is looking everywhere but at us. I feel really sorry for him, for I would die if it was me exposed like that.

'I'm sorry,' Nurse James says gently. 'I know it's difficult for you, but rules are rules and, there, we're nearly done.' She holds the flannel across to me, and I rinse it then hand it back. We move on to his legs and feet. 'Clean pyjama trousers please, Nurse,' she commands, and I pick them up from where I've placed them, neatly folded, on the locker top, next to a jar of early violets. A girl from the village brought them up yesterday. She got them down by the Abbey, she said.

'Careful,' Nurse James warns as we ease the pyjamas up round his waist. She ties the cord loosely above the dressing.

'Ah, that feels better,' he says, but the anxious look on his face is still there.

'Don't worry, Sister's going to do your dressings today,' Nurse James says, looking at him, and he lets out a sigh.

'No offence, girls, but I'm glad about that. If it's got to be done, then I'd rather it was her. She knows what she's doing, even if she is about as cheerful as a witch on a windy night.'

I laugh. 'That's quite enough hilarity,' Nurse James says as we bring up the blankets, and tuck him in. Then she passes Sergeant Webb his comb, and waits till he's tidied his hair. My fingers itch to do it for him. 'Sister Browning's one of the best. You'll soon learn that, Nurse Timms,' Nurse James says, looking pointedly at me.

'I reckon she's learned a good deal already, don't you, Nurse?' Sergeant Webb has recovered his composure now he's dressed and has the bedclothes pulled back over him. He's cheerful again, though he lies back, exhausted. I fold back first one part of the screen then the other, concertina fashion, the wooden frame gliding smoothly on its castors as I follow Nurse James.

'Stomachs are always difficult,' she says in a low voice. 'He's a brave man, but it'll be a good while before that wound's better, if I know anything about it. Which I do,' she adds. She walks up briskly to the next bed. 'Now, then, Corporal Dixon, let's make you more comfortable. Empty that water into the bucket, Timms. Come on, we haven't got all day.'

There's a letter waiting for me on the hall table when I get back to the hut that evening. I unbutton my coat, and slip the envelope into my apron pocket, opening it only when I am sitting down on the edge of my bed.

Chapter 21

Military Training Camp
Portsdown Hill
Portsmouth

February 28th, 1915

Dearest Maude

How is my little nurse getting on? I hope you aren't winning <u>too</u> many hearts? Mind you remember whose best girl you are! I have two pieces of good news to tell you! The first is that I am now 2nd Lt Wells-Crofton. Yes, I have been gazetted! What do you think of that? I am to have my own platoon. The second piece of news is that we're moving, leaving Portsmouth so that a second battalion can be set up. There's great excitement at the camp as you may imagine, although no-one seems to know quite when or where we're going. Please don't be alarmed, it won't be to the Front yet as we haven't completed our training, but we're to march out of Portsmouth with a good deal of pomp and ceremony all the same, and each man will have his own rifle by then, so we should look a pretty smart bunch. Will you come, Maude, when we march away? I should so like it if you did. It won't be for a few more weeks, I shouldn't have thought, but I will write and let you know the date just as soon as I know it myself.

You'll be pleased to know I have heard from Ralph again. He's training somewhere near Dorchester and already, he says, there's talk of them being mobilised by Easter time, though I think that cannot be true, for there's not even a whisper of <u>us</u> mobilizing at present. Everyone here is terribly keen to get to the Front, and I am no exception! I cannot wait to do my bit. My biggest fear is that it will all be over before we even get the chance to have a go at the Bosch!

Meanwhile, I am busy learning semaphore. It seems that I have a latent talent for communications, and am being pressed into all sorts of lectures and exercises. Every day, I get to practise setting up systems in the trenches we've dug, which is great sport, although it has to be squeezed in between marching and drilling and all the other daily things. Like you, I do not have much time left over for myself. But, I am becoming very fit, and quite the soldier these days. I am even able now to plunge my bayonet straight through the heart of the dummies here without flinching. So just you watch out, you Hun!

I have heard from my elder brother Aylmer, too. The business is continuing to feel the economic effects of the war. No-one, it seems, is buying much at all that isn't absolutely necessary. But I have told him that one can only cling to the fact that, war or no war, people will always need undergarments! So it can only be a matter of time before orders start to pick up again.

Do you remember me telling you about our 'housewife' sewing kits? You will smile when I tell you this, but today I successfully stitched on my first shirt button. There! What do you think of that? I must say that you women make these things look easy, but I broke the thread three times in all and also have a severely punctured finger!

Forgive me, I haven't thanked you yet for my scarf. The winds continue chill and bothersome, and so I am very pleased to have it, especially fashioned as it is by your own dear hands.

The last post is sounding, and I must hop to it. Good night and God bless you my dearest.

Yours affectionately

Hubert

Chapter 22

Military Training Camp
Portsdown Hill
Portsmouth

March 7th, 1915

Dearest Maude,

Thank you for yours of the third last. I must tell you straight away that there is great excitement here, for we're to be transferred to the 39th which is being re-formed, and our grand march out of Portsmouth is definitely to be in the next few weeks. I will let you know the date and time as soon as I know it myself so that you can book your leave and come and see me off.

You will, won't you dearest? Don't let them say you can't.

Affectionately yours,

Hubert

Chapter 23

I make my way through the crowd.

'Oi! Who d'you think you're pushin'?' A woman rams a large basket into my side.

'You're doing just as much pushing as me!' I say, as I duck past her to the front. I'm not the only one whose nerves are on edge, it seems. Policemen and army officials are tying tapes along the edges of the road, motioning people back onto the grass.

'Come along, now. There's plenty o' room for everyone,' a burly uniformed man calls as a group of girls behind me begins to shove forwards. 'They'll be marchin' right up the Common, all the way up to Hilsea. Plenty o' room for everyone!' he repeats.

A young woman shoulders her way to the front to stand next to me. 'But we wants to see 'em 'ere, down at the end they're startin' from, don't we, Grace?' She holds a little girl of nine or so by one hand, and with the other hand she steadies her hat against the wind that's gusting off the sea. She looks me up and down, taking in my uniform coat and hat. 'You 'ere to see your boy off, then?' she asks.

'My boy?' I think of Hubert, and what there is between us. 'Yes,' I say. A gust flicks wisps of brown curly hair round her face. 'My brother, too,' I add.

The words twist the pit of my stomach. Saying them makes it too real. If they're sent to the Front, they might not come back. The knot tightens. How will I ever bear it if either of them dies? God alone knows it was hard enough when little Horace went, but at least when death comes to you, there's some sort of natural order in it. But, healthy men going off so proud and cheerful, like our Arthur, just to be maimed and killed? What sense of order is there in that?

'Well, same as me then,' the girl says, 'except Donald's not really my boy, though he thinks he is, don't he, Grace? Won't let me be for a minute.' The little girl smiles and nods. 'An' I've got *two* brothers goin' off. We're t'either side of 'em in age, ain't we, Grace, squeezin' 'em in?' She's thoughtful for a moment. 'My ma wouldn't come, said she couldn't watch her flesh an' blood go off to be slaughtered.' The flag in her hand judders as the wind catches it. I think of Dad and Mother, back at Elmford, for they haven't come either. 'It don't bear thinkin' about, do it, not really?' the girl says, but her words are belied by the excitement in her face.

The discordant notes of a band drift up as instruments are tested. It can't be long now. Our men and boys marching away to God-knows-where, some to be killed, some injured. I swallow. Why don't they end it? This war, I mean. Why don't they stop the fighting before it gets worse? *Why* don't they?

I look down the line to see if I can see them, but there's nothing, so I glance back the other way. The crowd, six or seven deep in places, stretches up towards the town as far as my eyes can see, and it seems to me as if the whole of Portsea Island has turned out to wave our boys off. The mood's a festive one, too, as if it's a carnival or something

163

and I give myself a bit of a talking-to, tell myself to cheer up a bit. After all, our boys deserve a good send-off, don't they?

High above me, seagulls are swooping, and they add their cries to the growing restless chattering. They remind me, as they always do, of Arthur. How he'd have loved to be here, seeing our Walter off. He always liked an occasion, the chance of a bit of fun. The people opposite me part briefly to let someone through, and I catch a glimpse of the sea; the sun dancing on the swell of shifting green water. The music settles into a tune and I look back. There's still no sign of the band, but they must have started off, for people are waving handkerchiefs, and children are fluttering their flags. Then the excitement of the moment catches at me, and I feel my fears recede. The music is growing louder. They're coming! Anticipation swells and I lean across the tape, crane my neck to see.

Yes! There they are!

The sunlight, strong now, catches on the polished instruments as the band strides ahead of the men, leading the way. They're playing *Fall in and Follow Me*. Normally, I'd hum along, but my throat has tightened at the sight of them, and I can't. Beneath the music, there's the tramp, tramp, tramp of boots, rhythmic and urgent. Eleven hundred men, there are, leaving home. All those chairs and beds, empty. The sound of their marching swells as they approach.

Every head is turned to watch them now, the music growing with each step they take. Behind the band, a sea of khaki caps bobs along, keeping time with the music. Goodness. However will I be able to recognise two people amongst so many?

Louder and louder, the music grows. Louder and louder, the sound of marching feet. Crump-crump, crump-crump. Crump-crump, crump-crump. A figure of a portly man in a business suit steps in front of me, and I push the tape forward to see round him.

'Move back there, sir, please,' a military voice immediately calls. 'You too, miss.' But I hold my ground, for I haven't come all this way just to miss seeing Hubert, no, nor our Walter neither. 'The men need room to come through,' he says. 'Stand back. Stand back, I say!'

Finally, the business man steps back, so I do too, and there's the band now, right in front of us. I've always liked bands, ever since I was little and we watched them on Southsea Common. I stand still, watching as they pass, the men puffing their cheeks in and out as they blow into their brass instruments, the drums booming out the time, loud and insistent. It gives me a funny mix inside of pride and dread.

Then the band has passed, and it's the turn of the men. Our own Portsmouth boys. How handsome they look, their heads held proudly, marching off to glory, their rifles against their shoulders. How young they are. I knew they would be, of course, but somehow it catches me out. Some are smiling. Some are set and serious. All of them eye the crowd.

The first line of men is level with me, then quick as anything, they're past and the band ahead has struck up another tune, *It's a Long Way to Tipperary*. It makes me think of Hubert and the time we went to see the fleet, and suddenly I'm transported to the high wall overlooking the harbour where we watched it all. How long ago it seems already. My fingers tighten round the handkerchief inside my pocket, crumpling it into my fist.

The men are filing past – row upon row, upon row, upon row. The crowd cheers as more and more of them come. I recognise a group of men from the storeroom at the Emporium, Fred Johnston amongst them, then some of the boys from Elmford village, but no sign of the two faces I love so dearly amongst the hundreds of khaki caps.

Then I catch sight of our Walter. He's sandwiched between two other soldiers, his head set rigid, his face lit with pride. I can see him flicking his eyes from side to side, looking for me.

He knows this is where I'll be, for I wrote and told him so. I draw out my handkerchief then, and wave it in the air, and the sudden change of movement must catch his eye, for he turns and looks at me, and his face relaxes into a broad smile as he marches past, the curls beneath his cap bouncing on his forehead to the rhythm of his stride.

He holds himself as tall as his five feet and eight inches will allow, and he marches as if he's cock o' the roost. Khaki blurs and dances in front of me, but I won't let the tears fall, I won't. I blink them back, flutter my handkerchief with the rest of the crowd and smile, smile, smile, just like in the song. Children wave their flags. Men lift their hats. Everyone cheers. Then our Walter's gone, and I'm scanning the lines again, glancing feverishly from face to face looking for Hubert. I search until I grow dizzy, and panic begins to knot my stomach again as I think I must have missed him.

'Oh, there's Donald, Grace,' the girl beside me shouts in my ear above the continuing cheers of the crowd, and she raises her arm to wave wildly. It makes me more anxious still, for fear that Hubert might already be gone. The feeling grows but then, when the sound of the band has dwindled to a hum way ahead in the distance, I see him, a dozen or so rows from the rear. He's already seen me, and he locks his gaze on mine, just like he did at the meeting at the Union Hall, that first time. How blue his eyes are. I can see their colour even from here. I stand still, forgetting to wave and cheer as we look at one another, and it seems for a moment as if everything slows down, slower and slower till the sound of the marching is like the pause between heartbeats, and the thudding rhythm of the drums and the blasting, rousing tune of *Follow Me*, just an empty echo between now and what's to come.

Hubert gives me a kind of half smile, as if he knows the emotion that's turning inside me, then his boots have crumped their way past, and he's gone too, his head jogging in time

166

with the other men. I don't take my eyes from the black curve of his hair beneath his cap as he rocks and sways, no, not until he merges with the others and I can't pick him out any more. And even then, when the crowd surges forwards onto the road taking me with it, I stand and watch till every last one of the men has disappeared. Gone.

Gone from Portsmouth to a training camp, where they'll stay till they get their mobilisation orders. And then, if the war hasn't ended, off to the Front.

Chapter 24

'Nurse Timms!'

I look up from where I am sitting, rolling bandages. Sister Browning is staring at me. Why is it, I wonder, that she can make me feel guilty even when I haven't done anything wrong?

'Yes, Sister?' I jump up, and the bandage falls onto the floor.

'For goodness' sake, girl! That's another one that will have to be thrown away. Do you have any idea how the cost mounts up in a hospital this size? Waste not, want not, Nurse, remember that.' I look down at the bandage, unravelled now, snaked across the floor in a white, undulating line, and I curse myself for my clumsiness. Another black mark against me.

'I'm sorry, Sister.'

'Sorry's not good enough, Nurse Timms. 'Do you think we have so many bandages that we can afford to waste them? The next time, it will be marked up and deducted from your wages. Do you understand?'

I bite my lip. 'Yes, Sister.' How I'd like to jut my chin out like I used to with Dad, and shout how I'm doing my best, and working as hard as I can, and would a word of praise every now and then be so very hard?

'Now, pick it up and put it in the waste receptacle. Then I want you to go with Nurse James to meet the three-thirty. Nurse Robertson's busy.' She stares at me. 'Well, don't just stand there, girl. Hurry up.'

'Yes, Sister,' I repeat. She leaves, and I gather up the spoiled bandage then go and pull my cape from its hook.

'Come on, Timms.' Nurse James pokes her head round the door a minute later as I'm fastening the hook and eye. 'The train will be there before us, if we're not careful. We can't have wounded men on the platform with no-one to look after them.'

I hurry after her, and we go out of the ward and along the corridor, our footsteps falling in time as we walk, side by side. It might be April, but the day is not spring-like at all. It's overcast, and gloomy as November. There is a sudden chink in the cloud, and for a moment, the sun comes out and falls through the long window frames onto the polished floor, making arches of brightness on the gleaming chestnut surface. But it disappears just as quickly and, when we turn into the passageway that runs up from the back of the hospital to the station, it is overcast again. The gloom deepens as a grey mist begins to roll in from the water. I watch it for a moment as it curls across the pier and onto the grass. Sea frets come in quickly here, and by the time we reach the station platform, the mist is seeping through the budding branches of the trees, blackening their thrusting stems with moisture. Nurses have gathered in groups. One of them turns now and raises her hand to Nurse James. She waves back.

'For goodness' sake don't try to do anything on your own, Timms, will you?' she warns me as we walk towards them.

Nurse James is a regular, a QAIMNS nurse. A lot of them haven't got much time for us VADs, but she's all right really, for all she's a bit snooty. I'm lucky to have been assigned to her, really.

She joins the group. All the others are QAIMNS nurses, too. It seems that I'm the only VAD. Despite the surge of satisfaction I feel at that, I hang back from the others, for they won't want the likes of me joining them in their precious chat, that I do know, for they always fall quiet when one of us VADs comes near. I take the opportunity to stare around me. It's the first time I've had the chance for a proper look at the station and I think how, even though it serves a hospital, it looks much the same as any other railway station I've ever seen, except for the row of trolleys and wheelchairs at the back, of course. The canopy overhead even looks quite gay with its slatted white trim all round the edges. I lean against one of the wooden stanchions, and turn towards the back of the platform, where it's darkest. I can just make out a narrow bench against the brick wall where the orderlies are waiting. From here, in their khaki, you could easily mistake them for soldiers. I know that some of them are too young to fight, and some are too old, but I can't help being curious as to what reasons the others might have.

The mist is swirling around us now, slinking along the earth and pushing its damp fingers everywhere. I draw my cape close around me, losing myself in my thoughts. I think of the men who are on their way here. What would happen if I recognised any of them? I push the thought aside, think of the pair of socks I'm knitting for Walter – how I've only got to cast off and I've finished – and then of the list of things I must put in my letter to Hubert tonight.

When I hear the sudden whistle of the train, it makes me jump. I know it must have arrived at the crossing, for the trains always blow their whistles there, to say they're coming.

I wonder if anyone has come out to wave to them today? Probably not, in this weather. I step a little closer to the edge, and look up the track. Nothing but mist. I wait. Suddenly, a black shape appears, thrusting its way towards me. Closer and closer it comes until it's a thudding, throbbing monster, drawing its rattling carriages with their red crosses past me, before stopping with a hiss at the end of the platform.

An officer with a flushed face immediately steps down from a carriage. 'Serious cases first!' he calls to the orderlies who have come to line up at the edge of the platform. He ushers the first two in through the open carriage door, and they soon re-appear.

'Stand back.' The line shuffles back as the orderlies manoeuvre a stretcher out. They hurry with it down the platform, breaking into a half-run, not waiting even for one of the trolleys, but turning down the covered walkway towards the hospital. I look at the mound of blankets and the clay-like profile of a man's face.

'He looks a gonner to me,' I hear another of the orderlies say when they've passed. 'I'd bet five bob on it. I'd know that look anywhere.'

'I know what you mean, mate. Poor sod, eh? Gets all the way back to Blighty, then cops it.'

The platform gradually fills as wounded men are taken from the train, and for a moment it seems like chaos. Shouts mix with the groans of the badly wounded, while underneath it all, the soft voices of the nurses as they talk and reassure the men. But there's banter, too, the less badly wounded just pleased to be back home. They laugh and joke amongst themselves as they wait.

I hurry with Nurse James to the row of trolleys. Behind us, the engine gives a final belch, steam hissing from its black funnel into the misty air. Suddenly, the train judders forwards a little, then stops again and I hear cries of pain as the men are lurched about.

'For Christ's *sake*, man.' The uniformed officer strides up to the engine driver. His boots are covered with mud. I hadn't noticed that before. 'Lock those bloody brakes,' he shouts, then turns and strides, red-faced, back down the platform, looking at each of the patients in turn as they are disgorged from the train. The seriously injured are placed on the trolleys, their field dressings pressed on to various parts of their bodies, many soaked through with fresh blood the colour of the crimson of our capes.

There's a smell, too. All the men have it when they first come back. The smell of the battlefield, we call it. It's not just the stench of unwashed bodies, although that's bad enough. No, nor the inky smell of blood. Not the faeces, nor even the vomit, the stink of clay nor the thin, lingering smell of something scorched. It's something else, a mixture of it all, perhaps.

Nurse James leads me to a trolley. A soldier lies, unconscious, on it. She lifts the blanket that covers him and looks at the cardboard tag that has been tied to his boot. I look, too. *'Sergeant John Harris'*, she reads, peering closely in the dim light, *'Lancashire Fusiliers, Eleventh (Service) Battalion'*. His injured leg has several field dressings on it, so many that they merge, overlapping, one into another. From the knee down, there is nothing but blood-soaked gauze, and I realise with a shock there is a space where his foot should be. I feel a surge of nausea. It's not that I'm not used to wounds on the ward. I am. But, there is a sense of rightness about them there, a clinical orderliness. Here, it seems far more shocking.

Nurse James replaces the blanket and I force away the feeling of sickness, stepping closer. The man stirs, moves his head, and I wish I had a pillow to put beneath it. But then he's still again and I suppose it doesn't matter, not if he doesn't know anything about it.

'They'll have done what they can,' Nurse James says, 'but he'll need immediate attention. Take him with Bellfield down to Central.'

Bellfield, a dour middle-aged orderly with a crooked back, motions me to the front end of the trolley. 'Central' is our nickname for the reception area where the men's wounds are assessed and wards allocated, and we make our way there now, weaving our way around the walking wounded who are being helped out of the trains. Some of them have their arms across the nurses' shoulders as they're helped slowly along the platform. A wicker invalid chair creaks as it's pushed along behind us.

'Hold tighter,' Bellfield calls urgently to me. 'Watch his head!' I do as I am told, holding the front of the trolley and steadying the soldier's head across the uneven bits. Bellfield pushes from the feet end and does most of the work, steering it, easing back, then forging on again as we wind our way forwards.

I look at my soldier's face. His hair is swept back from his brow. It is a good face. It might even be a handsome one when it's washed clean from the mud and blood that smears it. He has a moustache, not a great bushy, pretentious one like a lot of the soldiers have, nor a thin, haughty one like some of the officers, but a homely one, friendly somehow. In fact, his whole face is friendly I think, despite the cheeks that are a little too sunken, and the dark circles beneath his eyes. His eyes. What colour are they, I wonder?

We make our way as swiftly as we can towards the hospital, and I glance down again at my patient. I get a shock then, for his eyes are open and he is staring at me, his forehead creased, as if he is in pain, or doesn't understand where he is or what's happening to him. But his eyes themselves are clear, and I can see they are half-way between green and brown. Hazel, Mother would call them. We are nearly at the sliding doors when he reaches out a hand from beneath the blanket. I know he wants me to take hold of it and I do, although I know that's another rule I've broken, for we're not allowed to give personal comforts. His hand is large and surprisingly warm. He's trembling.

His face creases in what I know is meant to be a smile, and I smile back. But then, when we jolt over a dip in the floor, the smile goes and his skin greys. I hear him groan, and Bellfield swears. 'Try looking where you're going, miss,' he says and I feel a blush rising, for I'd do anything rather than add to any of the men's distress. I know that I will always avoid that dip in future.

'I'll take him from here. You go on back,' Bellfield says as we go through the doors into the hospital. I give Sergeant Harris's hand a squeeze then let go, standing back as Bellfield pushes past me.

When I return to the station, I'm given another trolley to steer, and I do it a little better this time, with only the tiniest bump into one of the stanchions. This patient is completely bandaged, even his eyes. Burns, his label says. He moans softly all the time. I talk to him as we go, tell him about the hospital, about Walter and Hubert, about Elmford and the weather, anything, just so he can hear my voice. He doesn't answer but, gradually, the groans quieten.

Next time I'm sent back, I light a cigarette for one of the walking wounded who is waiting at the back of the station. His hands are both bandaged, and I have to place the cigarette in his mouth and hold the match to it as he draws.

'It's all right, love, I can manage,' he says, pushing the cigarette to the side of his mouth where he lets it sit, drooping, while smoke curls up. He half-shuts an eye against it, and smiles at me.

'Good old bloody England,' he says, drawing out the last word. He has a broad accent, Devonshire I think. He laughs.

'Who'd've thought I'd end up with a Blighty, eh?' He sees me looking at his hands and looks down, too. 'Shell exploded just in front o' the parapet,' he explains. 'I were blown into the damn can o' stew I were heating up for the lads. I were only out for a minute or so, but it were enough to turn my hands red, bloomin' raw.' He winces as he laughs. 'A stew burn, that's what I've got.' He laughs again, motions for me to remove his cigarette. I take it from between his lips, and he turns aside and spits. 'Better'n bein' back in that bloody trench, though,' he says. 'Beggin' your pardon, Nurse.'

'That's all right,' I hear myself say as I replace his cigarette. 'I'd be saying an awful lot worse if it was me. Stew or no stew, it's still a battle wound.'

'Ah, you're a good'un, you are, to say that.' He leans back against the wall, lets the smoke drift into his mouth and nose, and draws deeply.

'Get a move on there, Nurse.' A sister, in her grey cape with its red trim, calls out to me as she passes. She's supporting a soldier whose ankle is bandaged.

I take my soldier down to Central and when I return, the platform's almost empty. The last task I'm given is to try to persuade a young soldier boy to come out from where he's hiding beneath the seat at the back of the platform. But he won't come out for me, no matter how much I coax him. He has folded himself away, his knees touching his chin and his face tucked down, the way Florrie's little Horace curls up when he sleeps in his cradle.

'Stand aside, miss,' a voice commands behind me. I do as I am told. It's the officer with the muddy boots. His face still looks stern, though he's not so flushed as before.

'Get up from there, soldier!' he booms out, making me jump. 'You snivellin' little shirker, get up. Get up, I say!'

The boy slowly unwinds himself to stand, shaking, in front of the officer. 'Now go with the nurse,' he says, in a gentler voice. He turns to me. 'Don't stand any nonsense, or you won't be able to do anything with him.'

'No, sir,' I say, and lead the soldier by the arm.

He comes, meek as a lamb.

Chapter 25

Hut 49
Royal Victoria Military Hospital
Netley
Hampshire

April 30th, 1915

Dearest Hubert,

Thank you for your letter. I'm glad you like getting mine,
for I do so love coming off duty and finding something in
your dear hand waiting for <u>me</u>. The post was early today and
I was able to spend my afternoon break reading yours over
and over as I lay on my bed. That is how we often spend
our time between shifts nowadays, lying on our beds. Isn't it
awful? Ana has taken up smoking. She says that all
sophisticated women are doing it and, anyway, why should
the men have all the fun? She got me to try one, though I
can't say that I cared for it at all. It only served to make me
feel sick.

Yesterday afternoon, Sister Browning sent me up to the
station to escort the wounded men from the ambulance

train down to the hospital. I really rather think she must be pleased with my progress to have let me go, for I was the only VAD there. She would never give actual praise, of course. Hell would freeze over first! But it was thrilling, though upsetting of course, to see the suffering of the men. The first patient I had to escort was Sgt. John Harris. He lost a foot at Ypres, and has ended up on my ward. He had an operation today and the surgeon has taken the rest of his leg off below the knee, though he doesn't know it yet, and was still asleep from the anaesthetic when I came off duty. It must be very hard to lose a limb, though much worse to have one's mind affected, don't you think? There are plenty here like that.

Now for some news that will make you quite envious! I am going out on a boat trip one afternoon soon. Ana put my name forward, as she has made chums of a chap and his wife who have begun to take patients and staff out for a few hours on Southampton Water. I don't know how I will like it, for the only other time I've been in a boat is when I went on the Isle of Wight ferry, and I have to say that I felt rather seasick then. I only hope it is calm but, like Ana says, there's only one way to find out.

Oh, and another thing to tell you. I had to put my first-aid into practise this morning when one of the laundry girls here was knocked down by a coal lorry. She's ended up all right, thank goodness. Just a graze, but she fainted from fright, and who's to wonder? If one of those big locomotive vehicles came roaring towards me, I think I should faint too! They really ought to go a little bit slower, but perhaps she wasn't looking where she was going. You need to have eyes in the back of your head here sometimes, with the traffic going up and down our little roads all day the way it does.

In your letter, you say you are getting impatient to be off to war. I would say <u>please</u> do not be wanting to go too quickly, Hubert dear, though I do understand that you want to do your bit, of course. The men here are so proud to have served. But, as for me, I shall hate it when you go and are in the trenches, in danger.

To end, I will say once more how much I love getting

your letters. Sometimes I keep them by me in my pocket (well out of sight of Sister Browning of course!) and carry them around all day. Just so that I can feel you with me.

Yours,

Maude

Chapter 26

Training Camp
Winchester

May 4th, 1915

My Dearest Maude

I have stolen a few moments to dash off a quick missive to
you. Thank you for yours, which came yesterday. It's always
good to hear about your life at the hospital, for I almost feel I
am there with you when you describe it, and so don't miss you
<u>quite</u> so much. By the way, you can tell your Sister Browning
from me that she ought to appreciate you a little more! I think
she's jolly lucky to have someone like you.

What do you think of the war news? There doesn't seem to
be any chance of it stopping yet, does there? (Hooray!)

I, for one, hope it carries on, at least until I've had a go at the
Hun. Though, if I'm being perfectly honest Maude, sometimes,
in the middle of the night when everything is quiet and my
thoughts get a chance to be mulled over, I do wonder whether
I will actually have the courage when the time comes. It's one
thing sticking a bayonet into a sack of straw, but quite another

when it comes to doing the real thing, and I cannot help asking myself if I will have the requisite courage when I am actually faced with the enemy. Even Germans are human beings. Randolph says it's best not to think too much about that sort of thing, but I can't seem to help it. What if I'm not the example of courage to the men that I wish to be?

Please forgive me for writing so openly to you in this way, dearest. I trust that you will understand, and not think less of me?

No more now. I promise my next letter will be more cheerful than this melancholy one!

Yours ever,

Hubert

Postscript: There are rumours of another move, but not to the Front yet, I think. It is very frustrating.

Chapter 27

My brush catches on a tangle, and I tug absently at it, working it through till the bristles run freely again. I've perched myself on the window sill, and am drying my hair in a patch of evening sun, the window pushed back as far as it will go, propped there with a pile of books. A pattern of shadows from the trees moves gently on the top. It's the book Hubert gave me, the one with the poems in. How faded the red cover has become.

The May evenings have lengthened and, even though it's already half past eight, it's still almost as light as day. I continue brushing, rasping my scalp with each stroke, lifting the strands high time and time again, letting the warm air through. Outside, a pair of blackbirds flit backwards and forwards to the hedge. They take it in turns to alight a little way off from their nest, cocking their heads from side to side. Then, caterpillars and grubs dangling each side of their yellow beaks, they disappear, and I can hear the fledglings' tiny, urgent squeaks.

I glance down at Hubert's most recent letter on the sill beside me, re-read the bit that's got me thinking.

Talking of leave, Maude, I have had an idea. Since it cannot be too much longer, I shouldn't have thought, before our Battalion is mobilised, not with the way the war is stepping up, I was thinking how good it would be if we were to spend a couple of days together. We could stay at an hotel by the sea, perhaps in Brighton, or Worthing? Just you and I, dear – though separate rooms of course. Would you like that? Do write back and let me know, for I should like it above everything. Let me have your answer as soon as you can, and I will make the necessary arrangements.

I let my gaze drift out through the window again. Two days with Hubert. Just him and me. My mouth stretches softly in a smile. I am so deep in thought that I jump when the door opens. Ana comes in, unfastening her hairpins and drawing off her cap. Her hair is damp with perspiration, her dark curls flat.

'Well?' she says. 'What is it that's got you grinning like a cat that got the cream?' She's still got her uniform on, and her face is pink from the heat. She reaches out and snatches Hubert's letter from the sill. 'Aha!' she says, holding it high above her head. 'A billet-doux.'

'Give it back,' I laugh, trying to take it back from her. She goes over to her bed and flops down on it, waving my letter in the air. When the door opens again, she slips the letter quickly beneath her pillow. It's Susan. She walks towards us, flicking her eyes from Ana to me and back again. I sit down on my bed, brushing vigorously at my hair. Try as I might, I can't help wishing she'd turn round and go away again.

'God, what a day!' Ana says. 'Old Tompkinson had me running about all the bloody time. Do this, Nurse Pemberton, do that, Nurse Pemberton, hop, skip and jump, Nurse Pemberton.' I see Susan look at the corner of my letter that's sticking out from Ana's pillow. She picks up her cardigan from where it hangs on the end of her bed.

'You don't fool me, changing the subject as soon as I come in,' she says. 'That's not what you were talking about, and well you know it.' She flounces back towards the door. 'Well, you have your precious secrets!'

'There's no need to be like that …,' I begin, but she disappears as Kitty and Lil come in.

'What's up with Susan?'

I shrug. 'She feels left out, I suppose,' I mutter.

Lil has a pile of ironed laundry in her hands, and she places it on her bed then nudges Ana's feet away to sit down beside her. 'Yes, well, it's never very nice being the odd one out, is it?'

'That's her fault, I should've thought.' I bend my neck to brush upwards through my hair.' My voice is muffled beneath the curtain of hair. 'She doesn't exactly try very hard.' I sit up again, lifting the hair from my face with a sweep of my arm.

'She's a strange one though, isn't she?' Lil continues. 'Did you know that she stores food in her cupboard?'

'Food? Whatever for? There's plenty to eat here. That's probably why she's as thin as a rake then, if she's not eating properly.'

'It's not dinners or anything, of course, she couldn't do that. It's fruit and bread and pieces of cake that she wraps up. Her family live in the village. I think she takes it down to them in the afternoons, while we're lazing about.'

'And there's me thinking she's been meeting a boy!' Not that I believe what I say, not at all. Who'd want someone as miserable as her?

'No, I'm sure it's nothing like that,' Kitty comes to sit beside me on my bed. The sunlight catches the top of her dark head. 'Her father had an accident a while back. She told me the doctors have said he'll never work again. There are children still at home, seven of them I think. A lot of mouths to feed, anyway.'

'She'd be better off with factory work if it's money they need,' I say. 'They get paid a good wage. She'd earn a darned sight more than she does being a VAD.' I stuff my bolster into the small of my back. 'Fancy her telling you all that, though. She never tells me anything.'

'Well, she might do if …. Well, sometimes, you can be a bit ….' Kitty looks at me, her eyebrows drawn together in a frown.

'A bit … what?' I put my hairbrush down on the counterpane.

'Well, sometimes you can be a bit … *opinionated*,' she continues, 'and you don't always listen very well, either. I just think you could try a bit harder with her, Maude. She's all right, once you get to know her, you know.' I put my hairbrush down, and look at Kitty. It's not like her to be so serious. Come to think of it, she doesn't look at all herself. Now that I look, I can see that her eyes are rimmed red, as if she's been crying.

'What's up, Kit?' I ask, reaching out to take one of her hands. 'Lord knows, you're right. You want to hear what Dad says about me sometimes.' I grimace. 'I will try with Susan. You're quite right. Circumstances alter cases, don't they? My mother's always saying that, and it's true.' I watch as Kitty's eyes suddenly fill with tears.

'What *is* it, Kit?' Ana presses.

'I expect it's nothing.' Kitty twists the corner of the counterpane between her fingers, hesitating.

'Tell us!'

'It's just that I haven't heard from Conrad for nearly two weeks now. Two weeks, and he always writes! Almost every day,' she adds, and dabs at her eyes. We stare at her in silence.

'Look,' I tell her, 'just because you haven't heard for a couple of weeks, it doesn't mean anything. It's more likely that no news is good news, I should say. You'd've heard if something *had* happened, that's for sure. I bet they've moved him somewhere and he hasn't had time to write, that's what it is.' I look across to the picture that stands on Kitty's locker by her bed. Her Conrad's not the most handsome of men, not like my Hubert with his dark hair and blue eyes, but he's got a nice face all the same, and a lovely wide smile. He puts me a little in mind of Sergeant Harris, now I look. Yes, John has that sort of face too. Not exactly handsome, but the sort you feel comfortable with, someone you know won't let you down.

'Yes, well, it's all right for you to say that, Maude,' Kitty says. 'You're still getting your letters, aren't you? You're lucky. But then, your boy hasn't been in danger yet, has he?' I feel as if she's slapped me with her words, but it's true. I can't deny it. What would I feel if Hubert was overseas and his letters suddenly stopped coming? Despite the warm evening, a shiver runs through me.

'I'm sure everything's all right, Kit,' I say, but my words sound empty.

'I hope so.' She gets up, and Lil follows her out.

'Phew!' Ana says when they've gone through to the sitting room. 'Poor Kitty.' Her bed creaks as she rolls over onto her front. 'It's true what you say though, Maude. She would have heard if something had happened, wouldn't she?' I watch as Ana reaches beneath her pillow and draws out my letter, and I get up ready to snatch it back, but she only holds it further away. 'I'll let you have it,' she says, 'but only if you promise to tell what's made you so smug.'

'All right,' I say, 'all right.' Ana hands me back the letter and I fold it up, tuck it into my pocket.

'Well? What is it?'

'Hubert's asked me to go away with him.'

'No!' Ana screams out her delight. 'How absolutely, perfectly thrilling. But, how wicked of him.' She looks slyly at me and I start brushing my hair again. 'You *are* going, aren't you?'

I hesitate, torn between my desire to say yes, and my fear

of what might happen if I do. 'Actually, I don't know.'

'Are you mad? Good God, if I had a handsome soldier boy keen as mustard on me as your Hubert must be on you to write to you a dozen times a week ....'

'Hardly that, Ana.'

'Well, if it were me, I'd be straight out of this place on the next train and blow anybody who tried to stop me!'

I think of Mother and Dad, and what they'd say if they ever heard about it. 'You make it sound so easy.'

'Of course it's easy. Why wouldn't it be?' I look out of the window to where a bee is buzzing in the evening sun amongst the hawthorn blossom. 'You'll get leave,' she continues, 'bound to. You've hardly taken any of your allocation.' She sits up to kick off her shoes, and they drop to the floor with a thud. She lifts a foot, rubbing it between the palms of her hands. 'Ooh, if I'd have known how much my legs and feet would ache being a VAD, I'd have thought again before I signed up,' she says, lowering her foot and lifting the other one.

'It's not the leave, Ana.' I deem my hair dry, and put the brush down on the table beside the bed.

'What is it, then?'

I think of the day on Harting Down, the excitement I felt at Hubert's touch. 'It's just that ....' Ana raises her eyebrows at me. 'Just that I don't know if he'll be expecting, well, you know.' She looks at me and I feel a blush rise to burn my cheeks. She laughs.

'And how is that a problem?' she asks.

'It isn't that I don't want to,' I tell her. I leave the sentence unfinished, and she smiles at me knowingly.

'Look,' she says, growing serious. 'It's not as if it's a flash in the pan, old thing, is it? I don't know what the fuss is about. There are things you can do, precautions and all that, if that's what you're worried about. 'If it were me and I had the chance of a few days with a fellow I really liked, I wouldn't think twice, believe me.' She stares through the window for a while before looking back at me. 'Hubert's bound to be sent to the Front sooner or later, isn't he?' I nod briefly, wishing her words away. 'Don't take this the wrong way,' she continues, 'but there is a war on. You've got to take every chance that life gives you.'

'I know. It's just ....'

'Just what?'

'Well, if I make it easy for him, he might think I'm – well – maybe he'll think I'm not the right sort of girl.'

She laughs. 'That's balderdash! Listen, Maude. Everyone's that sort of girl beneath it all. The only people who say that kind of thing are those who haven't learnt how to live. Besides, I thought you were a modern woman, one who thinks for herself? Do what's right for you and Hubert, not what other people think you should or shouldn't do, for goodness' sake.'

'But ....'

'But?' She raises her finely shaped eyebrows at me.

'It's just that if I *do*, I'm afraid he'll stop wanting me. I couldn't bear that. I don't suppose there'll ever be a proper future for us, not with him coming from his side of things, and me from mine, but I wouldn't want it to end like that. And, before you say anything,' I add, 'marriage is definitely out of the question. His mother would never allow it.'

'His mother! It's not up to his mother, is it? If he loves you ....'

I think of the things he says in his letters. 'I think he does, Ana, in his own way. It's just that, well, there are too many differences between us, that's all. It's complicated.'

'Well, you don't have to have relations with him if you don't want to. There can be an awful lot between a man and a woman besides you-know-what. I should know.' I look at

Ana. I mean, really look at her this time, for there's a strange look on her face.

'What d'you mean?'

She sits forwards on the edge of her bed, and stares down at the floor. 'I was thinking of someone, Maude.'

'Who?'

'Someone I've known all my life.'

'Oh?' I narrow my eyes at her. 'What's his name?'

'Ashby.'

'I haven't heard you mention him before.'

'That's because there's no point,' she replies. 'Yours isn't the only relationship with no chance of a future.' She pauses. 'I've always loved him. Always. All my life.' She traces a pattern with the toe of her shoe on the floor.

'Why can't there be a future with him, then?'

'Because he's queer, old thing, that's why. He doesn't want sex with me. He prefers going to bed with boys, to doing it with me.'

'Oh.'

'So now you know. That's why I think you should take what happiness you can. I'd give anything, *anything*, to have that with him, even for a single moment.'

Chapter 28

August 25th, 1915

My Dearest Maude,

I can hardly bring myself to write this, dear, for I must impart some bad news. Father has telegraphed to say that Ralph has died. He was in the reserve trenches just outside Lens when he became ill. They took him to a military hospital, but it was all to no avail. Poor Ralph, he should have died gloriously, for he was such a gloriously brave chap, standing up to the world, believing in himself, even when his own family turned against him. Father said there was a mention of tuberculosis in the letter from his Commanding Officer, though I am at a loss as to why it wasn't picked up sooner.

Such strange thoughts have occupied my mind since I heard the news, and I cannot seem to settle to anything. Memories of us as children keep coming to me, the long holidays we spent in Dorchester, the games we played, the races we ran along the lane, and the time we found a hawfinch's nest in the orchard.

How can it be that he is not alive any more? I am sorry,

dear, to be so gloomy, but I know you would want me to share my deepest feelings with you, and I know, above all, that you understand, having lost two brothers of your own in Arthur and Horace.

There is, alas, more bad news, though it is of little significance compared to poor Ralph. It is just that the holiday we had planned will have to be postponed. We are off to Witley for further training and all leave has been cancelled until we are safely ensconced there. I am being permitted a visit home on compassionate grounds, in view of Ralph's death, but it is only for two days, and I have orders to report straight back.

Rumours are flying about of mobilization, but I will believe it only when it happens. I want more than ever to be out there in the thick of it now, for I have Ralph's memory to fight for, too.

So, I leave you, in the saddest of minds. Please say a prayer for us all, won't you? I hadn't fully realised till now how dear my brother was to me, and now it is too late. The night ahead seems so dark, dearest. How I wish you were here.

Your own

Hubert

Chapter 29

That letter of Hubert's was three months ago, and today's bright November day is a mere ghost of the summer long gone. There have been many changes at the hospital, men coming and going. Some have died, but many more have gone on to convalesce. As for me, I am still on Ward G.Eight. It seems that Sister Browning, for all her complaining, doesn't want to part with me. Sergeant Harris is still on our ward, too, for his leg is taking a long time to heal. I've heard Dr Edesworthy talking. He says he might have to amputate a bit more, though he doesn't want to, of course, not unless he has to. I suppose it's because of John staying, that he and I have become friends. I find I can talk to him. He's that sort. Yes, he's one of those people you can tell things to.

Hubert and I still write to each other, of course. Every day if we can. Many, many letters, though no meetings between us.

Until now.

I look around me as I wait on Brighton Station, searching the crowds for sight of him. So many people waiting, so many leavings. Sometimes I wonder if the government is purposely trying to keep people apart. Take our Walter. I haven't seen him more than once or twice since he enlisted, what with the battalion up at Witley and me at the hospital at Netley, and if he does make it home, I can't, and so on, and so on. It's almost as if nobody belongs to themselves any more. We're the sole property of His Majesty, King George V.

I look at the station clock as I clutch Hubert's latest letter in my hand, curl up my fingers till I feel the paper crumple. *I'll meet you off the train. Make sure you don't miss it,* he said in his letter. Miss the train! I would have thought he knew me better than to think I'd do that.

The clock shows a little wanting twenty-to-six. I watch the long hand register another minute, then search the crowds again. Most of the people here are in uniform but even those who are still in civvies, including the women, are in the sombre colours that have become popular since the outbreak of war. Not a single bright colour amongst them.

I sweep my eyes left, then right, watching as a train stops in a puff of steam. What if Hubert has changed his mind? I nearly did, for it still seems a bold thing, to come away with a man, even though we've got separate rooms in the hotel. Good heavens, what would Mother say if she was ever to hear of it? Or Dad?

Outside the station, through the archway that leads to the street, I can see the sky. There's only the slightest blush of light left now, and already the temperature's begun to drop, even here inside the station. I look around, glance up at the clock again. What will I do if he doesn't come? Will there be trains all the way back to Netley tonight?

I wait.

There he is!

'Maude? *Maude!*' he calls as he pushes his way through the crowds towards me. The joy I feel mixes with anxiety. He's changed. His face looks different, a little thinner perhaps? Then, suddenly, he's the same Hubert he ever was and my heart is racing as I push towards him, too, until at last we are standing together.

An elderly woman carrying a child jostles against us. 'Really!' she says, 'what a place to stand, right in the way.' Hubert steps back.

'I do apologise,' he says, but his eyes quickly rest on mine again.

'You want to look where you're going, dear,' she continues, then she's past and we move together again, this time his face is so close to mine, I can see the fine texture of his skin.

I know what I want my first words to be. I wrote them, but I want to say them too. 'Hubert,' I begin, 'I'm so very sorry about Ralph.'

He holds my eyes for a moment before looking down to take my bag. He puts his hand on my elbow, and silently leads me through the crowd. 'Thank you,' he says, when we're outside in the evening air. 'I can't believe he's gone, Maude, to tell the truth. It's as if he's away, on holiday perhaps, and that one day he'll be coming back.' The sky above us is dusted with the first of the evening's stars. 'But, don't let's talk of it now,' he says, drawing my arm through his. 'It doesn't do any good and, besides, we're here to enjoy ourselves! Just think,' he continues, smiling, 'two whole days, just you and me. My God, how I've dreamed of this!' He laughs and so do I, for I've dreamed of it, too. 'Come on!'

All thoughts of the hospital and of home disappear as I walk beside Hubert. I let him lead me down the hill, past hotels and guest-houses with their shadowy 'Rooms to Let' signs, down and down until we reach the seafront. The moon is rising; I can see its light on the sea, a soft shine as if someone has unrolled a glowing carpet towards us. We walk along the promenade until we reach some wooden steps, then Hubert lets go of me and treads lightly down before turning to lift me onto the sand. His hands grip me, and he swings me as if I weigh no more than a child. Then, pulling his cap hard down on his head, he breaks into a run, pulling me along after him. The moon casts rocking, silver lines on the incoming waves as we race together across the beach, my bag bumping between us against our legs.

I can feel the hard ridges of wet sand through the soles of my boots as I run. I keep running until I can't run any more, and the blood beats in my veins, making me as warm as if it were summer-time. I bend over and Hubert laughs, and when I have caught my breath, I laugh too. We stand together, watch the moon rise slowly above us as we look out across the wide expanse of sea. I press the moment into my mind, as you would a flower between the pages of a book, and the fancy comes to me that the line of moonlight is pointing to our destiny, a dark place that lies hidden beyond the horizon.

'Can you hear that?' Hubert murmurs, his arm encircling my waist, and drawing me closer to him. 'Can you?' he says.

I listen. There's the sound of the waves lipping the shore, the distant growl of a motor engine, the whinny of a horse as it trots along the seafront. Which does he mean?

'Hear what exactly?'

'The war, Maude. I can hear it, you know. Every now and then, I can. It's the guns. Listen.'

I listen again, concentrating, trying to hear beneath the sounds of the evening. I shake my head. 'I can't hear the war. Is it possible from here? Surely not.'

'Yes, yes,' he says, his eyes opening wide as he stares out to sea. 'Of course it is. I can hear it.'

Hubert has booked us rooms at The Corinth Hotel. It's a large, rectangular building, gaunt and dark with tall chimneys, next to the sea. As I gaze up at it, I can't help wishing we were staying in one of the friendly guest houses we passed on our way here. Supper is in a wood-panelled room, where sounds are muffled and the tables have vases of greenery in the centre. I manage the cutlery all right, despite my fears that I wouldn't and by the time we get to coffee, I feel myself begin to relax. It's good coffee, strong and bitter, nothing like the pale milky drink we get at the hospital.

We have a game or two of cribbage in the snug. Hubert taps his fingers on the arm of his chair as he waits for me to lay my cards, but I purposely take my time and drag out the game, for I still don't know what to do about tonight. He soon begins to yawn, and when I try to persuade him to have another hand, he only smiles at me, and packs away the cards. 'Too tired', he says, so we make our way to the lift in the foyer. Hubert pulls aside the grilled door, stepping back to let me pass inside, clangs it shut behind us, and presses the button for the second floor. Then he reaches out for my hand as the machinery whines and, with a small jerk, we're pulled slowly upwards. The lift stops on the first floor to take in an elderly lady.

'We're going up, I'm afraid,' Hubert tells her.

'No matter, dear. I'll go up with you, then down again.' She smiles at us, and we move apart.

'Well, goodnight to you both,' the old lady says as we get out at the next floor. She stares pointedly at my hand as I pass, and I feel myself blush. The concertina'd gates clang behind us, and we turn to walk along the worn red carpet that runs the length of the corridor. My palms are perspiring as I reach into my pocket to draw out my key. Engraved on the brass disk is my room number. *Thirty-Three*.

I fumble the key into the keyhole. My hands are trembling now, for my mind is full of Harting Down and what we did there. I feel again Hubert's fingers through my hair, the hard press of his body. The lock catches and clicks open. I turn back. Hubert is close beside me. I realise then what it is I want. I want him to want me. When he bends to press his lips against my cheek, my breath shortens, and I turn my lips towards his.

But, 'Goodnight, dearest,' he is all he whispers. 'Sweet dreams.' He steps back. 'I'll knock your door in the morning, shall we say, eight-thirty? We can have breakfast and decide what to do then.'

I am surprised by the strength of my disappointment. Ana's words come into my mind. *Take what happiness you can,* she said didn't she? Yes, that was it. But Hubert has turned away. And I have let him.

'Goodnight, Maude.'

'Goodnight,' I say.

'Well?' Hubert pushes aside his breakfast plate, smeared with yolk, a piece of bacon rind snaked at the edge. He draws his side-plate towards him and takes a piece of toast, spreading on a thick layer of butter, then marmalade. I marvel again at the quality of the food here. 'What would you like to do?'

'The weather's good,' I say, pouring a second cup of tea for Hubert from the china teapot, then one for myself. It reminds me of the time at the Culver Hotel in Portsmouth, when we had taken tea. We had only just met then. How strange to be sitting here with him all these months on. And at such an hour, too. If only it could always be like this! Bright sunshine strikes through the window, and touches his cap on the chair beside him and the webbing at his shoulders. The leather shines a ruddy brown, like conkers just split from their skins.

'Perhaps we could go for a walk?' Hubert takes a bite of his toast, and I spread some raspberry jam on my own. The jam is delicious, every bit as good as Mother's.

'That'd be nice,' I say. I listen to the soft morning-voices as I eat, and the clink of cutlery against china. I look around. We're down early, but we're not the first. Oh dear, there's the old lady from the lift. I know what she'll be thinking, but she's wrong, isn't she? I wish I could tell her so. I look away, watch a couple instead as they come into the room. They're young, like us, and the man is in uniform. The girl catches my eye and smiles. I smile back. Are they married? Does she think we are? What would it feel like if Hubert and I *were* married? What if he was bound to me, and I to him? I think of the limitless sweet, private hours we could spend together.

Hubert wipes his lips with his napkin, and leans back in his chair, turning to look out through the window. I follow his gaze to where a pair of seagulls hang upon the air. They dangle there as if they were puppets on strings.

The beach is deserted as, coats buttoned up and hats pulled firmly down on our heads, we descend the steps from the promenade. Hubert is wearing the scarf I made for him, tucked into the neck of his coat. I smile when I think of it pressed close against his skin.

Down beneath the rise of the wall, the wind is a little less blustery, and we turn and walk in the direction of the pier. How big it looks compared to the pier at Netley. And how blue the sea is. It's hard to believe that, on such a day and just across the stretch of water beside us, such awful things are happening. But I won't think of that today. No, not today.

I'll think how wonderful it is to be here with Hubert at last, with the wind stinging colour into our cheeks. And how sensible he was last night. I needn't have worried after all, but if it had been up to me, I would have kissed him, a proper kiss like the ones at Harting, and I don't think this time I would have stopped, for I've such a longing for him. How quickly he walks. I'll have to run soon just to keep up. Now the sun is catching him as he smiles. I'll remember this. Yes, I'll remember it always.

A cloud appears suddenly, as if from nowhere, and covers the sun as spots of rain spatter on my face. 'Come on,' Hubert calls, pulling me after him. We shelter beneath the great iron girders of the pier as the rain cloud passes over. There's no-one else for miles, and when Hubert takes off his cap and bends his head towards me, I turn up my face to meet his.

The rain stops and we continue along the wet sand, walking along the tide line where the waves play. My heart is still racing from the kisses and from the closeness of him. Hubert takes off his glove and motions for me to do the same, and our fingers entwine together.

'Remember the picnic we had?' he says suddenly, drawing me closer and slipping his arm around me.

'Of course I do.'

'That was November too. A whole year ago.'

'It was a bit warmer then.' He holds my gaze for a long moment. Are his thoughts the same as mine? Does he keep each detail of that day in his heart the way I do? The poems, the wine that was like sunshine, the nearness of each other?

We follow the shoreline, with its wash of brown seaweed, the cold wind full in our faces. Empty white cockle shells lie scattered like blossom, and the wet sand pales at my tread. We make our way towards a group of houses crowded together in a dip, and are soon turning up a tiny street towards a public house. Its sign, a ship in full sail, creaks in the wind.

Hubert holds open the door for me, smiling encouragement as I hesitate, and I walk into the dim, empty interior. I've never been inside a public house, for it's not at all the done thing, of course. But here, away from home, everything is different and, besides, I have to admit to being more than a little curious. I breathe in the musty odour of beer and stale smoke as I have a good look around me. The small leaded windows don't let in much light and, together with the low dark beams, give a sense of secrecy and gloom. There are several settles and tables and a small fitful fire burning in the hearth. Even though it's mid-day and bright outside, there's a lighted lamp on the wooden bar. Hubert ducks his head beneath the lintel behind me, and strides across the room.

'How may I help you, sir?' The landlord's voice comes out of the gloom. He's a large man, with grey whiskers. He puts down his newspaper, and gets up from his stool behind the bar.

'I'll have a stout for the lady, and a glass of your local brew for me, please,' he says.

'You sit yourselves down, and I'll bring 'em across.' Hubert escorts me to a tall settle that stands next to the fireplace where a pile of driftwood smokes in the middle of the grate.

'It's only just been lit but don't worry, it'll soon get going,' the landlord calls. We sit side by side on the seat as the landlord walks with a rolling gait towards us, spilling beer onto the flag floor. He places the glasses down on the table in front of us. 'There you are,' he says. Hubert hands him a half-crown, and we sip our drinks as we stare at the fire, a piece of driftwood glowing as it catches. The landlord returns with Hubert's change. 'You've come at the wrong time for this part of the world,' he says, standing with his hands on his hips as he stares down at us. 'Summer's the best time for visiting. It's grand then, it is. But winter down here?' He turns his thumb to the floor. 'Best left to the blasted seagulls.' He puts back his great head and laughs, a booming sound that reverberates around the room. His eyes come to rest on Hubert's uniform. 'Been to the Front?' he asks.

I see Hubert's face flush. 'Not yet, more's the pity,' he says. 'We're off soon though, I hope. We're expecting to be mobilized any time now.'

'You up at Salisbury?'

'No, no. My brother did some training there. I'm based at Witley, near Hindhead – in Surrey,' he adds. 'To tell you the truth, I can't wait to be off.'

'More fool you then. If the papers are anything to go by, the poor sods over there are being killed by the thousands. Canon fodder, that's what they are.'

I see Hubert frown, then he catches the landlord's eye, flicks his glance to me, and back again. The landlord nods and taps his nose with his finger. 'Right you are, sir,' he says, nodding as he moves away.

'You don't have to treat me like a child, Hubert,' I say coldly, picking up my glass of thick, dark stout and taking a sip. It tastes bitter on my tongue. Hubert reaches out, tries to take my free hand in his, but I draw it back.

'I was only trying to protect you. A chap can do that for his girl, can't he?'

'But I don't need protecting. You're not the only one this war has changed, you know.' I think of Private Willis's wound, and Sergeant Harris losing his leg, and of the men shut away in D Block. 'I've grown up in the last year, Hubert, and I've seen enough at the hospital for me to know what war's really about.' My glass jars against the table as I put it down too heavily. 'I've probably seen more than you have, truth be told.'

Hubert is quiet for a moment, his gaze somewhere by his boots. 'There was no need to say that, Maude,' he says after a while. He looks up, his eyes glittering. 'Do you honestly think I would still be here if it were up to me?'

I can't help thinking of how unhappy he was before he enlisted. 'No.' I sigh. 'I don't.'

There is a long pause, and I begin to wonder if I've spoiled it all, our precious time together. I'm glad when at last Hubert breaks the silence. 'I've never thought you a child,' he says. 'I'm sorry if you thought that.'

I feel a wash of relief that he's not angry with me. 'I'm sorry, too.' I pull a face. 'Me and my temper.'

The tension gone, we sip our drinks, enjoying just being together and watching as the fire takes hold while outside, the sign creaks out its slow rhythm. Eventually, Hubert drains the last of his ale. 'Come on,' he says. 'We'll walk back and get some lunch at the hotel. Then perhaps we can go to the show at the pier. Would you like that?'

I smile, glad to forget our rift. I think of the variety shows we used to see together before the war. 'That'd be grand,' I say.

That evening, we have supper again in the panelled room. I look at the menu, and it's hard to believe we're at war at all with all the things on offer. Hubert chooses for us. We have mussels, duck with orange sauce, followed by rich sherry trifle. I'll have so much to tell the girls when I get back.

Afterwards, we sit in the conservatory, drinking port beneath exotic, green-fringed plants. We're alone apart from a black and white cat curled up beside the radiator. I have on my best dress, a dark blue with pin-tuck pleats that I know becomes me. We sit silently together. Hubert's eyes are already bright from the wine at dinner. He drains off his glass, and holds up a finger to a waiter who is passing by the double doors that separate the conservatory from the lounge.

'Yes sir?' The waiter, stooped and deeply wrinkled, stands by us, an empty silver tray in his hand. I can't help noticing the way his black suit shines at the elbows as he places our glasses on the tray.

'Another port, I think. Make it a double. What about you, Maude?' I nod, for the first one has made me feel pleasantly relaxed. I haven't drunk port before. It's much nicer than stout. 'Two doubles then,' Hubert says.

'Straight away, sir.'

Hubert reaches for a newspaper. 'What are you reading?' I ask after a moment or two of silence. His brows are drawn together, making two deep furrows. 'Is it about the war?'

'Yes, it's about the war.' He gives me a wry smile. 'Everything's about the war these days, isn't it?' Suddenly, his smile turns to a laugh. 'I sometimes wonder what we found to talk about before.' The waiter arrives back and sets down two small glasses full of a dark red liquid that sparks in the light.

Hubert lifts his glass. 'To us, Maude, and our time together.'

'To us.' I lean back and my wicker chair creaks beneath me as I settle against the cushion. I stare across his bowed head, to the long windows beyond, the panes black with night. Laughter drifts in to us from the bar, mixing with the chink of glasses and the pop of a champagne cork. The war seems far away.

We finish our drinks. Outside, the wind gusts, rattling the windows in their frames. When, finally, we stand, I am a little unsteady. I take Hubert's arm as we turn towards the door.

We have the lift to ourselves tonight. We do not break the silence as we ascend to our floor, and as we walk along the corridor I measure my steps slowly, for I do not want us to part. My heart beats faster as we near our rooms. Will Hubert turn from me as he did last night? What if this is our last chance, and we waste it?

But tonight, there is no chaste goodnight kiss between us. Hubert takes the key from my hand, unlocks the door, and passes with me into my room.

Moonlight falls through the window onto my single bed, bleeding the room of colour, and giving the crimson eiderdown a bluish tone. It throws its veil over us, too. I do not put on the light, nor draw the curtains across the window. We stand together, the draught from the slit of open window, cold against my cheeks.

Hubert takes off his jacket and throws it onto the chair beside the window. Then he pulls me slowly to him, and I feel the warmth of him passing through our clothes into my skin. Suddenly, I am assailed by doubts. What if he doesn't like my body? What if I do the wrong things? What if I don't please him? But his lips are on my lids, my cheeks, my neck, and I can feel the trembling of his hands as he unfastens the buttons of my blouse.

Soon I am standing in my shift. I open his shirt, pushing it away and down his arms. The musky smell of his sweat mixes with my own lily-of-the-valley scent, exciting me. Slowly, he draws my shift from my shoulders and exposes my breasts. They seem large and full in the moonlight. I cover them with my hands, but he gently eases my fingers away, and a fire passes through my belly as he draws my nipples into his mouth.

Is this his first time, too? I cannot help but wonder as I run my fingers over the smooth, hard surface of his shoulders. But, from the confident way he unlaces my stays, I know it is not. I think a moment about the girls he has had before, until his stroking fingers send delicious ripples through me, and I am lost.

I press my lips to his chest. His skin is different there, covered over with dark, springy hair, silky-rough. He eases me back across the bed, and the headlights of a motor car travel across the picture rail. Below, on the road outside the hotel, there is a faint squeak of brakes, then voices, 'goodnights' being called. Then the bark of a fox from the hill behind the hotel. Then silence.

Hubert seeks my mouth, and I willingly give it. We struggle for each other, my heart heating wildly as I feel Hubert unfastening his trousers.

The moonlight strikes the side of his face and neck above me. He pulls me to him again, draws back the eiderdown, and I breathe in the crisp laundered smell of the sheets. I know I cannot stop. No, not even if I wanted to, for all that exists is this. There are no more regrets, no more fears, just him and me, the saltiness of his skin, his tongue probing mine. He takes my hand and traces the hardness of his erection with my fingers, then he is entering me, and I am shuddering against the first shock of pain. He stills, and kisses me. Only that. Then it is me who is moving, smoothing the firm roundness of his buttocks over and over again, pressing and kneading them gently till he moans. Still he does not move. As my pain recedes, I dip my fingers between his buttocks, pull him further into me. It's then that he moves. Oh, yes, he moves then. Gone are my fears of pregnancy, the shyness, the fear I might not know what to do. Gone is everything but the thrill of the moment.

We stay together the whole, long night. Sometimes we sleep, but I am aware of his body even when I am dreaming. We wake often and each time, one of us reaches for the other and our fingers search in the darkness. Then, my breath catches, quickening until it gutters like a candle in a draught. When he parts me and I feel him moving inside me, my back arches, my breasts lifting to him. His lips are urgent on my own as he moves, the rhythm like the waves that shush against the shore below. It takes me with it. On and on, those regular, shushing waves. I wrap my legs around him, pull him deeper within me. On and on we rock, until I am sensible of nothing but the breaking of our desire in the darkness.

The following morning dawns bright again. The air is cold, but the sky is a cloudless blue and the wind has dropped. We climb the hill behind the hotel to the Downs, and my breath comes heavily as I trudge upwards. Hubert races ahead, stopping every now and then to wait, hands on hips, as he laughs down at me. The tenderness of the night seems to have gone. Perhaps he doesn't want me now that he's had his way?

'What a slowcoach you are,' he calls. 'It'll be time to go before we reach the top at this rate.'

I stop, breathing deeply as I turn round to see the view.

Immediately below us, the edge of the town straggles out to evaporate into the sea. Sparks of sunlight dance on the waves; seagulls, far away, are tiny specks of white floating haphazardly above the water; ships, insubstantial blots of grey.

Thoughts spin in my head as Hubert comes back down to stand beside me. We haven't spoken of our night together. How does he feel about it? Does he think worse of me for it? He reaches out his hand and tries to pull me up behind him, but I shake my head, preferring my slow, steady ascent. He catches me to him, and kisses me roughly before releasing me and walking on. 'That's so you won't forget me, Maude,' he calls cheerfully.

Forget you? Forget you? Forget you? The words sound again and again in my head. I will never forget you, Hubert. Never. I try to imagine a time when he is no longer there. *No, it is impossible that I should forget you.* I look up to where he stands outlined, the bottom half of him against the green of the Downs, and the top half against the blue of the sky. There is a thin, gauzy rip of cloud at his shoulder. It's in this moment that all that there ever was between us, slips somewhere deeper, and I know my life has changed forever. I climb towards him but, each time I almost reach him, he withdraws, laughing, backing away until he's on the ridge. He waves his cap at me.

The wind is much stronger here on the top, and we shelter in a shallow dip, sitting on the springy, dry turf to eat the sandwiches the hotel has packed for us. The sun catches on Hubert's face as he unwinds the grease-proofed paper, then holds the opened packet out to me. I take a sandwich. Ham, with apple chutney.

I stare down at the town as I eat, my eyes drifting across the strip of sand to the sea. I avert my gaze. I will not let myself look at the horizon beyond.

Chapter 30

It's almost Christmas. Each day for the last two weeks, I have expected to feel the dragging sensation in my stomach that means the onset of my monthly, but each day there has been nothing. Despite having used the vinegar douche Ana got for me, I can't help worrying.

Christmas Eve, and still no sign. A package comes from Hubert, small, wrapped in brown paper and tied up with string. I put it on my bedside table, with my cards from the girls, to open in the morning.

Ana knows my visitor's late. We all know each other's timings. It's impossible not to, living together like we do.

'Don't worry,' she tells me. 'It'll be all right.'

'Don't worry! How can I help it?'

'When you were in Brighton, you used the stuff I gave you, didn't you?' I nod, and she shrugs. 'That's all right, then. Look, it's the anxiety that'll be delaying it. It's a well known fact.'

'It's all right for you to say,' I tell her, and the worry stays there, knotting my insides. It makes me clumsy and forgetful on the ward.

'For goodness' sake, what is the matter with you, girl?' Sister Browning says to me for the hundredth time that day. 'I'll set you to making paper chains with the men if you don't buck your ideas up.'

I half wish she would, but all I say is, 'Yes, Sister. Sorry, Sister.'

In the afternoon, the walking wounded on our ward go out into the woods behind our hut, and cut branches of evergreen. They bring long trails of ivy, and holly, lots of it, with bright red berries, like splashes of blood. I try to put aside my thoughts, and attempt to enter into the festive mood, but it's not until we give up our afternoon break, and stay to help the men decorate the ward, that I feel my spirits begin to rise. It's impossible to stay gloomy with so much laughter and jollity around me.

On Christmas morning, I sit up in bed, and open my present from Hubert. It's a pen, black, with a gold nib. Very nice. I'll buy some indelible ink from the Naafi, and write with it to thank him. I wonder if he likes the gloves I've made for him. I hope he got them in time, for I was still sewing in the loose ends when Austen arrived to take the parcel to the post-room.

When I dress, I decide that I had better wear one of my monthly towels, just in case, and I carefully fold and pin the napkin into my drawers. Half-way through the morning, we are sent off to the chapel for Holy Communion, and when we arrive back on the ward, we find that Sister has put out little presents for the men. Christmas seems to have softened her, and brought out a different side, for she's actually smiling!

There's something for every patient to keep him warm – a muffler, a pair of gloves, or socks. And some cigarettes too, and some sweets. They've been donated by the Red

Cross, but Sister has bought something else for each of them, too. Something special to make them laugh, like the dish mop she gave Corporal Smith, just because he's always helping with the clearing up. The men are delighted with it all.

As I go round the ward, I glance frequently at John. He is propped up in bed, his head resting back against his pillows, his sandy hair combed back from his forehead. I can see by the smoothness of his chin that he's had a shave, and his large moustache has been trimmed, too, showing the fine outline of his mouth. He's looking much better these days, fuller in the face, and his skin has lost its greyness.

'Hey, Maude!'

I hurry across to him. 'Hush, for goodness' sake!' I look round for Sister Browning, but she's busy at her desk, writing. 'Surely I can call you by your proper name on Christmas Day?' His eyes are smiling at me.

'You know very well you can't!' I say with mock severity. 'Now, what it? What do you want?'

'Besides you, you mean?'

We exchange a smile, then John reaches beneath the counterpane and draws something out, holds it out to me. 'What is it?'

'It's a Christmas present.'

'For me? You shouldn't have done that, John.'

He smiles again. 'It's all right. Go on. I made it for you.'

I take the gift in my hand, fold back the thin layer of cloth that covers it. It's a bird, carved from wood, with wings outstretched, as if it were flying. 'Why, it's beautiful,' I say, bending my head to look at the delicate way he has etched each feather, the whole thing polished to a deep chestnut colour. 'I didn't know you were so talented.'

He grins. 'It's surprising what you can do, given the opportunity and the inclination,' he says.

209

I place the bird in my pocket. 'I haven't got anything for you. I feel dreadful now.'

John smiles. 'I didn't make it for you just to get something in return. That'd hardly be in the spirit of Christmas, now would it?' Suddenly, his fair eyebrows crease together as he looks at me. 'You all right? You're looking a bit pale.'

'Yes, yes. Of course I'm all right. Excuse me.' I turn. 'Thank you, John, for the present,' I say, looking back over my shoulder. 'It's wonderful.'

We only just manage to clear up in time for Dr Edesworthy's round, although we needn't have worried, because even he seems to have the Christmas spirit, smiling and joking. And there was me, thinking he didn't know how!

We serve dinner for the men at twelve o'clock, turkey and vegetables, followed by Christmas pudding and mince pies. The sight and smell of the food isn't making me feel sick, that's one good thing, I think, as I help take it round. In fact, it's making my mouth water. I look at the clock. It's another two hours till my own dinner.

In the afternoon, there are entertainments in the hall for the patients, put on by some of the nursing staff. Even those who are too ill to go don't miss out, as each ward has a visit from the entertainers afterwards. Then there's tea, and when we've finished, the beds are pushed back for games. The last hour is the most riotous of all, when the night staff arrive, and we stay on for a bit, just for the fun. Sister stays, too, and even joins in with a game of musical stools. It's so amusing to see her scrabbling for a seat with the men! I don't think I'll ever think of her in the same way again.

Then, at last, we've cleared away, and I'm doing a final tidy of the beds before the handover. It's when I'm bending to strip Corporal Smith's blankets back, that I suddenly feel a low, dull ache deep in my belly. Another cramp twists my stomach, and I'm glad I thought to put on the napkin, after all. I straighten the counterpane, fold the sheet down over the top, and smooth it sideways, then turn to do the same for John. 'Thank you again for the present,' I whisper, tucking in the blankets around him. 'It's lovely.'

The familiar cramps deepen, and as soon as I've been dismissed, I hurry to the lavatory. Long griping pains are pulling at my insides, dragging them down. But, I still won't believe it, not until I check.

In the privacy of the cubicle, I look down at the bright holly-berry spots on the white towel.

I should be glad. And, of course, I am. But, deep inside me, there's a different ache. An unexplainable sadness. For something that might have been.

Chapter 31

Witley Training Camp
Surrey

February 22nd, 1916

My Darling Maude,

Such excitement! Finally, the news we've been waiting for, but which I know you will not like at all. The 39th is being mobilized, and we're off to the Front! Yes, it's finally come. It's to be sometime next month, although we haven't been told the date yet, and we don't know exactly where it is we're headed. I am permitted only to pass on that it's to be France.

As you may imagine, it is organised chaos here now with all the preparations. The men were most disappointed not to have been inspected by the King, but spirits are high nevertheless, and it is just one of those things in life that one mustn't mind too much.

I hope by now that your little sprinkling of snow has entirely gone. We are still knee-deep in it here, but I think Netley must be a little warmer, seeing as how it is so close to the sea. It has stopped snowing for the time being, although it remains bitterly cold. With March only a week away now, one wonders how Spring is ever going to push its way up through the frozen earth once again. It's strange to think that when it does come, I will be in France, isn't it? I wonder if French flowers are different to those here?

I was so interested to read about your work at the hospital. Please write and tell me more, especially about your Sergeant Harris, although – and forgive me for saying this, Maude – please do not get too fond of him, nor any other of your patients, dear, will you? I know what a kind heart you have and it will give me such comfort if I know it still all belongs to me! Say it does, dearest, for my affection is yours alone, as you must surely know by now.

It's almost certain that I'll be granted a short period of leave before I embark for France. Do not be offended when I tell you that I feel I must spend it with my family. You and I had such a time together in Brighton, but I must now look to my duties. Mother (she does not know about our little holiday of course) has been feeling somewhat low, according to Father's last letter. It is the awful news of Ralph I expect, and with me being away from home, well I'm sure it cannot help matters. Her situation is a hard one for any mother to bear, and I know you will understand when you see the position I am in? However, be that all as it may, I am wondering, dearest, if you will be able to take a small amount of leave to come and see me off at the railway station? I will let you have details as soon as I know them myself, but I would go with a lighter heart if I were to see you again, albeit briefly.

I kiss this letter as if I were kissing your own dear lips.

Yours ever affectionately,

Hubert

Chapter 32

A rifle clatters to the ground. The noise of it rises above the hubbub of voices to echo in the overhang of the platform.

'You want to look after that rifle, soldier!' a deep voice shouts. 'Your life's going to depend on it before long.' His words conjure up a picture in my mind of mud-filled trenches and guns and barbed wire, like the newsreel images they show in the hospital canteen. The wind cuts, raw and cold, from the open space beyond the station, and I shiver, shrug myself deeper into my overcoat, and tuck my hands into my pockets.

Hubert said two o'clock in his letter. I glance up at the clock. It's fourteen minutes past. Perhaps he's gone already? After all, they sent Walter's lot off early. I would have missed him if I hadn't been early myself. How excited he was. The way he was laughing and larking about you'd have thought he was off on the railway works' outing rather than to the trenches, and war.

If I can just get up onto this plinth, I might be able to see a bit better. There. Yes. That's better. My gaze slips across the sea of khaki caps. So many people are squeezed into the station, how will I ever spot him? I watch as an officer pushes his way through to the platform edge, then strides up and down it, shouting out orders. He's wearing a sword. How strange it looks, clacking against him as he walks, as if he's off to the Boer war, not this one.

I glance again at the clock. Twenty-two minutes past. A young soldier nudges past me. A woman, his mother I should think, reaches out her hand to him but draws it quickly back as the boy bends to pick up his kit bag from a pile on the floor. He's looking across to where a group of his friends are laughing, and tossing cigarettes to each other. The woman's eyes do not leave him as he slings his rifle over his shoulder and swaggers across to join his mates. Anger tightens my chest. Do his friends mean so much more to him, then?

A train pulls in, its whistle shrill and piercing, and the soldiers surge forwards. The boy is carried along. He backs up into the dark oblong of an open carriage doorway. It's as if his mother's not here. How can he leave her so easily? But, suddenly, he throws a nervous glance across his shoulder, hesitates, and jumps down from the train, pushing back through the crowd to where the old woman stands. He bends to whisper something in her ear, and presses a kiss to her cheek. She smiles, lifting her hand to touch the place, as if it were sacred.

Brittle sunshine flashes on the carriage windows as the doors slam. Girls and women stand on tiptoe beside the train, turn up their faces for farewell kisses. The engine hisses, and steam drops in a white shroud around the carriages as the huge iron wheels strain into life. They clank forwards, slowly gathering speed. A row of heads appears as the steam thins, thrust through the open carriage windows. I can't see the young boy any more. Some women are running. How undignified they look. They stop at the end of the platform, fluttering their handkerchiefs until the train has gone. How different their faces look as they turn back, blank and unsmiling.

More soldiers drift into the station. I think of the streams of khaki all over the country, flowing from towns and villages, bleeding them of life. The men heave their packs from their backs, and swing them heavily to the floor to take the place of those just gone. They laugh and talk together, strange, mysterious items jangling together from their belts. Some prop their rifles against the stanchions, some hold theirs loosely at their sides, butts on the floor, the rifle slings dangling like braces on a man's trousers. One of the soldiers leans on his gun, as if it were a shepherd's crook, and rests his hands upon it, one on top of the other. A girl is handing out flowers. She gives him a wild daffodil, and he places it in his barrel. His friends laugh, and reach for their rifles for her to do the same for them and she slips them in, one by one, until there is a blossoming of yellow against the muddy-brown of their uniforms, transforming the scene, like a church at Easter-time. At the edge of the crowd, an officer accepts a posy of primroses and tucks it into the band of his cap. I want to scream. What do they think this is? A carnival?

'Stand back! Stand back!' A porter makes his way through the crowd, a cart behind him piled high with packs and boxes.

'Not this train, Sam! The next one!' a guards shouts. There are so many soldiers leaving, it seems that the trains are behind schedule. He points to the back of the station, and the porter parks the cart beneath a hoarding with an advertisement for Bovril. Will these boys drink Bovril out in the trenches, I wonder? If not, what will they drink? What will they eat? Will there be enough? Will they get the sleep they require? Sister Browning says that sleep and good food are essential to health. Will they survive? Will they?

A young lad, not more than seven or eight, suddenly levers himself up to stand on top of some milk churns. He's come to watch the fun, I expect. Of course he has. It must be exciting at that age. How can he possibly know what it all really means? I think of the broken men at the hospital as I glance again at the clock. Twenty-eight minutes past.

It's as I'm turning back that I catch sight of him. I know it's him from the blackness of his hair peeping beneath his cap. He's moving towards me. I stand on tiptoe and wave. He sees me, but he doesn't wave back. It's not him, after all. The man smiles at me, and I blush at my mistake. How could I ever have thought it was Hubert? He might be the same height, and his hair as dark, but his eyes are pale, not the kind of blue you can see across a crowded hall.

Then, I really *do* see him. He appears at the top of the steps with a group of officers. How smart they all look with their caps and gleaming boots. Their presence seems to fill the station. I come down from my ledge. Whatever would he think to see me up there? That I'm no better than the boy on the milk churn, I shouldn't wonder.

But he's noticed me after all, and a minute later I hear his voice behind me. I turn. 'You came, then,' he says.

The bonds that tie us together tangle between us. 'Of course I came. I said I would, didn't I?' My voice sounds cold. How is that possible when my heart is on fire? I stare at him. He has a new stripe on his sleeve. He reaches out, steers me to the edge of the throng.

Another train arrives, chugging in slowly to take the empty space by the platform. I see Hubert glance from it to his watch. Carriage doors slam. A vicious gust of wind sweeps into the station, shreds the puff of smoky steam that lifts from the engine. It blows it towards us, bringing with it a smell of scorching oil. We stand and stare at the train, wasting our last few precious minutes.

'Come on, Hu, old chap. This one's ours,' a voice calls. 'Is your platoon here? Soldiers surge towards the carriages. There are sounds of scurrying boots and more doors opening and shutting. This is it. This is where we part. I look up at him. I wish now I hadn't come. How *can* he smile?

'Stay still,' he says.

'What? What is it?'

He reaches into his pocket, cupping my face in his hand as he wets the corner of his handkerchief with his tongue. His handkerchief is khaki, regulation issue. He wipes the hem across my cheek, and I feel the soft ridge of the stitches on my skin. 'A smut,' he says, and I breathe in the closeness of him. Tobacco. Soap. A trace of aniseed.

We move apart. I haven't said any of the things I've meant to say. None of them seem right here. I am unable to utter a single word. Suddenly, he pulls me to him, here, in full view of everyone. The hubbub of the crowd dips as he bends his head to mine. I can feel his belt buckle hard against me. His lips are warm, despite the cold of the day. He kisses my cheeks. When I close my eyes, he kisses my eyelids, then my mouth, and desire mixes with anger and grief at his going.

'Hu! Come on! We're off!'

Then Hubert is turning from me, running towards the train. A scream sits impotently in my throat, large as a flint from Bent Meadow. I see hands reach out, pull him in. The door swings closed.

He's gone.

There is a slow, drawn-out chug from the engine. Then another, and another. Finally, it catches its rhythm, and I'm walking along beside the train. I'm not so very different from the other women, after all. We walk faster and faster until we are running.

There he is! His face, at the window. He leans out. 'Write!' he calls.

'Yes,' I shout back. 'You, too.' It's all I can think of to say.

'I will. Every day, if I can.' His voice is distant already, taken by the space between that is growing with every second. At the end of the platform I am forced by the barrier to stop.

I stand and watch as the carriages grow smaller and smaller, until, one by one, they curve and disappear.

Chapter 33

France

March 6th, 1916

My Dearest, Darling Maude,

It was a bitter thing to have to say goodbye to you, dear, although I am very grateful to you for managing to come. If only we had had a little time <u>alone</u> together, it might not have been so hard. But then again, perhaps it would have been worse, who can tell?

The journey to Southampton was uneventful, though we had a bit of a wait once we got there, and did not embark until after midnight. But, they gave us a good meal, so it wasn't too bad, and afterwards I sat on the dockside and watched the evening star appear. I wished upon it, dearest. Yes, I wished that it might keep us both safe until we meet again. I should like to think of it as 'our' star, dear. Will you look out for it each night, as I will, and think of me?

The crossing was better than I thought it was going to be, despite the weather worsening (thick clouds and a north-easterly wind). My platoon was placed on deck, and we had to spend the entire time outside! We were each given a blanket, but it was perfectly inadequate for the task, and you may imagine how glad I was of your scarf. It is wound around my neck as I write, and I'm sure it keeps me all the warmer knowing whose fingers fashioned it! When we got out in the Channel, the swell increased, and some of the chaps were seasick, but you will be pleased to know that I managed to hold on to my supper. Once, when the moon came through, I could quite clearly see the destroyer that was accompanying us, and I must admit that I began to get a bit worried then that the enemy would see it too. But the clouds soon came back and we travelled on in darkness, arriving at Le Havre quite safely. I am, at the moment, sheltering with my platoon beneath an overhang on one of the dock sheds. Ah, must stop. We have been ordered to move.

Here again, dearest! It is now late in the evening and I am tucked up in a cosy billet. After stopping off from writing, we left the port and marched to the railway station where we entrained, making for the spot where the Division was assembling. There we were given a sandwich of cold bacon and a mug of tea before entraining again. The next bit of the journey took up most of the day as the jolly old train kept stopping and starting for no good reason that I could see, and it seemed to take forever. There were no clues at all to where we were (which perhaps was just as well, dearest, for I wouldn't be allowed to tell you anyway), and each village we passed was as nameless as the rest. Then, to cap it all we were put in a siding for a couple of hours. When eventually we started again, a few miles down the line we stopped again in a field covered with snow, God only knows why. But at least there was one good thing – we were packed in like sardines, so we were warm enough!

Eventually, we arrived and, although there was still a four kilometre march to get here, it was good to get moving again. An enemy aeroplane was circling above the station, so low that for a moment, even in the fading light, I could see the pilot's face, and even the buttons on his flying coat. My first glimpse of the Hun! It was all rather thrilling to tell the truth.

We could also hear the barrage of guns in the distance, and occasionally there were flashes lighting up the sky. I had dreamed for so long of arriving, that it all felt rather unreal.

It was stranger still a little later when we came to one of the villages, for we had to march past a church with a large crucifix outside (the churches here all seem rather grand – does it pronounce the importance of their faith to them, I wonder?). Anyway, the moon came out and it looked so peaceful, this slump of suffering Christ, bathed in moonlight, that it almost seemed as if we were receiving a blessing.

I am billeted with several other officers in a farmhouse and the old woman whose house it is, is cooking me up some eggs. It's warm as can be in here with the range going, despite the snow still falling outside. I am to share a bedroom upstairs with some chaps – we have straw pallets on the floor – but I am so tired that I think I could sleep anywhere. Now my eggs are done, so I will say 'bonne nuit'.

Yours ever dear,

Hubert

Chapter 34

Somewhere in France

March 12th, 1916

Dearest Maude,

I hope that you are well, and quite over your cold. I am in the best of health, although tuckered out after another long and wearisome march with full packs, and this time as many extras as they could find for us to carry! We still haven't quite made it to our final destination, but have got pretty close to the Front at times. The nearer we get, the more deserted the towns and villages become, and there is much evidence that many were once in the line of fire. One town was completely destroyed, with only a pile of rubble and plaster to remind us that people used to live there.

The village we are bivouacking in tonight, is still fairly intact, although it is more or less deserted of civilians. One does wonder where they could all have gone. The buildings themselves are laid out as most of them here seem to be: there is a long main road with houses strung out along each side like clumps of reed along a river, not clustered together like our English villages. We arrived at our billet here, late-afternoon. The whole Battalion has been crammed into a large store, a kind of barn. We can hear the guns from here. Indeed, we are never far from that incessant rumbling now. I can't help wondering, if we can hear it like this here, six miles away, what must it sound like to be in the thick of it?

Will you believe it if I tell you that it has begun to snow, yet again? Although I do not think it is cold enough to settle now the ground has thawed, it nevertheless feels as if we have been plunged right back into Winter. Is it any better at home? The roads here are in the most appalling condition. Everything takes five times as long when you have to push through several inches of mud, and it gets everywhere, on our uniforms and into our kit. We are constantly plastered in the stuff, and are not permitted to bathe or change our undergarments, until we are off duty. It is forbidden to remove even a single item, so I will leave it to your imagination how much our ablutions are needed by the time we get them!

I have just eaten what one can only suppose is meant to pass as dinner (what wouldn't I give for a roasted pheasant and one of Cook's fruit pies, or some of the wonderful food we had at Brighton), but it seems I must learn now to make do with a diet consisting mainly of bully beef and boiled potatoes. The evening has turned to night, and the lamps have been lit. It is really rather festive the way the men have placed them here and there on the tables, and more hung from the rafters. There is hay, large loose bales of it, and some of the chaps have already made themselves comfortable for the night, though most of us are employed as I am now, balancing their writing tablets upon their knees. Please continue writing to me won't you, Maude? Every day if you can, for I long for letters from home, especially yours, and the post travels along behind us when we move, so never worry about them not reaching me.

Take good care of yourself, and pass on my best wishes to your family, as you see fit. How is your young nephew? He must be quite a big boy now.

Affectionately yours, my dearest,

Hubert

Chapter 35

Somewhere in France

March 15th, 1916

Dearest Maude,

I have had my first introduction to war! When we arrived here at camp yesterday, the Germans decided to send over some shells to welcome us. Unfortunately, one man from my platoon, Sergeant Charles Pearce, was killed. We buried him this afternoon. I have had to write to tell his wife, and to send her his belongings. It was a terrible letter to have to write, for it wasn't as if anything had been gained at all by his death, though I couldn't say that to her, of course. It has put a damper on all our spirits as Pearce was well liked in the platoon, and I had got used to relying on him, too. He was what I'd call an 'old hand', and he will be missed. The CO's ordered a get-together this evening to raise morale, some communal singing. The last thing I feel like, but the best thing for the men, I think.

Also, our Company's rations were destroyed in the

bombardment, so we have had a very much reduced supper. It seems it was a random attack, but the CO is taking the precaution of moving the camp back out of the range of the German guns, and so we have got to all heave-to and help re-establish camp tomorrow, a couple of miles back.

But forgive me. I haven't thanked you yet for your last letter. It really is most wonderful to get such a regular supply of news, and I look forward to your missives so very much. Mother has sent a letter, too, to say that Aylmer is now up at Witley and that he has already been gazetted. If you knew Aylmer, you would know how much amusement it gives me to think of him being put through his paces. But, perhaps it will be the making of him, who knows? It is hard to think of him as part of Kitchener's Army and serving our country, though I am sure the men under him will have a thorough knowledge of how to dot their I's and cross their T's before he's finished with them.

Do write and tell me all that is happening at the hospital. It really does seem a jolly place to work, apart from your Sister Browning, of course, and it may just be that it's a case of her bark being worse than her bite. A lot of the higher ranks are like that here, you know. All part of the discipline. You must try not to mind too much.

With much affection,

Hubert

Chapter 36

The porch door of the hut is ajar, letting in a thick slice of evening sun. I stop, and my shadow drops across the little table where the post boy leaves our letters. There are three envelopes today. I feel my heart beat fast as it always does as I pick them up, and I cannot help offering a silent prayer that one will be from Hubert. A prayer. Me, who jumps between believing and not, like a cricket in a cornfield! Yes, there it is, at the bottom. *Thank you God, Thank you God, Thank you God.* I put the other letters down, and stare for a moment at Hubert's looping hand. Then I lift the envelope to my lips and hold it there for a moment, breathing in the scent of it. It smells as the men's letters always do that are sent from the trenches. Musty. A little sharp. Like the pages of an old book.

I lean against the lintel for a moment. I love this sense of anticipation, the moment between seeing a letter from Hubert, and opening it. I have finished my afternoon shift, and the May sun is warm and gentle on my face. The wood beyond the hedge is a canopy of fresh green, and through a gap in the hawthorn I can see a sweep of blue. But the faint, sweet smell of the bluebells is mixed with something more astringent – ramsons, wild garlic. Someone must have been walking amongst it and crushed the plants underfoot. I stand on tiptoe to look, but there is no-one there now. Some of the men, perhaps, have walked there in the day. They like to do that. It gives them a sense of peace, they say.

A man died on my ward today. First Lieutenant Grover. I helped Nurse James to lay him out. His skin was so smooth and white, still warm. It was hard to believe he wasn't still alive. There are bluebells this side of the hedge, too. I look at their arching stems and they remind me of home, of the copse up by the station. I picture the thick carpet there's sure to be there now. I haven't been able to pick any this year to put on Horace's grave, no, nor primroses neither. Suddenly, I long to walk along the lane from the station, up through the little town, past the post office and Mrs Lawson's shop with its bobbins and bright cotton threads in the window. I close my eyes, in my mind seeing myself turn down the hill towards the cottage set back from the road. I can hear the big mill-wheel turning, splashing the churning water through the culvert to run beneath the road to the pond.

I sigh, opening my eyes again to step from the porch into the sitting room. I am the first back this evening, and everything for the moment is still and quiet. In the bedroom, I unfasten the windows, pushing them each in turn to catch on the furthest hole of the long latches. The metal is warm against my fingers. Everything I touch today is warm.

Faint footsteps sound. They grow louder and Kitty comes in, waving a piece of paper. 'This,' she says, planting it down on the sill beside me with a flourish, 'is the programme for Sports Day.' There's been talk of nothing else for days, but I hadn't thought it could actually be true, for how can there be a Sports Day for men who are maimed as badly as the soldiers here? I lean with my back to the open window and look at her as I push Hubert's still unopened letter into my pocket.

'Well, I think it's cruel, a Sports Day for injured men,' I say. I can't help thinking of John, the friendly droop of his moustache, and the kind expression always to be found in his eyes.

'It's not cruel, you chump.' Kitty looks at me and her cheeks form two deep dimples as she smiles. She reaches up to pull out the pins that secure her cap, tosses them one by one onto the table by her bed. I look at the pile of things there, the knitting patterns, the needles and wool that she hasn't bothered to put away, the cold cream she uses on her face at night, the packet of Woodbines she's taken to smoking. Her bit of the room is always a mess. The Commandant would have a fit if she suddenly came in for one of her surprise inspections, not that Kitty would care much. Not like me. I wouldn't sleep for a week if I got caught like that. I look across at my table, the stack of books and writing things, my sewing kit and empty glass, all neatly placed. Kitty adds her cap to her pile of things, then flops down on top of her bed, rucking-up her counterpane with her feet.

'There's lots they can enter,' she says, placing her hands beneath her head. 'It's not just running, you know. There's tug-o'-war and wheelbarrow races, lots of things. Perhaps the men who can't walk can be the ones to sit in the wheelbarrows?' I think of some of the dreadful injuries in our ward, and shake my head at her. 'Anyway,' she says. 'There are loads of games they can join in, even those who can't get about. Austen said there's to be one where you have to get a stick through a hole and if you don't, a bucket of water comes down on top of you.' She squeals with laughter. 'Oh, it'll be grand!' She turns to lean on her elbow, looking at me and shaking her head. 'We've *got* to take part, too. Sister

Atwood says so. Got to make it a happy occasion for the men, she says. I'm going to enter the three-legged race, and the egg-and-spoon, and I'll help with teas or something, although they won't get me running full-pelt down a race track, not with this lot they won't.' She looks down at her large bosom, and it shakes as she laughs. 'I'm hardly built for racing, am I?' Suddenly, she sits up. 'I say, why don't we do the three-legged race together?' she says. 'That should be slow enough, even for me. We've all got to do something, after all. Oh, go on,' she prompts. 'I need someone who'll do it properly, for I'm sure I won't know what I'm doing at all. I'll even practise if you say yes.'

I pick up the typewritten page. I think of Arthur and the races in the village square. He always chose me for the three-legged. It was because we ran in rhythm. We never strayed our pace, not once. 'If you like,' I say. 'When is it?'

'Next month. They're going to have two dates, and if it rains on the first one, they'll move it to the second. We've got to check the notice board in the refectory.' I wonder how it is that Kitty seems to find out such things, for she always seems to know what's going on. She flops back down again and stretches out her arms in a cross shape, closing her eyes. 'This is heaven, Maude. Absolute heaven. I've been looking forward to this all afternoon. God, I'm so tired.' She yawns.

'That's your own fault, Kit,' I tell her, coming to sit on my own bed. She opens her eyes, and puts on a pained expression as she watches me. I look back at her. 'What was it Sister Tompkinson said to you the other day?' I wag my finger at her in mock sternness. '*If you were in bed at a decent hour, Nurse Brown, instead of staying up all hours dancing, you would be bright and fresh for duty, wouldn't you, as you should be,*' I say.

We laugh, for it's not a bad take-off, and there's more than a bit of truth in it, too, although Kitty's not the type to take much notice of such things. I lift my feet to undo my laces, and my work shoes fall heavily to the floor. I push them with my toes so they're neat together, then lean back against my bolster. Hubert's letter crackles softly as I move, and I am just reaching into my pocket for it when the door opens, and Ana comes in. How pretty she looks in her uniform. But, then, Ana would look good even if she was wearing a potato sack. She just can't help it. I glance at the long streak of blood that stains her apron, just beneath the waistband where the material gathers. Even that seems to have been placed there, just so, to make her look like a heroine. Her cheeks are flushed, as if she's been hurrying.

'Heard about Sports Day?'

'Too late, Ana,' Kitty murmurs. 'I've already bagged Maude for the three-legged.'

'I don't care about that. I'm going to see if I can get tied up to one of the doctors,' she says. 'Dr Edesworthy, I think. Hmm. Yes.' We laugh. Dr Edesworthy's an elderly man, come out of retirement to offer his services for the duration of the war. 'I would have thought that you'd have chosen your good-looking Sergeant, Maude,' Ana says, looking at me slyly before lifting her apron over her head. I feel a blush rising to my cheeks. 'Well, perhaps not the three-legged,' she says hastily, rolling her apron into a ball, but I know what she's driving at.

'John and me are just friends, you know that,' I say. I take Hubert's letter from my pocket and deliberately place it on the bed beside me.

'Anyway, Ana,' Kitty says, yawning. 'The races are segregated, so you'll have to think of other ways to wheedle your way into the good books of the doctors. Even if I could, I wouldn't touch any of them with a punt-pole. Give me one of the soldiers, any day, Corporal Titherton on Ward E. Seven, now. I wouldn't mind *him* being tied against me!'

'You really are awful, Kit,' I say. 'You'd better not let Sister

'T catch you talking like that.'

'Oh, don't start, Maude. God, I can perfectly see why you used to be a suffragette, you know.'

I sit up, arranging my bolster behind me against the iron bed-head. 'I still *am* a suffragette,' I tell her. 'Just because we've stopped campaigning while the war's on, it doesn't mean we're finished. It'll start up again, I'm sure it will. The war can't last forever, can it, even though it feels like it sometimes?'

'You could always join the NUWSS.' Ana kicks her shoes beneath her bed. 'They're still pretty active.'

'Go over to the NUWSS? Not likely! No, I'll wait until the war's over, thank you very much.'

'I wonder if it the war will change things for us women?' Ana continues. 'I suppose we won't know till it's finished, but we're doing all sorts of jobs the men used to do, aren't we? Look at the way women drive the trams and work in offices, and clean windows and deliver coal – there are even women fire-fighters, you know.' She pauses. 'Actually, when I think about it, I don't see how men will ever be able to say they're better than us, ever again.'

'Ah, but they will, even though some of the jobs we're doing are really dangerous. Look at the girls in the munitions factories. If you ask me, that's almost as dangerous as being in the trenches. They're always getting sick from it. Either that, or blown up.'

'I wouldn't do it – work in a munitions factory, that is,' Kitty says, 'not for anything. I couldn't bear it if my skin turned yellow. Whatever would Conrad say?' She giggles, and I frown at her. She turns to look at me. 'Do you know something, Maude?'

'What?'

'I think you're getting too serious. You're becoming maudlin.'

'Don't be silly. I'm not a bit maudlin.'

'Yes, you are. At least, you have been lately. What you need is a bit of fun. Come to the dance on Saturday night with us,' she says. 'Go on, do. A girl needs a bit of relaxation from time to time.' I hesitate, thinking of how I *would* like to. 'If it's Hubert you're worried about,' she continues, 'don't. He'll be having what fun he can get.'

I glare at her. 'That's a rotten thing to say, Kitty. They're out there fighting, not having a good time.'

She turns to look at me, drawing her eyebrows together so that the ends turn upwards even more. 'Sorry. No offence, Maude. I'm only stating facts.'

'What facts?'

'Well ....'

'Go on, what facts?'

'I was just thinking of the diseases some of the men come back with.'

'Diseases? What diseases?'

'You know.'

'Oh, those.'

'Yes, those. Where d'you suppose they get them from, if not from having fun? French country air? The men aren't always in the trenches, you know. They have to pass through towns and villages, and they're billeted there sometimes, too, aren't they? And there are girls in those towns, wives who are lonely. I've heard the stories the men tell each other.'

'Then you shouldn't eavesdrop. Besides,' I say, a haughty note creeping into my voice. 'You can't really blame them, stuck out there like that. They're only human, and everyone needs a bit of comfort sometimes.' I see her eye my letter, and shake my head at her. 'I'm not talking about Hubert!'

'Why should he be any different?' Ana says suddenly, rolling her eyes. Then she laughs. It's a frank, open laugh and infectious and Kitty joins in, and after a minute, I do too.

'Come on, Maude, what d'you say?' Kitty says. 'The dance

on Saturday night. I know some other girls who are interested, some chaps too. We can take the ferry across to
Southampton. Go on. It'll do you good.'

'Oh, all *right*,' I say. Then, so they can see, I pick up
Hubert's letter from the bed beside me, and sit up to open
it. Kitty and Ana fall quiet as I read. It's our unspoken rule
where letters are concerned.

Chapter 37

Hut 49
The Royal Victoria Military
Hospital
Netley
Hampshire

May 30th, 1916

Dearest Hubert,

Thank you for your letters of 23rd and 25th inst. They arrived in
the post together. I'm glad that you've had some time out of the
trenches, and also that you are having a little good weather at last.
It's been the same here, sunshine and rain on and off, but not like
a proper Summer at all yet.

Now, the most marvellous thing. I have been to a dance, in
Southampton. I had quite forgotten what fun it could be! We had
to have special passes, and went across on the Woolston floating
bridge. It was very exciting, and wonderful to put on something
other than uniform for a few hours. We had to take our dresses
with us and change at the hall, because of course we aren't allowed
in or out of the hospital if we're not in uniform. Like I said to

Ana, it's a good thing we didn't lose them then, or they mightn't have let us back in!

The women outnumbered the men at the dance, by half again at least, so you may imagine how we danced them off their feet with all the turkey-trots and bunny-hugs we did. They didn't get a minute's rest. Many of the men were soldiers who had been wounded and who were waiting to be sent back to their regiments, though there were some home on leave and some boys in reserved occupations, too, plus one or two older types. I danced with whoever asked me, and even had one or two waltzes with Ana, for she knows the men's steps as well as her own, which is very clever of her don't you think? Oh, and she has started to teach me the tango, which some people think is very daring, but really it's just good fun. You should see us practising up and down our little sitting room to Lil's gramophone records!

I had tea in one of the cottages at Houndgate the other day. Kitty's chummed up with a lady, Mrs Cook her name is. Her husband has a builder's yard up by the incinerator (how I hate those great tall chimneys with their horrid clouds of smoke – I can never see them but wonder at what it is they might be burning). Anyway, the cottages have gardens that run right down to the railway line. It was very odd to be sitting having my tea and to look up to see a train going past behind the runner beans. I have to say I rather liked it.

There is a lot of talk at present of Sports Day, and the word is that they are looking for volunteers to make bunting. I think, as I am good with my needle, I shall put my name down. You can see there is never a spare moment these days. Susan has come in to say that a troop ship is mooring up and that always means lots of patients, so I must get ready. I'm due back on duty in twenty minutes anyway, and I still have to tidy myself and scrub my nails ready for Sister Browning's inspection, so had better finish or I shall be late, which is strictly forbidden! Please take good care of yourself dearest Hubert.

Yours affectionately,

Maude

Chapter 38

Goodness, that's all I need, Sister Browning on the war-path! We thought if we came out for a Sunday stroll, we'd be safe from her watchful eye for a minute or two. I watch as she hurries across the quadrangle behind the main building, to where I'm standing with John's weight against me.

'Sergeant Harris!' she calls out. 'What *do* you think you're doing?' I slip my arm around John's waist to steady him, planting my feet firmly apart. Whatever I do, I mustn't let him fall. It flashes through my mind, as I stand there, how it seems the most natural thing in the world to be holding him. The thought brings with it a rush of guilt, which I quickly brush aside. Now is not the time for all that. I can feel his warmth now through the blue wool of his hospital uniform. How tall he is. It's the first time I've been next to him when he's stood upright. Why, he's taller even than Hubert. Over six foot, I should have thought. He reaches for the pair of crutches we've borrowed from the store and slips them beneath his arms.

'As for you, Nurse Timms,' Sister Browning says, reaching us and looking with her wide grey eyes first at the empty invalid carriage on the grass beside us, then pinning them on me, 'I would have thought better of you.' A shadow passes over us as the sun goes behind a cloud. I can tell from the expression on her face that I'm in for it.

'I'm sorry, Sister,' I say, 'I thought ….'

'You're not here to *think*.' Her voice is clipped. 'Get back in your wheelchair, Sergeant. Nurse, get the other side of the patient.'

'Now then, Sister, don't I have any say in the matter?' John stays upright, leaning on his crutches. 'It's the first time in months that I've been on my feet.' He gestures with his head at his left trouser leg pinned across his stump, at the gap between his knee and the floor. But the movement throws him off balance and he staggers. Sister Browning puts out her hand and, together, we steady him. Fear sweeps over me. If I let him fall, I would never forgive myself.

'There you are! That's what you get for not following the doctor's orders.' We lower John into the wheelchair, and Sister Browning takes hold of the crutches. He winces as he eases himself back.

'Sergeant Harris,' she continues, her hands clasped in front of her, her arms rigid against her apron, 'you've had several severe infections, and if Dr Edesworthy thought you were ready to walk, he would have said so. He's a man of considerable experience, and not one to trifle with. If he says you are not ready for mobility exercise, then you are not.'

'I can't sit on my backside, begging your pardon Sister, any longer. There are mates of mine still out there, and I'm here doing nothing! It's high time I was useful again, and the Doc said I could start getting about soon.' I can't help wishing he wouldn't talk about being useful again, for it brings with it the fact that he will soon have to leave. Suddenly, I realise I don't want him to go. I want him to be better, of course I do, but I want him to be here, too.

Sister Browning's eyes grow more kindly. 'Soon is not *now*, is it, Sergeant? I haven't nursed you for the past months only to have you undo all the good I've done.' A lorry chugs its way up the road towards the station, the sound echoing off the buildings surrounding us. Sister Browning places a hand briefly on John's shoulder before she turns to me, and her eyes harden again. 'When Sergeant Harris has finished taking the air, report to my office, Nurse.'

'Yes, Sister.'

'In the meantime, I'll take care of these.' She gathers up the crutches so that they clack together, and we wait, watching as she walks across the grass of the quad.

'That's done it, Maude,' he groans. 'Now you're in trouble, and it's all my fault!'

'Don't be silly, John. How can it be your fault? I've got a mind of my own, haven't I? You asked me to help you, and I said yes.' I shrug. 'It's quite simple.' I don't add that I'd do almost anything for him if he asked me, for it wouldn't be right to say such things with Hubert away in the trenches, facing danger every day. And, besides, it would make things too complicated by half. I grip the handles of the invalid chair and give it a big push. The wheels begin to turn, and I manoeuvre us back onto the path, the carriage rattling on the hard surface.

'Well, I'm sorry, anyway,' he says. He turns to look up at me, smiling an apology, then winces as his stump knocks against the side of the chair.

'Are you all right?' He nods. 'Don't worry about me,' I continue, 'she'll just tear me off a strip, then it'll be all done. That's one good thing about Sister Browning. We're all afraid of her tongue, but once you've had your punishment, there's an end to it.' I stop as we reach the edge of the quadrangle. 'Now, where to?'

'The pier. Let's go to the pier.'

Once we've left the protection of the buildings, the wind

gusts against us, flapping my dress wildly against my legs and tumbling John's hair. As he lifts a hand to push it back from his forehead, it's all I can do not to reach down and entwine my own fingers with his. I reach up instead to press my hairpins in more securely around my cap.

We pass the huts, where the bed-cases have been wheeled out to take the air in the lee of the walls. The walking wounded lounge in chairs beside them, and as we pass I try not to dwell on how their lives have changed for ever, how they'll never go back to how things were, with a leg or an arm missing, or blinded, or burned. We meet other invalids as we walk, and exchange smiles with the patients and nurses as our chairs pass. All the while, rooks wheel and caw round their nests high in the old elm trees behind us.

I continue pushing steadily. We pass the signs for Essex Hut and the Electrical Treatment Hut, then head towards the tennis courts. They're empty for once, and there's nothing for John to watch, so we continue on to the little golf course where a group of men in plus-fours are bent over their clubs. John motions for me to stop, and his head turns towards them. I can't help but wonder what's going through his mind, for it can't be easy for a man, wounded like he is, to see able-bodied men doing such things.

'Did you like your work on the estate, John, before you joined the Army?' I ask, as a golf ball rolls quickly towards the hole, tips the rim and jumps back out again.

I have to bend to hear his reply above the groans and laughs from the players. 'It was all right.'

'What made you go into it?' There is a faint click as another player taps at his ball.

'Father worked all his life on the Fletchlings Estate just outside York. So, when I got to fourteen and it was time to leave school, it seemed natural that I'd go there too.' I watch as his broad shoulders shrug.

'Was it what you wanted, though? What about your own ambitions?'

'Ambitions?' He shakes his head. 'Can't say as I ever had any. Where I come from, lads leaving school don't have much say in the matter. They have to get out in the world and earn a crust. I've always been a practical person, and soon got used to the work. I liked it well enough. I can turn my hand to most things, you know. It's book-learning I've not got much of a head for.'

We watch the men finish their putts, then turn to look at the ragged line of visitors that have begun to drift towards the hospital entrance. I often think that Sunday should be the most cheerful time of the week being the day of rest, but for me it's the saddest: relatives coming in their Sunday best, the children up from the village with gifts of flowers and fruit, and soldiers travelling across to visit their mates – it all takes the men away from us. All week they belong to us, relying on us for almost everything, then suddenly they become different people, with parents, sons and daughters, brothers, sisters and friends to change them. But, I've never liked Sundays, not even when I was little; the quietness of them, only being allowed the dullest of occupations and folk shushing you all the while so that every sound was magnified, like the buzz of a fly on a hot summer's afternoon.

I stoop down beside John, and he smiles at me. 'Are you expecting any visitors, John? Do you want to go back to the ward?'

He shakes his head. 'Who is there to come? It's too far for Mum and Dad to make regular trips, and with George in France now and my sister Dollie so near her confinement, I can't think what other visitors I could expect.'

'Your brother's in France? But I thought he'd only just got back from Italy?'

'I had a letter from him yesterday. All leave's been cut short.

There are a lot of rumours going around.' Something about the way he says it, makes me suddenly shiver.

'Rumours? What sort of rumours?'

'There's to be a big push, so George says. Keep it under your cap, Maude, won't you? There's probably nothing in it, an' it'll only scare folks here half to death.'

Well, the thought of it's scared me half to death, and all. My thoughts fly to Hubert and Walter. They're in France. I try to picture them somewhere safe; in billets perhaps, or resting in camp, smoking, reading, writing letters home. Anything, anywhere, rather than in those awful trenches filled with death.

'Did your brother say where the push was to be, John?'

He shakes his head. 'The Army doesn't work like that. Look, I really shouldn't have said anything, I've worried you. It's probably nothing, you know. There's always a rumour of one sort or another.'

We remain quiet for a little while, me standing beside his stationary chair, watching as the golfers walk off the green. 'It's a shame they didn't let George come and see you before he went.'

John gives a little shrug. 'Yes. Yes, it is.'

'It'd be funny if your brother bumped into Hubert and Walter when he's out there, wouldn't it?'

John laughs then, and the seriousness of the moment is broken. I turn to take the handles of the chair again. 'It'd be very funny. In fact, it'd be a chance in a million!' he says. 'France is a big place. And even if they did ....' He laughs again. 'How would they know each other? It's not as if they've met.'

I laugh too. 'No, of course it isn't, you're right. How stupid I am sometimes.' But the truth, I suddenly realise, is that I never feel stupid when I'm with John, no matter what silly things I might say. It's different when I'm with Hubert. Even though I adore him, and I do, I never quite feel that I measure up. A steamer sounds its hooter up the river, and John pulls himself a little more upright in the chair.

'Now then!' he says, rubbing his hands together, 'let's get moving.' He leans over, pointing ahead. 'Forward!' We join the avenue of trees, and make our way down a tunnel of green. A large troop ship is moored beyond the pier, sunlight sparking on the surface of the water beside it.

The salty tang in the air grows stronger as we approach the shore. I walk slowly, for it's good to be out in the fresh air. But, even when the weather is bad and we have to stay inside, afternoon duties are still my favourite. The men are always good company. Sometimes we play bezique, or I take them to the building at the back of the hospital where they make baskets, or to the needlework hut with its cupboards full of embroidery silks and wools, and its shiny, wooden floor. But, most of all, I like walking in the grounds. You can really get to know a patient then, when it's just you and him, and no Sister Browning looking over your shoulder all the time. And Nurse James assigns John to me whenever she can, too. She's a good sort, really. She knows we've become friends.

Even though it's June, my skin gooses in the breeze as we near the shore, and I stop the chair to ease the woollen rug from the seat back, unfolding it across John's lap. He watches me as I tuck it carefully round his leg. 'Thank you, Nurse,' he says, and I can tell without looking up that he's smiling.

'Just doing my job, Sergeant,' I reply. I start to push again. 'By the way, what exactly did Dr Edesworthy say to you this morning?'

'It depends how I get on over the next couple of weeks, but he seems to think I've turned the corner at last, and that I'm on the last leg of my recovery.' He pats one side of the blanket, well above the stump, and laughs at his own joke. 'As long as it carries on healing as it is.'

'But, that's wonderful!' We come to the bottom of the path by the entrance to the pier. I lean forwards and place my hand on his shoulder, feel the stir of his strong muscles as he reaches up to cover my hand with his own. He quickly takes it away again, and points to the right.

'Let's not go on the pier after all. Let's go along here.' I follow the line of his hand, and turn in the direction of Netley village. The thick trunks of the fir trees make the troop ship appear to flick in and out as I push the chair. Slowly, John's words sink in, and I realise with a jolt that if he's almost better, it won't be long before he leaves.

'I'll miss you when you go, John.' The thought is out before I can stop it.

'Will you, Maude?' He hitches himself round in his chair to look at me. His hazel eyes are serious.

I nod, serious too. 'I can't imagine the ward without you now.'

'Ah, the ward. The thing is, Maude, I can't imagine *anything* without you.'

Chapter 39

Somewhere in France

June 8th, 1916

My Dearest, Darling Maude,

I have decided to write you a few lines, for I find I cannot sleep, and I know from experience that if I just lie here, I will begin thinking wretched thoughts.

Last night I led a raiding party and we captured a German. I suppose it is the excitement of that which is keeping me awake. You should have seen your best boy, crawling across no-man's-land to capture one of their chaps for questioning! The men were marvellous – a better bunch I couldn't wish for, but the strange thing was, dearest, when our Hun took off his helmet, if it were not for his uniform I would not have known him to be the enemy. I'm not sure what I expected, but there was no difference at all between him and one of my own men. It has quite unsettled me.

The weather has turned hot, and I am sitting outside my dugout, thinking of you, and making the most of the sunshine. If only I could take off my jacket and roll up my shirt sleeves so as to feel it better, but of course we're not permitted to do such a thing as we have to be ready for action at all times.

We lost another chap this morning from a sniper shot. However many times one tells the men to keep their heads down, there always seems to be one of them who does not. As for myself, I think, when I come home on leave, I will be permanently walking down the road with my shoulders stooped and my head bent. But perhaps I should not talk of home and leave and get our hopes up, dearest, for there is not even a whisper of it yet.

We have had a longer stint than usual in the Front Line this time. The reserve trenches have taken a bashing, and they have had to bring up more men. We're being relieved tomorrow, however, although we will still have four more days in the new reserve trenches before being sent back to billets for a rest. It's funny how time seems so much slower at the beginning of a stretch of duty. That's the hardest time, when one first arrives back in the trenches, although it soon speeds up and goes quickly enough once one gets through the first couple of days.

Ah, you will not believe this, dear, but a pigeon has landed on the parapet, just down the trench from where I am sitting. We're both engaged in giving each other a staring match! It seems too exhausted to move, poor thing. It's one of ours, I can see that from the little container it's carrying. I'll let it rest while I write this then encourage it on its way, for the message must be urgent otherwise they would not have made use of it. I wish I had my very own pigeon to send to you, dearest, to tell you how much I am missing you, but the jolly old post will have to do instead and, indeed, it does us well enough I think.

I'm hoping that a missive from you will be waiting for me when the rations are brought up later. I do so love that time in the day, when I am handed an envelope bearing your dear script. Then, for just a few moments when I open it, it's as if I'm back in England with you. Mother's letters have such a sadness to them these days that was not there before Ralph's death. It has shaken her dreadfully. I would ask you to visit her, if only I had had the courage to have taken you home. It is a great regret of mine, Maude, that I did not do so before I came away.

How I wish I could look up from writing this, my darling, and see you standing before me. But even as I write the words, I know that isn't true, for I would not have you here in these trenches, nor have you see and hear the things I have seen and heard. No, not for anything. Better, I think, if I were to look up from writing this and be back on Harting Down or in our hotel at Brighton. How often I think of those times, and how little I knew of the reality of war then. But, there will come a time when I return home for a spot of leave, and perhaps we can be together again? As I sit here in the midst of all that is uncertain, it is the thought of that which gives me courage.

Now my little pigeon has flown, and so must I if I am to try again for a little sleep before I have to wake the men for more trench repairs. How they will curse me for it!

God bless you and keep you, dearest.

Yours ever,

Hubert

Postscript: please excuse the shakiness of my writing. My hands have begun a dance of their own of late. A lot of the chaps are the same - it is the effect of the shelling, I suppose.

Chapter 40

June 15th, 1916

My Dear Sis,

I reckon you'll be in for a surprise, getting a letter from me, heh? Before you think of telling me off, I do write to Mother and Dad every Sunday when I can and Mother writes back, and I know you'll be pleased at that. However, I thought it was high time you had a letter, too. It's good of you to send yours so regular, with me like I am, but writing was never my strong point, was it? Do you remember trying to teach me my letters when you was a helper up at school? How you used to shout at me when I'd do anything and everything not to get down to it? It fair makes me laugh just to think of it. You always did have a bit of a temper on you. But I'm glad that you did make me now, for out here getting the post is what we look forward to all day, and the men get very low in spirits if they don't get a letter or two, even them as can't read and has to have theirs read out to them.

You say that you worry about me. Please do <u>not</u>, for I'm

247

having the time of my life out here. Lt Allen, who's in charge of our platoon, says I'm the most natural soldier he's ever come across. Despite being in danger from time to time (which so far I haven't minded too much) I find the life suits me. I want for nothing apart from some of Mother's home cooking and a few extra fags. I sometimes see your young man, by the way. When he joined C Company, he made a point of seeking me out, and now he always has a word when our paths cross, which is very decent of him, being an officer and all that.

I wonder if you might see your way clear to knitting another of those balaclava helmets? (Not such a tough soldier after all, I hear you thinking.) It's all right now, being summer and all, but it won't be so very long before I'll be needing to keep my neck and ears warm of a night, and if you start now, perhaps I'll get it before the nights turn cold? The last one you made got snagged on some wire and unravelled quick as that, so I sent it the way of most things here, and fed it to the mud. Oh, and an ounce or two of baccy and some A.G. papers wouldn't go amiss, neither, when you're sending.

Ah well. That's all for now.

Your loving brother,

Walter

Chapter 41

June 26th, 1916

My Dearest Maude,

Thank you for your parcel. The cake you bought at the NAAFI went down a treat.

All is quiet at the moment. The day is fading, and the evening quite beautiful. The barrages will begin soon, so I must write quickly before they do. I have come out of my dugout to watch the strip of sky above the trench, for it is turning from rosy pink to the palest green, the colour of a wheatear's egg. I found a nest of wheatears' eggs once, did I ever tell you? It was on the cliffs at Lulworth Cove. I took one for my collection. How long ago all that seems now, a different lifetime.

Ah, there is the first star. I will send all my best love across with it. Do you still look out for our star, Maude? I do hope so, for you will know then that I am thinking of you at that very moment. All too soon it will be dark, and then someone will send up a Verey light, and the stars will be lost in the eerie brightness of it. Then the shelling will start, explosions of sound that I cannot begin to describe, but which take away one's thoughts as those great flashes of red spray out into the night.

I have just stopped to light a cigarette. Who would have thought that I would find solace in such a thing? But that lick of smoke somehow makes things not quite so bad. Even a trench like this one, with the stench of the latrines close by, is made a little better for a smoke. I don't know why, but I am feeling more confined than ever tonight. It seems to my imagination that all it would take to make this trench a coffin, is a lid. Forgive my sombre thoughts. They do plague me so. Sometimes I think that I would go mad if I did not have you to confide in.

The sky is darkening quickly, and I can hardly see now to write. Soon the moon will rise. I know where it will appear – above the parapet at the end of the trench, just where a curl of wire is sticking up like a pig's tail beyond the sandbags. Yes, there it is now, right on cue, a tiny arc of brightness. I must stop or you will never read what I have written. Now the Jerries have started with their guns down the line. They have got in first tonight, and the allied guns are replying, BOOM-BOOM-BOOM, echoing louder and louder as the order to fire creeps closer to us. What hell it all is.

Goodnight, dearest, and God Bless.

Hubert

Chapter 42

Sports Day. The weather has kept fine after all and the sky is a cloudless, dusty blue. The loops and strings of bunting flap between the marquees and around the edges of the sports field.

I'm standing by the tape, waiting, for I made it through the heats yesterday, and have been called to the final of the egg-and-spoon race. I rein in my thoughts, and concentrate. A shout, and we're off. I run as fast as I dare without losing the wooden egg from my spoon, holding my arm out rigidly in front of me. I'm doing all right, though I'm not in the lead. I glance up at the length of white tape at the end of the track, see the rows of men in their blue patients' uniforms beyond, and my egg thuds softly in the new-mown grass. Damn! I quickly stoop down to place it back on the spoon, and hear groans and laughter behind me as others lose their eggs, too, but now I'm racing forwards again. I pass some St John's nurses in their grey uniforms, and then there are only two other girls left in front of me, a nurse from Medical Ward Three, and Gladys from the canteen. She's quick as lightning, is Gladys. The nurse from Med Three stumbles, and I overtake her, concentrating hard, but Gladys is too far ahead and pushes through the strip of bandage they're using as a finishing tape. A cheer goes up from the crowd. I cross the finishing line, too, and then we're all grouping round, and laughing together as if we were children while I fight back the annoyance inside.

John comes towards me, taking his weight on his crutches. He's getting quite expert on them these days, easily swinging his good leg through to take his weight.

'Well done!' he says.

'Pooh! Second!'

'What's wrong with second?'

'I didn't win, that's what's wrong!'

'We can't always win, Maude.'

I reach out my hand for the programme he holds against his crutch handle. 'What's the next race?'

'Orderlies' One Hundred Yards.' I glance at the programme before handing it back. He folds it awkwardly in half against him, then in half again before putting it in his pocket. At the far end of the field, the orderlies are warming up as if their lives depend on it. John turns to watch them for a moment. 'Come on,' he continues brightly, 'we've got half an hour before your three-legged at quarter to three. Time for a cup of tea.'

I reach out and touch his arm for I like being here, just him and me. 'Let's see this one first, shall we, then we'll go?'

We make our way to the tape as the men line up in the sunshine, their different heights forming a ragged outline. A group of Indian soldiers with white turbans stand beside us watching too, talking in broken English as they watch the orderlies take their places.

Suddenly, the deep voice of Sergeant-Major Braithwaite booms out. 'On your marks, gentlemen!' he shouts. Sergeant-Major Braithwaite's on Kitty's ward. He lost an ear and an eye at Loos, and the left side of his head is badly burned. It's still bandaged. 'Get set!' he roars. His wounds don't seem to have affected his voice. The runners crouch down, and steady their poses. 'GO!'

'Why didn't they use a starting pistol?' I ask as the men sprint forwards.

John shakes his head. 'They're scared of setting the patients off. You know what some of them are like. You only have to drop a book in the ward, and they're under their beds.'

'Oh.' What he says is true. I'm always coaxing one or other of the men out from hiding.

'If I could've got off the bed myself when I came here, I expect I'd have been the same,' John says in a quiet voice. I think of the weeks he lay in the ward, his fever stripping him of strength, his face pale and sunken. I think, too, of the fondness I feel for him. Is it for no other reason than that I was the one who rescued him from the railway station? Or has something else grown in my heart?

The men are neck-and-neck as they race down the track, but then Bellfield begins to edge in front. 'Goodness, look at him go,' I say, laughing as the elderly man sprints past his younger competitors. He lifts his head and pushes his chest forward as well as his bent back will allow, and crosses the line. John turns to me, smiling, the sun catching on a tiny patch of stubble to the left of his chin that his razor has missed. It fills me with a sudden tenderness.

'Who'd have thought the old devil had that in him, then? It just goes to show – you can't tell a spud by its skin.'

I laugh then, doubling over, I can't help it. 'That's the sort of daft thing my Dad would come out with.' Suddenly, I'm lost in his gaze, and there's such a feeling between us that I have to force myself to look away.

We wander along in the sunshine, looking at the crowds. It's mostly patients in their blue and red uniforms, some walking, some with crutches, others in chairs being pushed by nurses. But there are hospital personnel, too, and people up from the village, and some soldiers in khaki, come to visit. And, everywhere, children running backwards and forwards, their faces bright and excited.

Suddenly, a group of sailors pushes through, laughing, their caps at jaunty angles on their heads. My heart quickens and, even though I know our Arthur's gone, I can't help looking for his face amongst them as they pass. He's not there, of course. He never will be, will he? I force myself to turn back to nod at a family I recognise from Netley village. A band, up from Aldershot, strikes up next to the big marquee, their brass instruments and drums sounding out, *If You Were the Only Girl in the World*, and my heart slowly returns to its normal beat.

Beside me, John hums along. 'It's a shame your parents aren't here, Maude. I'd like to have met them.' I have a sudden picture of John at home, introducing him to Mother and Dad. I see him smiling as he dips his head beneath the scullery lintel, then he's listening patiently to Mother's sharp words before sitting down with Dad to put the world to rights.

'I didn't even mention it to them,' I confess, 'but they wouldn't have come, even if I had. Dad always says there's no need to go gallivanting off anywhere when all he wants is right there at home.'

John laughs. 'Sounds like my old man,' he says. 'He's never been further than his home town, either.'

'Selby, you mean?'

'Aye,' he says, smiling.

We pass a sign set up by a small green bell tent, *Madame Marvel - Fortune-Teller*. 'Oh,' I exclaim, stopping.

'No, no, no!' John shakes his head. 'You can have your palm read if you like, but I'm certainly not going to!'

'Go on, it'll be fun!'

'It's a lot of stuff and nonsense. You go,' he nods towards the tea tent. 'I'll wait for you there.' He turns away. I hesitate for a moment, a picture of Hubert filling my mind. Even though I'm not sure I believe in God, I'm one as thinks there's got to be more to life than we can properly know about, for existence is bigger than any human mind can understand, after all. Perhaps Madame Marvel really has got the gift, and can tell me whether he'll come home or not? I take a deep breath, then turn to duck my head beneath the entrance flap.

I enter an underwater world of filtered green sunlight. In the centre of the tent, a plump grey-haired woman sits behind a table. The lantern on the table in front of her flickers softly, and gives the interior of the tent an atmosphere of intrigue. She's dressed in a mix of bright colours, and has a red scarf folded and tied around her head, with layers of necklaces, and brass curtain rings dangling beneath her ears. Despite the jollity of it all, I feel a surge of disappointment, for I can see it's Captain Solbank's wife.

'Come in!' she calls, beckoning to me and smiling. Ah, well, it's only a bit of fun, after all, I tell myself as I walk forwards and sit down.

'Cross my palm with silver, dearie,' Mrs Solbank says, her eyes crinkling. 'It doesn't really have to be silver,' she whispers, 'just a donation for the War Fund.' I dip beneath my apron into my dress pocket, and come up with three pennies. 'Thank you,' she says. 'Now, give me your hand. I really do read destinies, you know,' she adds, smiling reassuringly.

I do as I'm told, and she bends over it, tracing the lines on my palm. Then she turns my hand a little and looks along the edge, then back at my palm again. Eventually she speaks. 'I see good fortune,' she says. I hadn't realised I'd been holding my breath until I hear myself sigh with relief.

'There's nothing bad, then?' I ask, thinking of Hubert, deep in the French countryside.

'There are always challenges in our lives, dear,' she says gently. 'There's no escaping those.' She holds my gaze for a long moment, then she smiles again. 'But I can see happiness. And children.'

'Children?'

'Two.' The sounds outside the tent fade as I take in her words. 'And a handsome husband, too.' Hubert. I feel a sudden surge of joy. He'll be coming home!

She closes her eyes. 'He's working, turning something in his hands, though I'm not sure what it is. And there's water. You're going to live by a lake perhaps, or near the sea.' She frowns. 'You have a sister. Her name begins with an 'F'. Frances, perhaps, or Fanny?'

'Florence,' I smile. If she knows about Florence, it must be true then, what she says. 'Can you see anything else?' I ask.

'You want more than that, then, my dear?'

Yes, I'd like more. I'd like to know what will happen to John, for one. Will he walk out of my life for ever? But, 'No,' I say. 'No, I suppose not. Thank you, Mrs Solbank.' I stand up.

'Madame Marvel, if you please!' She gives me a theatrical wave.

I smile. 'Thank you, Madame Marvel.'

Outside, the sunshine seems harsh again as I walk towards the tea tent. John is sitting at a table beneath a striped parasol, his crutches propped beside him. I sit down, and he pushes a cup of tea towards me with a biscuit balanced on the spoon in the saucer.

'What did Madame Marvel have to say?' He grins.

Excitement about my future with Hubert mixes with

sadness. I don't know how to tell John about Hubert and me getting married, having children and all that, for we've grown so close of late, and it might only serve to hurt him. So I say, 'Oh, just the usual old rubbish. It's a money-spinner, that's all, for the War Fund,' and let my eyes slip to the sea in the distance. For a moment or two as I sip my tea, we watch the tug-of-war that's taking place on the shore, and the people swimming in the water beyond.

'Maude?'

'Mmm?' My mind is still on Madame Marvel and what she's told me.

'I've got something to tell you.'

'Oh?' Have his parents decided to visit at last? Or perhaps he's heard from George again, or his sister's had her baby? The bunting between the marquees flaps gently in the breeze above our heads. 'What's that?' I ask.

'It's my marching orders. They've come through.'

'Marching orders?' Startled, I look at him, see the serious expression that's come into his eyes. 'Surely they're not sending you back to the Front? I mean ....'

'No, no. Not that. They're never going to want me to fight again,' he says, looking down at his leg. 'How could they?' Inwardly, I curse myself for being so clumsy, and he guesses my thoughts, as he so often does. 'It's all right,' he says, 'don't worry. What I meant was – they're sending me home.'

'Home?' I frown. Sending him home! But, of course. He's been doing so well recently.

'I've got to go to York first, to see about a peg-leg. Then I'll be demobbed. They need the bed, Maude.' I lift my cup to my lips but put it down again without taking a sip.

'I don't know why it's come as a surprise,' I say. 'Silly of me.' The CO suddenly appears with his wife and we look up to watch as they walk past us. He looks so smart and upright, his long boots gleaming in the sunlight.

'You can always come with me,' John says when they've gone.

'Come with you?' I shake my head, but my heart is leaping at his words. 'To Selby?'

'Yes, why not?'

'Why not?' I look around me at the men I see broken by war. 'Because I'm needed here, John, you know I am. Besides ....' I think of Hubert, and what Madame Marvel has said.

'Ah, your young man. Of course. It's serious, isn't it?' I nod, smiling an apology to him. 'It could be serious between us if you wanted it to be, Maude.' I look down at my tea.

'No,' I say softly, shaking my head. The silence that comes between us is filled with the clink of cups from the marquee and the buzz of voices around us. There are children's squeals and the hoot of a ship from beyond the pier, one of the Union Castle boats, perhaps. I look back up at him. How well Mother and Dad would have liked him. Kitty and Ana reckon he's handsome, and I suppose he is, but his lips aren't Hubert's, nor his eyes, however kind, the ones I drowned in when we went to Brighton. I think of Hubert, fighting, risking his life for his country. For all of us. How could I possibly let him down?

'I'm truly sorry, John,' I say, and reach out my hand across the table.

He could have got up and walked away, then. A lesser man might have, after being knocked back like that, but he just takes my hand and holds it in his for a moment before letting go.

'Come on. Drink up. There's Kitty looking for you. Quick, or you'll miss your race.'

Chapter 43

I've been summoned to see Sister. I clutch the towel I've been using, squeeze it tightly as I hurry through the ward. Whatever can I have done this time?

'Nurse Timms,' Sister Browning says from behind her desk. I stand in front of her, listening to the sudden burst of summer rain on the window. I search my mind for recent wrongdoings but, for once, I can think of nothing. Her next words make me start. 'Your mother is here to see you.'

'My *mother*?' She must have got it wrong. It must be someone else's mother who's come. Mother never comes here. I open my mouth to tell her so.

'Matron has just telephoned through. You're to go to her office straight away.' She holds out her hand for the towel I still have in my hand. 'Nurse James can finish what you were doing.' The gentleness in her voice is unnerving.

'Yes, Sister. I was doing Corporal Mackay's feet.'

'We'll see to it. Off you go, now.' I have to go back through the ward to change my apron, and I smile an apology to Peter Mackay as I pass. He smiles back, a strange, uncertain smile. Is he reflecting mine back to me, I wonder?

Mother? Here? Why ever would she be? She never leaves Elmford. Not unless it's an outing or an emergency, like the time she had to go to St Mary's Hospital for some stitches when she cut her hand on a tin lid. And the memorial for Arthur, of course.

My stomach turns as I walk down the corridor towards Matron's office. There must be something wrong, or she wouldn't have come, not all the way over here, would she? Has Dad had a turn, perhaps? He's not as young as he used to be, and it's true he hasn't been the same since our Arthur died. But, why didn't she use the telephone? I feel a surge of irritation. I don't know what she's so afraid of. Does she think it'll bite her?

The corridor seems longer than ever today. The sun, fitful between the unexpected July showers, makes arched window-shapes on the floor as I walk. The patterns fade, then brighten again. If Mother's come just for a visit, she'd have been asked to wait till I was off duty, wouldn't she? Yes, of course she would. Perhaps that's what I'm being sent to Matron for. Mother's come and broken the rules and I'm in trouble for it? No. It can't be. They'd never call me off the ward for that. It must be bad news, then. I suddenly remember that it's what happened to Lil when her father died. She was called off the ward, just the same. My stomach turns. It must be Dad. I quicken my steps, resisting the impulse to break into a run. Will this bloody corridor never end? But, *why* didn't Mother telephone? I could have gone home and saved her a journey. I've told her a hundred times what to do. She's got the number. Didn't I show her where I put it, under the tea tin on the dresser? And Mrs Spinks at the Post Office said she'd help her, didn't she?

I reach the opening in the corridor, and turn into it. The door opposite me is marked 'Matron' in large blue letters. I stop in front of it, take a deep breath, and knock firmly. Matron's voice calls out straight away.

'Come!'

I push open the door. My throat catches to see Mother. She's wearing her best hat. The feather at the side has come loose, and flutters.as she turns her head to look at me. Her face is grey, her as always has such a high colour. Is it Mother who's ill then? Is that it? Her green eyes are like marbles as they stare at me.

'I'll leave you for a moment, shall I, Mrs Timms? Give you some time together.' Matron, her clean starched uniform rustling, bustles away. She places a hand on my shoulder as she passes, then I hear the door close behind me.

'What is it, Mother? Is it Dad?' She bends her head forwards for a moment, and I wonder if she's going to faint. But Mother never faints and, instead, she pushes back her chair and draws herself up straight. We stand looking at each other. She holds her handbag in both hands, her knuckles white as my apron as she grips the thick handles. I watch her mouth working.

'It's Walter,' she says finally.

I don't know why I haven't thought of Walter. My hands fly to my face. 'What about Walter?' I ask. 'He hasn't been hurt, has he?'

'Not exactly,' she says and the words come out slowly, and seem to echo as if she's in a tunnel. 'You'll have to be brave now, my girl.' She pauses. 'We 'ad one o' them telegrams this mornin',' she says. "E's gone. Killed in action, so they says. Down at the Somme. His Commandin' Officer says 'e died bravely.'

I stand stock still. Walter dead? I see him flick back his hair, give me his cocky smile as he turns at the door. I hear us arguing, throwing hot words like cinders across the scullery at each other. Then I feel the closeness of him, his head almost touching mine, as he shows me the redstart's nest in the station wall. It isn't possible that he's dead. It isn't! How can he be? He's just a child. My dear, sweet child of a brother.

I stare past Mother then, at the high window behind her. Outside, the sun suddenly breaks through the dripping pane, turning the tiny droplets to a burst of glittering shrapnel. Mother points to a seat as if she wants me to sit down, but I don't want to sit. I want to walk in the sunshine. Yes, if I do that, what she's just said won't be true. It's only here, in this room with its four walls squeezing in on me where the words have been said, that they have any meaning. I feel a surge of anger. Why did she have to say them, then? I have to get outside in the sunshine. That's it. That's where I have to be. If I can just get outside into the open, I can save Walter, and none of this will be true.

I turn and go out through the door. Matron is outside in the corridor talking to Sister Tompkinson, and they both look up as I start to run. I don't care about stupid hospital rules any more. If I'm to save our Walter, I have to run. Run! As I pass them, I hear Sister Tompkinson say 'poor girl' and something about 'brother'. I run up to Reception, and turn through the big double doors, race down the avenue towards the pier. The rain has stopped. I splash through the puddles in my haste to get away, and my wet hem catches at my ankles, making me stumble. I steady myself, and carry on down between the trees. The sun flickers through the dripping branches as I run. I don't stop. No, not until I get to the pier. Then I lean over the side, and my breath comes in great gasps, as if I've run the whole length of the hospital, not just from Matron's office. The grey water heaves and rocks beneath me, and the sun is hot on my back. It penetrates my dress and my cap. I turn and close my eyes to it, let it burn through my closed lids.

There! It can't be true, for here I am, outside, where the sun's shining, and the ugly words that hung between Mother and me are still in Matron's office. And that's where I'll leave them, and never go in there again. No, never. They'll disappear if they're left alone with no-one to listen to them. Yes, disappear, like an early morning mist on a May morning.

I stand, feeling nothing but the sun, and hearing nothing but the lap of the water against the pier. Nothing, that is, until I hear footsteps. A slow, steady scrunch of gravel. The steps come on and on, and echo as they pass onto the wooden boards of the pier. I know it's Mother. I'd recognise her footsteps anywhere in the world, eyes shut or blindfold, I would.

'Maude,' she says, but I won't open my eyes. I mustn't, if I'm to save our Walter. 'Look at me, girl.' I wait, not looking nor answering. 'Maude!' I cling for a moment longer to the sunshine, then open my eyes. Her image jumps and blurs. How old she's become. The hair beneath her hat is snowy white. How did that happen without me noticing? But her eyes are dry and it makes me feel ashamed, for if there are to be any tears, they must surely belong to her, for hasn't she lost all the sons she ever had?

I wipe my eyes with the back of my hand, leave the rail and go towards her. We haven't held each other since I was a little girl, but we hold each other now, and I feel her body shake with my sobs. Then we turn from the pier, take the path that runs by Southampton Water. Above us, a robin flicks the dampness from its wings.

I wonder how it is, that he can sing so.

Chapter 44

Somewhere in France

July 20th, 1916

My Dearest, Dearest Maude,

I am so very sorry to hear about Walter. I have just seen the lists and, despite death being such a constant companion here, it was nevertheless a shock to see his name appear amongst the many. What can I say to comfort you, my darling best girl? There are no words that come near, are there? I know that your parents will have received a letter by now, and probably his things too, but if there is anything – anything at all – that I can do for you or for them, please write and let me know. It seems this war is taking all that is dear to us, and I cannot help but question the human ideal that justifies such a price. Can one possibly exist?

There is one small comfort I can offer you, and that is that I know where Walter is buried. I have been there – it is a spot near where he fell. There are others with him, so he is not alone, and the co-ordinates have been recorded. So many families have not nearly so much, for it often happens that men have to lie in unmarked graves or, God rest their souls, make-do with the battlefield as their final resting place.

When it is all over, this wretched war, I will bring you here, dear, and your parents and Florence and Tom and baby Horace, too, if he is old enough for such a journey. Yes, I will bring you here, to these fields and woods I have grown to know so well. I will lead you down the lanes and across the mud that will one day be meadowland again, and together we will lay some flowers there.

Remember – he is not dead who lives on in our hearts.

With fondest love,

Hubert

Chapter 45

I am crouching on the floor bathing Corporal Mackay's feet, passing the flannel carefully across his swollen toes, when I feel eyes on my back, the way you do sometimes when someone's staring at you. I look up quickly, knocking against the bowl beside me, and a spill of soapy water lands with a splosh on the polished surface of the floor.

It's John. I was half thinking it might be. He's standing in the open doorway of the ward, the sun from the corridor lighting him up from behind. It makes me feel suddenly shy to see him in khaki, as if the uniform has put some kind of barrier between us.

Sister Browning comes up to him, and I look back, dry my patient's feet, then mop up the water I've spilled, hoping she hasn't seen. When I stand up, I can still see them both out of the corner of my eye, looking across at me.

I know why John's come. It's to say goodbye. He warned me it might be today, though it all depended on the doctor's final say-so. I spill some more water as I lift the bowl. My mind's not on what I'm doing at all. This time it goes down my apron. It's fresh on, too. John's talking to Sister now. Whatever can he be finding to say to her? I glance again. She's shaking his hand, and smiling. Yes, really. Smiling.

I hear the familiar clomp of crutches as John makes his way down the ward. The leg of his trouser beneath his knee swings, empty. He needs that pinning up, he does. When he slows to a stop at the end of the bed, I make a show of arranging my things on the trolley. When, finally, I look up, he's leaning on his crutches, smiling at me.

I risk a smile back, glancing across to see if Sister Browning is watching, but she's not there. I hear her voice from the corridor giving someone what-for, and I breathe a sigh of relief, wipe my hands, then place the towel beside the bowl. Behind me, there's a sudden groan.

'You all right, mate?' John calls.

'Now then, Corporal Mackay.' He is trying to get back onto his bed. 'Why are you trying to do that on your own? Here ....' I hurry to take the weight of his legs, lifting them gently until he's lying full-length on top of the blue-and-white counterpane. 'You should have waited for me, you know.'

'It's all very well for ye to say that, lass, but it comes a bit hard when ye've been used all your life to doing for yeself. It's a bugger, aye it is, having to rely on others.'

'I'd make the most of it, mate, if I was you,' John says, trying to make light of it. 'They'll have you back on the Front Line before you know what time of day it is.' The men exchange a smile, and John waits while I make my patient comfortable.

When I have finished, he beckons me to him. 'I've come to say goodbye, Maude.' Even though I've already guessed it, my stomach sinks at his words. 'I've got to report at two o'clock, down by the pier.'

I glance up at the clock. 'It's nearly half past one already! I don't get off till two.'

'It's all right, I've had a word with Sister. She says she'll let you off early, just this once.'

My mouth gapes open, and John and Corporal Mackay laugh. 'Let me off? Sister Browning's never let me off anything since I've been here, not a single thing.'

'I promise you, she said so,' John says. 'Come on, hurry up. I'll meet you in the corridor.' Sister appears from behind a screen, and bustles up to where we're still standing.

'Off you go, Sergeant Harris. You're making my ward untidy.' She turns to me. 'You can finish what you're doing here, nurse, then you can be excused. Just make sure you're back for duty at the normal time this afternoon,' she adds, before turning away.

'Yes, Sister. Thank you Sister,' I say, and scarper as quick as I can before she changes her mind.

John is waiting for me as I go out of the ward. The doors have been propped open, so the sunshine can reach in. It's the only bit the wards ever get, for they've all been built on the shady side of the hospital, I don't know why. As many patients as can be, have been wheeled out into the corridor where summer brightness streams in through the windows, and chatter fills the air as we weave our way round them. As John calls out his farewells, I search my heart for the words with which to say goodbye, but find none. He stops at a cage that's been hung by one of the windows, purses his lips and makes little squeaking noises at the goldfinches inside.

'I'd set them all free if it was up to me,' he says. 'I suppose it's good for the men's morale, but birds should be flying off across the fields, not cooped up.' He shrugs his shoulders, and we continue down the long corridor. Fresh air wafts through, competing with the smell of antiseptic that is everywhere in the hospital. The antiseptic wins. It always does. A group of patients, in their dressing gowns, are sitting in wicker chairs round a table, playing cards, and they lift their hands in salute.

'Lucky bastard, going home,' one calls, and 'good luck,

Johnnie boy,' from another. 'Have a pint or two for me!' John lifts his hand and salutes them back.

We go through the big swing doors and out of the hospital, walking together across the lawn. The sun sparks off the sea, setting it dancing with light, and sailing boats pass across it, far out beyond the pier. Patients and nurses dot the lawns on each side of the avenue, the sun catching on the nurses' white aprons and caps as they flutter gently in the breeze. It's only the movement of air that is making the heat bearable. I feel it lift the long folds of my cap, and flap them against my neck.

We walk without speaking. An invalid carriage squeaks its way past us. One side of the pier is full of men with fishing rods leaning across the railings, trying for a catch on the changing tide. Everyone's making the most of the perfect weather. I look around for somewhere for us to sit, but all the seats and benches are full. Then a group of soldiers by the pier entrance gets up to leave, and we take their place. It's the same seat I sat on the day I arrived. How long ago that seems. I think of the man, Colin, from D Block. I never saw him again. Did he get better, I wonder, and get sent back to the trenches? Or do you really ever get better from injuries of the mind? I don't know the answer to that.

John and I sit close, but not touching, the slats of the seat hard against my back. The waves on either side of the pier shoosh gently against the shingle, tumbling the pebbles, and cigarette smoke drifts towards us, mixing on the air with the salty tang of the sea. At the very end of the pier, just where the boats moor, a figure dives off and for a brief moment he's suspended in the air, like a punctuation mark on an instruction sheet. Then there's the faint splash of water, and soon a tiny head bobs on the surface as the figure strikes out for the shore. A group of off-duty nurses crunch across the pebbles in their swimsuits and stand at the edge of the waves, shouting encouragement.

'I'll be sorry to leave all this,' John says. 'I expect that sounds daft, being a hospital and all that?'

'It's not daft, John. Netley's much more than that at the end of the day.' I try to think ahead to a point in the future when this will all be a thing of the past, a shadow, and the sunlight will be able to fall on other things. But it is impossible. The hospital, like the war, is too big. It has taken us over. The slow chug of a trawler drifts across the sea to us.

'You can still come with me, Maude, you know.' I turn to look at him. I can see from the set of his features that he's serious and, suddenly, I feel as if there is nothing I would like more. To walk away, out of the hospital, away from Netley, and Portsmouth and Elmford, go far away with him, and wipe my life clean of all the horrors and the sadness, like a child wiping a learning slate clean at school.

I look back. 'You know I can't, John.' My heart beats hard as I wonder – would my answer have been different if I hadn't known Hubert first? 'What will you do, once you've got your new leg?' I ask.

John sighs. 'It all depends how I get on with it, I suppose. I might see if I can get my old job back on the estate, though I'm not sure they'll want me like this.'

It's hard to picture John, independent and isolated, making his way through woods and across fields, a gun or an axe across his shoulders, for I've only ever known him here, with the men, laughing and chatting, with the busy-ness of the hospital all around. Besides, without his leg, how will he ever manage such a job?

As he so often does, he guesses my thoughts. 'I might do some sort of factory work,' he continues. 'I'll find something to help with the war effort. Losing a leg doesn't stop you from being useful with your hands, does it?'

'They'll be fighting over you,' I smile and I know that it's true, for men like John are not commonplace. The breeze stops, and the hot sun hits hard at us. When he reaches out for my hand and draws it to him, I don't take it away. I feel perspiration pricking beneath my dress.

'Will you write?' I ask.

'No.'

'Oh.' I pause. 'Why not?'

'It won't do either of us any good. It's better this way. Every friendship has its time, Maude. This has been ours.'

A feeling of panic surges up in me at the thought of losing him. I turn to look at him. 'But I don't see why we can't still be friends, John. Why can't we? Why?'

'You know why, Maude.' John reaches out and pulls me to him, his new jacket rough against my cheek. I reach out and slip my arm around him, and I feel him press me to him. But then he releases me and levers himself up, reaching for his crutches. I stand up, too. I am trembling. Before I can stop myself, I reach up and press my lips against his. It's not a kiss the way Hubert and I have kissed. No, not that, but it is a kiss nevertheless. He looks at me in surprise, confusion darkening his green-brown eyes.

'Goodbye, John,' I say.

'Goodbye, darling Maude,' he whispers. I remain where I am standing, watch as he walks toward a lorry that is waiting in the shade of the trees. He must have left his kit bag there earlier, for now he picks it up from the grass, and tosses it up to one of the soldiers. Then he hands up his crutches too, heaves himself up on his good leg, and swings round to sit down. He does not look back.

The driver inserts the starting handle into the bonnet, gives it several sharp cranks, and I hear the engine sputter into life as I start back up the avenue, alone.

Chapter 46

Somewhere in France

July 27th, 1916

My Dearest, Darling Maude,

I have some more sad news for you, although you may already have heard it. Your Fred Johnston, who used to work with you at the Emporium, has been killed in a mine explosion.

Unbeknown to our own chaps, the Germans had tunnelled their way beneath a stretch of our line and laid explosives, and when they detonated them, the whole bally lot went up.

I confess I find myself in an increasingly sorry state about things over here, and I cannot help but feel that each death I see, each one I hear about, is moving me a little nearer to my own. What a wretched, cruel war it is. How different from our vision of glory when we enlisted. I do not think that I would even have come this far were it not for you, my darling Maude.

God bless you, and keep you.

Yours ever,

Hubert

Chapter 47

'Tom? Is it you?'

I peer at a stretcher the orderlies are taking from the train, and drop to my knees beside it as they lay it carefully on the damp platform floor. I could have sworn at first glance it was him, but it's not, for this soldier is far thinner than Tom ever was. Somewhere in the back of my mind is the thought that if it *was* my brother-in-law, he might have news of Hubert, for I haven't had a letter for nearly three weeks now. The last one had been so gloomy, and since then there's not even been so much as a field postcard. All around me are stretchers and walking wounded, and chatter fills the air. The men are always happy to have got a 'blighty', even those really badly injured. They're just glad to be out of it, I suppose.

Above, the overhanging branches of a tree drip moisture from limp green leaves onto the roof of the train. 'Are you all right?' I ask, gently lifting the blanket to look beneath.

'Right as ninepins,' comes the slurred reply, though he clearly is not. Thoughts of Hubert fade as I take in his condition. He is caked in mud and has a bloodied dressing on his thigh and several covering his right arm which is strapped across his chest.

He opens his eyes and looks up at me, and a shock of excitement runs through me, for it *is* Tom's face I'm looking at. It breaks into a smile. 'Well, I never,' he says. 'I must've died and gone to Heaven if I'm seein' angels.' His empty sleeve hangs loosely down the side of the stretcher to crumple beside him on the station floor. He begins to shiver, and I get up to fetch an extra blanket from the pile stacked on the table behind me, unfold it and lay it across him.

As I tuck it gently round him, I feel his eyes on me. His face seems sunk into itself, not like Tom's bright face at all. It's the pain I expect. I've seen pain in the eyes of all the soldiers here, of one sort or another, and sometimes it's accompanied by something else, something darker that I've come to recognise. I search his face for the darkness, sighing with relief when it's not there. I let go of his gaze then, and pull the blanket closer round him, cursing myself when I touch his arm, for he gasps and closes his eyes, his mouth falling open.

'I'm sorry, Tom,' I mutter, and take his good hand, holding it for a moment. 'I'm sorry.' The stretcher wagon rumbles back up the path. 'Here!' I shout. 'Please!' A QUAIMNS sister hurries across when I shout, checks the tag that's been tied to Tom's foot, then motions that we can go. Bellfield stoops down to take one end of the stretcher and a young boy takes the other. He must be new, for I don't recognise him. Perhaps he's the lad who took Austen's place when he went off to enlist? Whoever he is, he looks as if he should still be in school. They lift Tom onto a wagon, and we start off down the pathway to Central. I walk beside him, positioning myself where he can see me. The big black wheels turn quicker and quicker till I'm almost running to keep up.

'Thought I was invincible after I got through Gallipoli, Maude.' Tom's voice is faint. I bend closer to hear him better.

'You'll get through this, too,' I tell him. 'It's a marvellous hospital. They'll get you better.' His good hand's on the side I'm walking on. I take it and squeeze it gently. 'They'll need to register you first and assess you, then they'll get you to a ward, and make you more comfortable. Who knows, it could even be G. Eight. That's mine! That'd be nice now, wouldn't it?' I smile, but Tom has closed his eyes. 'I'll find out where they've put you, and come and see you when I get off duty tonight. How's that?' He nods, then slowly opens his eyes again.

'Let Flo know I'm here, Maude, will you?'

''Course I will.' We go through the big double doors at the end of the covered walkway, and into the hospital. When we reach the large room that serves as a sorting area, I have to let go of Tom's hand as he's wheeled away.

'I'll telephone Mrs Spinks,' I call. 'She can get one of the children to run down with a message. Our Flo'll be here in no time at all, you'll see.' Then he's gone, and the doors swing shut again.

'Mrs Spinks?' I shout into the telephone receiver. There's a loud buzzing noise coming from the earpiece.

'Yes, yes. Who is it? You'll have to speak up.'

'It's Maude Timms, Mrs Spinks.'

'Young Maude? How are you, my dear? Still at that hospital of yours? Your mother was in the shop yesterday with your nephew. Grand little chap. What's his name, now?'

'Horace.' I pause. 'I need to get a message to our Florrie. Is she still at the cottage with Mother, do you know?'

'Of course, dear. Yes, she is, though for how much longer I'm sure I can't say. According to your mother ....'

I interrupt her. 'I haven't got much time, Mrs Spinks, I'm sorry. I've got to get back on duty.'

'How can I help you then, dear?' The buzzing fades to a soft crackle.

'Would you tell Florrie that Tom's here, up at the hospital?' I hear her intake of breath, and imagine the look of interest that will have appeared on her face at the thought of a bit of gossip.

'Oh dear, dear, dear,' she says. 'Not too bad is he?'

'No, he's not too bad, but tell Florrie he's asking for her, will you, and to come as soon as she can? He'll settle better once he's seen her, I think.'

'Right you are then, dear. I'll send one of the girls down directly. Remember me to him, won't you?'

'I will, Mrs Spinks. Thank you.' The click on the line tells me the line has been disconnected.

As soon as we've handed over to the night staff and Sister Browning has said I can go, I hurry to find out where they've put Tom. I run my finger down the list in the assessment room, stopping at his name. He's been put in Berkshire Hut. Outside, a thick fog is sweeping across the lawns from the sea. I make my way carefully up the busy main path that everyone here knows as Piccadilly, then turn off onto a smaller path. How welcoming the hut looks in the eerie whiteness, with its chinks of light already showing between the curtains. I push open the door and slip inside. Sister Dorling immediately strides towards me, motioning me to wait. Over her shoulder, I can see the doctor's long coat. He's still doing his rounds. There are screens around some of the beds. Even when I explain why I've come, she won't have any of it.

'Come back tomorrow, Nurse,' she says. 'We'll know a little more by then. I'll tell him you called by.' I hesitate. 'Off you go.' Her tone is firm.

Next morning, I slip out of Ward G. Eight as soon as I can,

on the pretext of going to the lavatory. The mist from the night before has almost cleared, and the sun is trying to come out. I take a short cut, hurry across the lawns, trying not to think of the deep trouble I'll be in if I'm caught.

Inside Berkshire Hut, half-way down the ward, I see Tom lying in one of the pink-counterpaned beds. There's a small cage beneath the blankets over his legs, but it's not that that my eyes are drawn to. It's his arm, for it seems huge in the clean white bandages that run from his shoulder right down to the tips of his fingers. How black his nails look against it. He reaches out with his good arm and takes my hand.

'I can't stop long,' I tell him. 'Nurse James is covering for me as it is, and Sister Browning'll have my guts for garters if she finds out I'm here.' I smile at him.

'Did you get a message to Flo?' he asks.

'I did. I spoke to Mrs Spinks on the telephone. Don't worry, our Florrie'll be here before you know it.' I pause. 'What did the doctor say?'

'Well, the leg's not a problem. I just have to rest it and let nature take its course. He reckons it'll heal all right if I do that. No, the trouble's the arm.' We both look to where it lies motionless beside him. 'He says he'll do what he can.' The sun blazes briefly through the windows of the hut, then just as quickly fades again. 'The thing is, Maude, it's half gone already.' A nurse brings a vase of flowers and places them on the table in the centre of the room. It's Betty Quinnel who's in the hut next to ours. She looks across at us and gestures with her head to the door, frowns a warning that Sister Dorling's not far away.

'I'd better go, Tom. I'll come back this afternoon, shall I? For a proper visit?'

'That'd be nice, Maude.'

I hesitate. 'You haven't got any news of Hubert, I suppose, have you Tom?'

He gives me a steady look. 'That officer friend o' yours, you mean?' I nod. 'Ain't heard from him lately, then?' He pauses. 'I wouldn't worry over-much, if I was you. It's bloody chaos over there, an' no news is good news, after all. I expect he's on the move. Messes up the post wholesale, that does.'

Despite his words, doubt fills my stomach, heavy as lead. 'Yes, yes. That'll be it. Of course it will, Tom.'

It can't be more than four hours before I'm back in Berkshire Hut, but in that time they've moved Tom from where he was, and put him up near Sister's desk. Everyone knows that's a bad sign, for they always keep those places for the serious cases. Our Florrie's there, sitting in a chair by the side of the bed.

She looks up as I reach them. Her face is anxious, her eyes wide, and I glance quickly at Tom. He has two patches of high colour on his cheeks that weren't there this morning, and his eyes have taken on a feverish look. Florrie holds tightly to his good hand, as if she's never going to let him go, her wedding band catching in the light that drops through the window behind.

'They want to take his arm, Maude,' she says, looking up at me. Tom tries to hoist himself up on his pillows, but the effort is too much and he falls back, closing his eyes.

I reach down to give Tom a kiss, then I give Florrie one. Tom opens his eyes again. 'It's the only way,' he says to her, then turns his head to focus his eyes on me. 'It's the infection,' he says. 'They did their best at the field hospital, but the dirt's in deep, and it's gone bad. The doctor says if they don't take the arm off, I'll probably be done for.' He eases his hand from Florrie, makes a pretend cut across his throat with his finger, and attempts a smile.

'I wish you wouldn't talk like that, Tom.' Florrie dabs at the corner of her eye with her handkerchief.'

'Come on, love,' he says. 'Got to make the best of it, haven't we, eh? Plenty worse off than me.'

'I really don't see how.'

'Lots of the men in here have lost limbs,' I tell her, thinking of John. I try to sound reassuring. 'They get on perfectly well. It's not the end of the world.'

'But how will he work?' she asks, her forehead creased into a frown. 'The farm will never want someone with only one arm.' She makes me wince, saying that in front of Tom. One day, perhaps, she'll learn to think before she speaks.

'Tom's strong and fit. There are lots of things he can do,' I tell her. 'He doesn't have to go back to the farm. The main thing is for him to get better, isn't it?' I draw out the little canvas stool from the beneath the bed, and sit down next to Florrie. I look more closely at Tom. I must admit I don't like the look of him. I've seen enough since I've been here to know that he's going downhill fast. Beads of sweat have appeared on his forehead in just the time I've been here.

'When do they want to operate?' I ask.

'Today. This afternoon. Soon.' Florrie begins to cry. I want to shake her.

'The sooner they do it, the better it will be for Tom,' I tell her briskly, though my heart goes out to her all the same, for it's an easy enough thing to say, isn't it? We both turn to watch as two orderlies come through the open doors into the ward and make their way towards us.

Chapter 48

The day's post is waiting on the table in the little porch of our hut. I pick up the bundle and leaf through it, but slowly my heart sinks with disappointment. Still no letter from Hubert. It's nearly six weeks now. I tell myself for the hundredth time that it only means they're on the move like Tom said, and of course it must be a right old muddle, mustn't it, with all the battles that are going on? And besides, my letters haven't been returned, which they would be if ... but, I won't think that, I won't. I leave the post neatly on the table, and turn into the sitting room.

The next day there's no letter, either. Nor the day after, nor the day after that. Each day the anxiety's worse until by the end of another week, I'm hardly sleeping. I haven't told anyone about the letters not coming, for I don't want to hear my thoughts turn into words. Words make things too real.

But I might as well have done, for the girls have guessed, of course. I suppose if I saw one of *them* sitting on the edge of her bed just staring into space, I'd know something was wrong, too. That's where I am when Ana comes in – sitting on the edge of my bed. I haven't taken off my uniform, nor my cap, nor even my shoes, which are usually the first things to go. Ana's not one to tiptoe around people. She comes in and stands in front of me, her arms folded.

'Still haven't heard, then?' she asks.

I bend forwards to unlace my shoes. 'Don't know what you're on about.' I slip out my feet, catch her look as I sit back up. 'Oh, all right! No, I haven't,' I add as I rub my toes. 'There! Satisfied?' I make a show of inspecting my stockings, look closely at another hole that has appeared in the thick black reinforced toe. 'Christ!' I say, trying to divert her attention, 'another hole to darn.'

But she refuses to be put off. 'He's probably on the move, Maude. You know that letters are difficult sometimes when they're on the move.'

It's what I've been telling myself for weeks. 'It shouldn't stop them getting through for this long, Ana,' I say.

'It does sometimes. Remember what happened to Kitty?' I look up, hope surging through me. I was quick enough with the good advice then, wasn't I, telling her not to worry?

'That's true.'

'Yes, it *is* true.' The sun has come round, and cuts low across Susan's bed. It doesn't reach as far as mine, like it does in summer. I wish it would, then I could curl up in its warmth. I pull off my other shoe and scrutinize the stocking on my other foot. 'My God! I've got a hole in this one too.'

'Maude!'

'I can't talk about it, Ana, I'm sorry. I just can't.' She looks at me a moment, her eyes soft with compassion and understanding. Then she turns away.

Another week has passed since that conversation, and now I stir my food round my plate as I stare down at my dinner. The girls have already finished theirs, and gone back to the hut for a rest and a smoke. The dinner's good, steak-and-kidney pudding with the suet crust just right, crisp and golden, but I can't eat it. I haven't been able to eat a thing since yesterday, for the very thing I'd been dreading, happened. One of my letters was sent back to me. It was dirty and dog-eared, as if it had been sent round and round until someone just decided to return it.

The worst thing is, I don't know how to find out what's going on. I could ask one of the men, I suppose. They might be able to suggest something. But that's the last thing I want to do. We're here to be a support to them, not the other way round. If only John were here, it would be different. He'd know what to do. The thought of him gives me an ache in my chest. I've never missed him more than I do now.

Perhaps I should write to Aylmer? Even though I haven't met him, I think he would probably know of me. Surely he wouldn't mind just telling me if Hubert's all right? But then again, I don't know his Army number or anything. No, the best thing is to go to the factory and ask to speak to Mr Wells-Crofton, ask him outright. I groan aloud. I can't just walk into a great big factory like that and demand to see the owner! The very thought of it makes my stomach somersault. No, that's the worst idea of all. I push my plate away, stare out of the window at the overcast sky. It's a uniform dull grey, the colour of the battleships that come and go in Portsmouth Harbour. It presses down on the buildings that surround the quadrangle and on the scattering of autumn leaves on the grass. If only Hubert's mother was kinder, I'd ask her. Of course, Mrs Wells-Crofton! My heart thuds as the thought takes possession of my mind. What does it matter whether she's kind or not?

It's the only way, if I really want to know.

'Well, she can't eat you, Maude,' Lil says.

The four of us, Kitty, Lil, Ana and I, are walking across to the hospital to start our shift the following morning. Our shadows are long, and the maple leaves down by the cottages are tinged with red and yellow. I breathe in the cool air.

'Can't eat me?' I remember the time at Arthur's memorial, how Hubert's mother wouldn't shake my hand, and could hardly even bear to look at me. 'Huh.' I feel Kitty link her arm through mine. 'You haven't met her!' I say, managing a laugh, for it's a relief at least to have a plan.

'It's the only sensible thing to do.' Lil takes my other arm. 'Seriously, Maude, it's not good for you to be worrying like this when you really probably don't need to. And anyway, better to know, that's what I say.'

I look down, watch our stout rubber-heeled shoes marching, left-right, left-right, in time with each other. The dew flicks up and makes them glisten, as if we'd spent hours with spit and polish, which none of us have. We turn onto the path that leads down to the main hospital block.

'I think you're doing the right thing,' Kitty says, 'I mean, she'll know, won't she, if, well ....' Her words hang, unfinished, on the air. I see Ana nudge her, then frown. But, it's true what Kitty says. If anything has happened, whatever it is, Hubert's mother will know, won't she? They always let the next of kin know.

'Well,' I say, 'I can either stay here and worry, or I can take a day's leave and go and find out. I've got several days owing, and it's not as if I don't know where they live.' I remember how Hubert and I went past The Gables on the tram once. He'd pointed out the apple trees, the big gravel drive and the garage where his father kept his motor car. It's a big, new house, I tell them, with grounds all around it. Very grand.

When I ask her, Sister Browning says I can have the following Monday off, and in my dinner break, I go down to the office to fill in the form. I'll go and see Mrs Wells-Crofton in the morning, then perhaps I'll have time to see Mother and Dad before I come back, and even if I get a letter from Hubert before then, I'll still go to Elmford, for it's ages since I've been.

Each day, when I've finished my morning shift, I come up the little path to our hut, but still there's nothing. I've come to hate seeing the pile of letters, feeling that surge of hope, only to have it strangled as I go through the envelopes, one by one, with no sign of Hubert's hand. I've even started saying my prayers again, though it doesn't seem to have done much good. I've stopped writing to Hubert, of course, for where is the point? Every day I re-read his last few letters, looking for a clue as to what might have happened but, despite the obvious darkness of his thoughts, there's nothing in any of them to suggest a reason for him to actually stop writing to me. Kitty says, what if he's been injured, his arms perhaps, and is lying in a hospital bed somewhere and *can't* write? Well, if that was the case, I tell her, he'd get a nurse to write one for him, wouldn't he, for isn't that what we do for the men here? Besides, if he'd been injured, he'd be mentioned in the lists, and he hasn't been, for a day doesn't go by that I don't visit the library to look at the papers.

So, if I still haven't heard by Monday, I'm off to Portsmouth to see Mrs Wells-Crofton, and I'm that worked up about it that I'm not going to let her shut the door in my face, either. And if she's not there, like Lil says she might not be, well, I'll sit down on the step and wait.

I'm not going anywhere until I know what's happened to him.

Chapter 49

The dahlias are wonderful, with the sun lighting up their bright heads like that. I must remember to tell Hubert about them.

I push open the green side-gate of The Gables. I had meant to walk up the main drive, but those big iron railings put me off. This little gate here is far more friendly. The path narrows, and I duck my head beneath an arch of roses so my hat doesn't catch on the stems. There are a few late blooms, single yellow ones, with cups of rain in the petals.

I cast my eyes around, trying to take my mind off the reason I've come, and glance up at the house. Which is Hubert's room, I wonder? All those windows! However does his mother manage such a large house these days, with staff so hard to get? She's probably having to pay above the odds in wages, I should think. I can't see the likes of her rolling up her sleeves at the wash-tub, or getting on her hands and knees to black the grate!

The path divides at the small orchard, and I hesitate. Shall I continue on to the back, or turn right and go to the front as I'd intended? I stand there, my insides churning. But then, suddenly, it seems as if Hubert's beside me. He'd have walked this path a thousand times, wouldn't he? The thought gives me courage. I draw in a deep breath, then turn past the windows and French doors, and climb the steps to the front porch. An iron bell-pull hangs down beside the door, a long black rod with a ring attached. I reach up and close my fingers around it, the ring hard through my gloves. There's a faint tinkling sound somewhere deep inside the house.

I step back, watching as a squirrel skitters across the lawn. It stops to scrabble at the grass for a moment before bounding off across the gravel, scattering stones in its haste to climb to safety in the branches of a tree. I can hear nothing from the other side of the door. I lean my head against the pattern of iron-studs as I listen. No, there's no sound at all. Perhaps I should just go? Who am I, after all, to be calling here for all the world as if I were invited? A busy person like Mrs Wells-Crofton, with all those committees Hubert told me about, well, she's most probably out anyway. I'm just stepping backwards, when I hear the sound of a key turning and the door swings open. I smile at the young girl who stands there. She must think I'm someone, for she bobs me a curtsey.

'Can I help you, miss?' she says. I square my shoulders.

'I've come to see Mrs Wells-Crofton.'

'Yes, miss. Would you step inside, please?' She pronounces her words carefully, as if she's been schooled in what to say. I wipe my shoes on the doormat before stepping across the threshold into the dark hall. The door shuts with a thud behind me, and the girl shows me into a room that overlooks the front garden, indicates a chair with a tapestry seat that stands by the side of the empty fireplace. I cross the room towards it, my footsteps muffling on the rug. So this is Hubert's home. I look at the pictures and the expensive furniture, everything neat and in order. There is a smell of chrysanthemums. A vase on the mantelpiece is full of them, big copper-gold globes. They remind me of Dad. He always grows a few for Mother. They're her favourites.

'I'll tell Madam that you're here,' the girl says shyly. She bobs another curtsey, then turns from the door, leaving it ajar. Her light footsteps grow fainter and fainter until I can't hear them any more.

I wait. Outside in the hall, a grandfather clock ticks with deep, steady beats. I count them for a while, listening for the footsteps to come back. When they don't, I get up and walk across the room, stand and stare at a painting that hangs on the wall between the windows. It's of a young woman. Her hair is dark, like Hubert's, and she's dressed in a blue ball gown. She has a posy of flowers in her hand, and she's smiling. Is it Hubert's mother? If so, she was very beautiful then. I go back to my seat and sit down, pinch my cheeks to bring a bit of colour into them.

Why is she taking so long? I clutch the handles of my bag, running my fingers backwards and forwards along them, then get up to walk across the room again. This time, I stop by the sideboard and look down at the sepia images in their silver frames. My heart jumps when I recognise Hubert in one of them. There are two young couples, dressed for tennis, their rackets at their feet. He has his arm around one of the girls. She's tall. I feel a surge of jealousy as I pick up the photograph to look at it more closely. It's Clara Fotherington, I'm sure it is. I fight an urge to throw it across the room.

I can hear someone coming down the stairs. I put the photograph down quickly, and it clatters onto the surface of the sideboard. I haven't got time to worry about that now. I hurry back. The footsteps are crossing the hall. I get to my chair just in time, so that Mrs Wells-Crofton can see me stand up as she comes into the room. It wouldn't do for her to think I was having a good nose around, would it? My stomach is full of butterflies as I watch the open doorway for her to appear.

'In future, Mary,' I hear her words before I see her, 'make sure you ask the visitor's name,' then the reply of the girl, too soft to hear.

Mrs Wells-Crofton's appearance takes me aback when I see her, for she's changed a great deal from the woman I saw at the memorial service. Her skin is very pale and she has dark circles beneath her eyes. She's thinner, too. She looks me up and down, and I see a flicker of recognition in her eyes.

'How may I help you?' she says, her dress rustling as she comes into the room. She tips her head and looks down at me like I'd look at a pile of mouse droppings in the ward.

'I'm sorry to disturb you, Mrs Wells-Crofton,' I begin, hating the way my heart hammers inside my chest. 'My name's Maude Timms. I'm a friend of Hubert's.'

'Ah.'

I feel my face flush, but I'm determined to continue. 'I was wondering if you've had news of him lately?' Her eyes narrow but she doesn't answer. 'It's just that I haven't had a letter from him for over two months.'

'My son has been *writing* to you?' I feel the colour flush my face again.

'We've been writing to each other,' I say, and have the satisfaction of seeing her face flush this time.

'Indeed?' Her eyelids droop, veiling her gaze.

'Yes.' I can still feel the heat in my face as we stand, looking at each other. I don't think she looks at all well. But, unwell or not, I'm not being the first to look away, and adding to her advantage over me. We stare at each other until, suddenly, she opens her eyes wide, seeming to make up her mind about something.

'Wait there!' she says, before turning from the room. I can

hear sounds from the next room, of a drawer being pulled open, then shut again. She comes back a moment later with an envelope. I feel my heart give a lurch, and I reach out to steady myself against the chair, for the envelope is like the one we had for our Arthur, with its typed words and official stamp. She holds it out, and flicks it impatiently for me to take.

'It's what you came for, isn't it? Read it.' I sit down.

She stays standing over me, and I feel her eyes on me as I slip out the page. The words dance in front of me. 'Missing?' I say. 'Believed killed?' I look up at her. 'It's not true! It can't be.' I can feel the blood draining from my face, and the room seems suddenly dark.

'His name hasn't been in the lists. I've looked in the library every day,' I choke out as I stand up. 'I'm sorry, it can't be right.'

'The authorities are not in the habit of getting these things wrong, Miss Timms, I can assure you. Perhaps if you were able to read properly?' She holds out her hand for the telegram, and her eyelids droop again. 'Now, if there's nothing else I can help you with ....' She indicates with her hand towards the door.

I stay where I am for a moment, clutching the handles of my handbag tightly. I won't let her fob me off like that. 'There *is* one more thing, Mrs Wells-Crofton, if you please.'

She raises her eyebrows. 'Oh? And what is that, may I ask?'

'It's only that, if you get any more news of Hubert, would you please let me know? I don't believe he's dead. It's not as if they've found him, is it? Just because he's missing.' I shake my head. 'It doesn't mean anything. He might be in a hospital somewhere, with his memory lost.' She looks at me then, and it seems as if her eyes are just a little kinder. 'Would you let me know if you hear, Mrs Wells-Crofton? Please? You could write to the Royal Victoria Hospital up at Netley. I'm a VAD there.' I hate the pleading I can hear in my voice, but the truth is I'd get down on my hands and knees and beg if I had to, if it meant I could find out what's happened to Hubert.

She looks at me for a moment more without answering. Then she nods, a sharp, abrupt movement of her head, before reaching for the bell pull that hangs on the wall.

'Back entrance, Mary,' she says when the girl appears. Mary gives me an apologetic half-smile, and leads me down a passageway, which passes the length of the house. A smell of frying onions grows stronger as we near the kitchen. She stops at a bare wooden door and holds it open for me as I slip through into the garden. The sun strikes me as I emerge, and I shade my eyes.

'Down as far as the orchard,' Mary calls as I begin down the path, 'then left.' I lift my hand in thanks, turning just in front of the apple trees. There are bruised fallers everywhere. I step over a large fruit that has been squashed flat on the path, taking care not to slip on the brown mess. I won't believe that telegram about him. No, I won't believe he's dead. I won't.

At the bottom of the path, by the hedge, a bicycle has been propped against the little gate. It slides to fall sideways. Whoever it belongs to ought to take a bit more care of it. It's when I'm squeezing past that I feel my stomach turn over, for it's one of those bicycles the telegram boys use. I stop, turn to look back to the house. Yes, there he is, the post boy, in his uniform, walking up to the front door. I hate the sight of them, everyone does these days, though it's not their fault, poor things. They're just lads, earning a wage as best they can.

But I needn't have worried. It's not a telegram he's carrying after all, but a parcel. I breathe out a sigh of relief as I watch him balance it in one hand, and reach up to pull the bell with the other. Yes, it's only a parcel, so that's all right. It's telegrams you have to worry about.

I walk along Laburnum Grove, turning towards North End.

I'll catch the tram back to the station, that's what I'll do, then get a train to Elmford. I have a sudden, overwhelming longing for home, to walk up the path and in at the scullery door, to sit with Mother and Dad in our little living room, as if everything is still right with the world.

I don't have long to wait for the tram. It draws in, and I step on, choosing a seat where the sun comes in. I won't let myself believe Hubert's dead. Missing, the letter said, didn't it, that's all? They shouldn't send letters like that without knowing. It's not fair.

Chapter 50

A letter from Hubert!

It's waiting for me a few days after my visit to The Gables. As I see his handwriting, my heart thunders against my chest as if my whole body will explode. I reach out my hand to steady myself. See? I told Mrs Wells-Crofton he was alive! She didn't believe me, but I knew! I knew! The envelope's on the top of all the others, and I can see it's from him, plain as day, even though the words are scrawled and untidy as if he'd written them in the dark. I knock against the porch door in my haste to reach it, jarring the door against the wall, and the envelope trembles in my hand as I tear it open.

France

October 20th, 1916

My Dearest, Darling Maude,

Knowing that you will only read this if I have died, gives a strange release from all those bonds that tie one so terribly in life. It is an odd sensation, waiting to go over the top. One sees one's life so differently. I want you to know that I love you, Maude, with all my heart, dearest.

You will be wondering why I have not written to you of late. It is, quite simply, that I have not been able to bring myself to. My mind is cracked wide open, Maude, and sanity so far away now that I know I shall never again reclaim it. I find myself in a no-man's-land, a dark hell from which I can see no way out. For me, mine is the worst kind of weakness, for I am not only letting down myself but, more importantly, my men. They are good men, Maude, who deserve a better leader than I could ever be.

I have been looking back on my life a great deal of late. My one real regret is that we had not been married. There, that is the truth. If you are reading this, it will already be too late for such a thing, but it gives me peace to pen it. How wrong I was to allow convention to dictate to my heart, my darling, how I have hated my lack of courage, for you are everything I want, and have ever wanted, and what are manners and expectations when held up against such feelings? Perhaps it is a sad fact that it is only with death at one's shoulder that one is able to see clearly?

But, what's done is done, and it cannot ever be otherwise, wish as I might. I have quite lost my bearings, dear. I have seen and heard things that can never be erased, and they are too much for my mind to bear, and my body shakes constantly, day and night. I can, even now, hardly hold the pen to form these words.

I hope you will find it in your heart to forgive this mixed-up soldier boy of yours for all the worry he has put you to, and show that you do, by being happy in the rest of your life. I can see you now on the Downs, taking down your hair for me, and in Brighton, too, with the moonlight soft upon you. It is hard to think that such moments will not come again. When you find someone else (as I know you will my darling, for who could not love you?) let memories of me be only that – and <u>live</u>.

Yours, forever, and until we meet again,

Hubert

In the silence, I hear the distant hoot of the hospital train. Then the porch is rocking around me, and I am falling. Pain explodes in my head as I strike my temple against the door frame, taking me to darkness beyond.

Chapter 51

I turn to look up the track in the direction the train will come, pace slowly up to the white wicker gate, then back again. The new station-master comes out of his office. I never thought I'd miss old Mr Coggins marching up and down, calling out to folk to mind the doors, and to stand back from the edge. His son was killed over in Arras. It broke the old man's heart, Mother told me, and he died himself before the month was out. I didn't know he had a son. A lot you know, then, she said. Went off when he turned seventeen. You was only young then, o' course. He lived in Cornwall. Worked in the mines there.

I move to the back of the platform, and sit on one of the benches. The late afternoon sun slants up beneath the canopy and I close my eyes, letting my thoughts drift. So many things have changed. Take Clara Fotherington, for instance. When I bumped into her in Portsmouth the other week, I hardly recognised her. She's had her hair cut into one of these new bobs. It suits her long face. She even looked, dare I say it, pretty? She was the one who recognised me, actually stopped me in the street. She was with a woman who I felt I knew but couldn't quite place.

May I introduce Mary Stacey? she said, and it was when I heard her name, that I remembered her. She was the woman Hubert had pointed out at Arthur's memorial service, her children filing along behind her like little ghosts. Mary's the trade union representative at Crofton's, Clara said. Of course, there's still a lot left to do for The Cause.

Yes, there have been many, many changes, and not only that so many men won't be coming back. Miss Fotherington would never have stopped in the street to talk to the likes of me, for one. She spoke of Hubert and her eyes were filled with tears all the while, though my own stayed dry. She probably thought I'd got over him, bearing in mind my condition and that. Did I know Randolph St John, and Archie McFadden? I told her that Hubert had mentioned Randolph in his letters, and I had met Archie once. They were both killed in the Third Battle of Ypres. Yes, I said, Will – Captain Lawrence – told me. He came to see me after the war. Did he? That was nice. Yes, Roger Hunter came too. I was still at the hospital, then. We had tea in Netley village. Will still comes to visit from time to time. His scar has quite healed now. I'm glad of that, Clara said. Nasty injury, on his face like that. She and Aylmer are courting, she said shyly after a bit. It's strange to think that. He won a medal for bravery. They're going to be married in Portsmouth Cathedral, a big society wedding, and she rolled her eyes when she said it, which made us laugh. She didn't mention Mrs Wells-Crofton, and I didn't ask.

They've started up the WSPU group again at the Union Hall. Why didn't I come along? We need good, strong people like you. We might have won the vote, but the battle's not over yet! She'd smiled when she'd said that, but her eyes were perfectly serious and earnest. There's an awful lot that still needs doing, you know, an awful lot. We're not stopping here! Then she'd laughed that big horsey laugh of hers. Good, strong people like you. That's what she'd said, and she wouldn't have said it if she didn't mean it, would she? Good. Strong. Is that how Hubert saw me, too?

The sound of a baby crying brings me back. A family's come to sit beside me on the bench. The mother and I exchange a smile. I look up at the big station clock that hangs down from the canopy. The trains aren't so dependable since the war. I lean forward to rub my back. It's been good to spend time with Mother and Dad, to sleep in my old bed again, but I'm looking forward to getting back to my own home. We've got a little terraced house near the dockyard, with a nice big scullery with running water. We've got a bathroom, too, and a water closet. I smile as I recall Mother's face when I first showed her. How she jumped when I flushed the lavatory! Gawd, girl, she said, whatever next?

When I was up in Commercial Road, I stepped into Mason's Emporium. I don't often go in there now, for usually I use the little drapery in Cameron Avenue. But it was good to go to the old place again, even though the only person I recognised from my time there was Rose. She's in millinery, now. She's got my old job, senior drapery assistant. Did I hear about Mr Arnold? No. Well, he volunteered in nineteen-seventeen, went as a stretcher bearer, something to do with a white feather he'd been given. Would I ever credit it, Mr Arnold with his stuffy ways going off to be in the war? He must have lied about his age then, I told her. He was far too old to enlist. Anyway, she said, he was sent to France but was killed in the battle of Amiens. Blown up trying to help get the wounded back to the field hospitals, dear oh dearie me, was there ever such a thing? And wasn't it a shame about young Fred Johnston, and all the others too? She was so sorry to hear about my young man, Hubert wasn't it? She'd looked slyly at my belly then. Her and her husband haven't been blessed yet with children, she said.

The station clock gives a low click as it passes the hour, and

I shift on the bench. Yes, it's been good to come back. A whole week's been like a holiday to me. Well, all right for some, Dad said, each time I sat down. He's never had a holiday in his life. But for all his grumbling, he's changed too. Mellowed, Mother says, like a bit of cheese. Mellow is one word for it, I said to her. But, still, he *is* easier these days and often comes with Mother when she visits us, and Florrie and Tom come too when they can, with their Horace and little Ethel. That Ethel's the apple of her father's eye, her grandfather's, too, blonde curls, just like our Florrie, but with Tom's big brown eyes. She'll break some hearts when she's grown, that's for sure. I like it when they come, but I don't let it be us women in the scullery working and them sitting down reading their papers all the time, mind. Oh no, I won't have that, and I don't care what Dad says about it neither. We all help, and after dinner we go for a walk if the weather's good, along Southsea Common and down onto the beach. I like to see Mother link her arm through Dad's, with the children running around them.

Tom's back at the farm, too, in charge of the dairy, so all Florrie's worry was for nothing. It's surprising what you can do with just one arm, he often says, with a wink at her. And what does it matter, if things take that little bit longer? Who's to count the minutes when it's the fact you're alive that matters?

I hear the whistle of the train. It always does that when it's about to round the bend, so I get up and walk towards the platform edge. Soon, the engine's snorting past and I'm looking into each carriage window, trying to see them.

The doors are pushed open, and people step out. My heart beats quickly, and I feel the baby kick inside me. There's no sign of them. Have they missed the train? I turn to look up the platform again, then there they are, right up behind the engine, the last to alight. John, with our little fair-haired boy. Bertie, we call him. It was John's suggestion to name him after Hubert, and it means the world to me.

They've been up to Selby to see John's parents. I'll be able to go again next year, and we'll take the new baby too, to show them. If it's a girl, we're going to ask Kitty and Lil to be godmothers. Ana's Bertie's godmother. Spoils him something terrible with all those presents she sends. Don't you expect any more babies after this one, I told John. Two is quite enough for a modern family, and perhaps then I'll have some time left over and can help Miss Fotherington? You're ahead of your time, woman, John said to me, but he smiled, so I know it'll be all right.

Yes, I wrote to John after he'd left, to tell him about Hubert, and how his mother had found the letter in the parcel amongst his things, and sent it on to me. Even though John had said not to write, I couldn't help myself. Not that I got a reply, though. No. He came instead. Came to help me through those dark days. Got a job at the hospital, helping the men make things out of wood, toys and that, up in one of the huts. He met me each day at dinner-time, and again when I finished in the evening, and we went for long walks along the shore. It didn't matter what the weather was. He said it was so he could get used to his new leg, but I knew it wasn't that. It was to help me get right again.

John works down at the Docks as a carpenter now. He learned a lot up at the hospital and they're paying good wages, too, for skills like that are scarce now. He's even built a shed at the bottom of our garden, and makes things, furniture and the like, and some of it he sells. Whenever it's quiet of an evening, I know that if I walk down the path, past the peas and the beans with their orange flowers and winding tendrils, I'll find the both of them there, John turning something on the lathe, a table leg perhaps, pushing with his good foot against the treadle, and Bertie playing with the wood shavings on the floor. I've never told John that part of my grief was that I was half out of love with Hubert, and half in love with him. I didn't know it myself until I got the letter. It was the guilt, I suppose, as made it all so hard.

Now Bertie has seen me and struggles to get free from John's hand. He's running down the platform into my outstretched arms. I look down at my little boy. He's talking nineteen-to-the-dozen about the train ride and his other Grandma and Grandpa. Did I know they were very, *very* old and that Grandpa tucks his whiskers into his belt? I smile as I bend to kiss the top of his head. His silky hair is warm in the sunshine and, as I whisper his name, I think as I always do, of his namesake.

A bit of me's buried with Hubert over in the fields of France. Perhaps if he'd come back from the war, it would have been different. Perhaps I'd have had that little piece of me back, and given it all to John. Or perhaps, when I saw Hubert again, everything would have returned to how it was. I'll never know, will I? And nor will a million others like me. That's the thing about war. It takes away the natural order of things, and makes our decisions for us.

The knowledge that Hubert is never coming back is gradually becoming easier to bear, but I still can't bring myself to look at his photograph, nor walk along the harbour like we used to, though one day I will. Yes, one day, I'll go and stand on the wall and look out across the Solent to where we first saw the fleet review. I'll choose a hot day in July, when I'm able to bear the feel of his hand on my waist again. And when that happens, perhaps I'll be able to say goodbye at last, and be the wife that John deserves. One day. Yes, one day.

When the sun is back where it should be in the sky.

Notes

(1) From the song, 'It's a Long, Long Way to Tipperary', by Jack Judge & Harry Williams (1912)

(2) From the hymn, 'Abide With Me', by Henry Francis Lyte (1793-1847)

(3) From the poem, 'A Clasp of Hands', by Algernon Charles Swinburne, (1837-1909)

(4) Poem, 'Love and Sleep', by Algernon Charles Swinburne

Acknowledgements

There were so many books I found helpful when I was researching material for 'Dearest Maude'. The following are just a few:

1915 – The Death of Innocence by Lyn Macdonald (1993)

All Quiet on the Home Front by Richard van Emden and Steve Humphries (2003)

Chronicles of The Great War – The Western Front 1914-1918 by Peter Simkins (1997)

Forgotten Voices of the Great War (In Association with the Imperial War Museum) by Max Arthur (2002)

Keep the Home Fires Burning – The Story of Portsmouth & Gosport in World War 1 by John Sadden (1990)

Major & Mrs Holt's Battlefield Guide Ypres Salient by Tonie & Valmai Holt (1996)

World War One – A Narrative by Philip Warner (1995)

The First World War – An Illustrated History by John Keegan (2002)

The Royal Hampshire Regiment 1914-1918 by C T Atkinson (1952)

The Trench – Experiencing Life on the Front Line, 1916 by Richard van Emden (2002)

Living History: 1914, by John Canning (1917)

One Hand Tied Behind Us, by Jill Liddington and Jill Norris, Rivers Oram Press (2000)

My grateful thanks also go to:

The Army Medical Services Museum, Aldershot
The Hampshire Record Office, Winchester
The Heritage Centre, Royal Victoria Country Park, Netley
Sanctuary Wood Museum (Hill 62), Ypres Salient
Petworth Cottage Museum, Petworth
Portsmouth City Museum
The Royal Hampshire Regiment Museum, Winchester